ICED

ICED

Julie Robitaille

St. Martin's Press
New York

Production Editor: David Stanford Burr

Library of Congress Cataloging-in-Publication Data

Robitaille, Julie.
    Iced / Julie Robitaille.
            p.   cm.
    ISBN 0-312-11434-6
        1. Women journalists—California—San Diego—Fiction.
    2. San Diego (Calif.)—Fiction.   I. Title.
    PS3568.03175I26   1994
    813'.54—dc20   94-19688
                                                              CIP

First Edition: November 1994

10 9 8 7 6 5 4 3 2 1

For Bob

1

The two fifteen-year-olds who stumbled onto the charred remains had seen enough cop shows to know what to do. They yanked their curious retriever away from what was left of the body, scrambled back up onto the street, and ran to the nearest phone. The discovery was the lead story on the local edition of the Sunday evening news. Yes, the police confirmed tersely, the killings did appear to be following a pattern. No, they said, as of now, there were few clues to go by. The investigation was ongoing, active.

HARD TIMES ARE HARD TIMES, it's as simple as that. Recession, unemployment, pollution; disease, hunger, the homeless; political corruption, domestic violence, soaring crime. A regular litany of misery, even here in San Diego, a city that is supposed to be some sort of national ideal, the cheerful bellwether of a bright financial and successfully melded ethnic future for the U.S. Booming growth, growing business, temperate climate, and low crime statistics, right? No. Not exactly. Hard times had hit here, too. And even the news business, which is usually able to achieve a viewer-friendly if artificial balance with its stories (two more dismal economic forecasts with a found puppy or a successful bone-marrow transplant), was finding the gloom-and-doom attitude difficult to offset.

Given the prevailing social and psychological climate, it was inevitable that staff meetings at KSDG would vary in tone from 100 percent grim to defensively black humored, depending on the specific news item being discussed. I must confess that in my dual role as newswriter and sportscaster I was often the one to provide both the ugly stories and the comic relief. My name is Kit Powell, and I carry a notebook.

"MAX," Doll said, reaching for a bear claw, "what's happening with the transient murders investigation?" Doll Garr is our sharp, diminutive station manager, and he'd opted to begin the Monday morning staff meeting with questions about a story that might well ensure his pick of the freshments. At least, as soon as I conjured up mental images of the burned bodies, I shoved my uneaten bagel back toward the middle of the conference table.

The murders had begun five months ago, and with the discovery of the latest victim, the body count was now up to five—strangled, set on fire, and left as a sick warning to other homeless people. The message was clear: leave town. Head for Los Angeles, where the streets are equally dangerous, or Santa Barbara, where they'd be faced with a city ordinance that forbade them to sleep in local parks, or even San Francisco, where if random violence didn't get them, inclement weather just might do the trick. Anywhere but here.

"Actually, there *is* something new," Max Flores replied. Mildly hopeful interest perked up around the conference table. "The police are working on a tip they got that it's a group of skinheads who're behind the killings. But that's not for public consumption, not yet anyway." Max's deep, modulated voice was as calm and reassuring as ever; he was always the consummate anchorman.

"Skinheads . . . like white supremacists?" I asked.

"They call themselves white 'separatists' these days," Max said with a wry twist of his mouth. "But yes, those are the folks."

"Is that all?" Doll demanded, annoyed. "What are we supposed to go with in the meantime? While they're out beating the bushes for neo-Nazis, we're getting *hundreds* of calls after every broadcast. . . . Our viewers are panicking about this!"

"Aren't they confusing us with the police?" Alan McGill, senior staff writer, asked mildly. "Or do all authority figures look alike?"

Max nodded in agreement with Alan. "We can't do anything about that, Doll," he said. "I mean, face facts—it's not like there aren't plenty of other equally gruesome stories to report."

"Amen," Dewey Andersen, our weatherman, chimed in. He looked around the table and shrugged apologetically. "We're on a flash-flood watch as of six this morning."

"Oh, that's just great," entertainment reporter John "Pat" Patterson sighed. "Something else to worry about. If it's not the damned drought, it's floods. . . ."

The five-year drought Pat was referring to hadn't forced San Diego to resort to the stringent water rationing that Los Angeles and Santa Barbara Counties had endured. Our neighbors to the north had had to deal both with toilet-flushing restrictions and an exorbitant hike in rates—this despite the obliging response from a public who had let their cars and sidewalks get filthy and their gardens wither. In Santa Barbara, some entrepreneur had actually started a business spray-painting brown lawns a perky green. But here to the south we'd gotten nervous, too, and people had been— up until the recent rains—hoarding massive quantities of Sparkletts bottles in our garages. Having been raised on the belief that any day a gigantic earthquake was going to split the state into jigsaw-puzzle pieces and bury most of its population, all Californians resort to siege mentality pretty easily.

"If it's not transient murders, it's gang murders or drug murders. . . ." Patterson continued, shaking his head sadly.

"Jesus, Pat!" Doll snapped, his blue eyes annoyed. "Could you stop being the voice of the apocalypse, at least until this meeting's over? You're supposed to be entertainment. If you have to moan about something, moan about bad movies!"

But Pat's bleak attitude reflected pervasive feelings, not just around this table but all over town. Home burglaries were up a whopping 37 percent from the year before; violent crimes up even higher. Murderous rages erupted on freeways, on the increasingly gang-ridden streets of the city, in fast-food restaurants. Local news had been covering what could only be described as carnage—it gets to you.

People who had spent their entire lives in San Diego without ever getting up in the middle of the night to check that the front door was really locked now had armed-response security systems; newer cars yapped and howled and told you that you were invading their perimeters in parking lots. Locals also possessed an impressive array of weaponry with which to fight off potential intruders—not that you could really blame that on the national recession and its fallout. San Diegans have always held that particular constitutional right in very high regard.

"Speaking of murders, what about you, Kit?" The question came from Tricia Blaize, news coanchor and full-time pain in the ass.

"What about me?" I echoed the question, puzzled. "I'm not on the transient story."

"I know that." Tricia made no attempt to pass her smirk off as a real smile; she saves her best (potentially wrinkling) efforts for the time she spends in front of the camera. "But you have a *source*," she said pointedly, "in the police department. Don't you?" Her green eyes bored into mine. "Couldn't *he* provide you—provide *Max*, I mean—with the inside track?"

I made a concerted attempt to force my own face into a serene mask, not my normal expression. "My source, as you call him, is out of town," I said calmly. Nick Strummer was most definitely not what I wanted to be thinking about right now, and even less what I wanted to be discussing at a staff meeting.

"Well, when will he be back?" Tricia prodded.

Getting away from her is never that easy; she may not be smart, but she's tenacious. "Um . . . I'm not exactly sure," I hedged. "There's some sort of big law-enforcement convention in Phoenix, new findings on the DNA matching process, stuff like that. And then he's got some vacation time coming. . . ."

"Don't you two keep in touch?" Tricia asked, arching one penciled eyebrow knowingly.

"Well, *you* know how men are," I said sweetly. "At least, that's what I've always heard."

"Tricia," Doll said, intervening before our edgy little exchange could turn into something more unsheathed and unpleasant, "let's talk about your stories. Are you going to lead with the cross burning in Pacific Beach or the sewage cleanup?"

"Cross burning," Tricia replied. She brushed her streaky hair back, tapped her crimson nails on the table, and pretended to think. "Yes, definitely," she said finally. "It's more colorful, don't you agree?"

"Colorful. Nice choice of words, Trish." Alan's voice dripped with false sincerity. There's no love lost between Alan and Tricia; for that matter, I doubt if there's love lost between Tricia and any creature with warm blood running through its veins.

"Well, excuse me!" Tricia said snippily. "And don't call me Trish." She turned her attention back to Doll. "Personally, I think the sewage spill has been done to death," she said.

Doll ignored Tricia's editorial opinion and turned his attention back to Max Flores. "Even if we can't reveal what the police are investigating, we still need to stay with the transient killings. Public interest is too high to let it slide. How about doing a background story on the homeless, Max? You know—tying it in to profiles of the victims, that sort of thing?"

Max nodded. "Okay," he said obligingly. "But don't get your hopes up too high. I don't think we're going to discover that any of them were actually long-lost millionaires or Rhodes scholars with amnesia. Better be ready for some plain old hard-luck tales." He glanced down at some scribbled notes. "No ID on this last one yet, but three others were just garden-variety transients—one drifter from L.A. and two locals."

"Alan," Doll said, "I want you on this one with Max."

"Oh, good," said Alan. "I just love researching depressing stories about people who died because they couldn't get a job."

A gloomy silence fell at the conference table.

Unemployment was at an all-time high, at least for those of us who weren't old enough to remember the Great Depression. And naturally California, the state hovering perennially on the cutting edge of any and all trends, was leading the nation in those statistics. Here in the very southernmost part of the Southland, aerospace and microchip jobs were disappearing as fast as any other endangered species. So the overqualified unemployed, desperate for any kind of work, were snatching up service and blue-collar jobs wherever they could find them. Ergo, the famous, now-defunct trickle-down theory translated locally into the working poor becoming the nonworking poor, with the welfare lines swelling accordingly.

And despite the undeniably grim national economic picture, illegal aliens kept crossing the border in record numbers. There was a new method now: swarming. Instead of sneaking across the border in twos and threes in the middle of the desert in the middle of the night, groups of fifty or sixty people would simply race across the border en masse and onto the highway. The border patrol had decided to force traffic to slow and let them swarm, hoping to catch up with them later, rather than allow a bloodbath on the freeway. It was a surprisingly logical and humane response, but it wasn't getting the kind of moral support it needed from the irate community who felt that their jobs and their futures were even further threatened by this influx of people willing to work for minimum wage. Or less.

It was all getting too damned depressing for words.

"I don't suppose anybody at this table has anything cheerful to contribute?" Alan asked rhetorically.

"Actually, I'm working on a story that could be a nice change of pace," I volunteered. This probably sounded like it came from left field, since I'm not exactly a Pollyanna by nature. And nothing that had happened recently in my personal or professional life had made me any perkier than usual. "The Bethlehem Pro-Am Invitational Skating Championships are here, with all the attendant hoopla. The press conference is this morning. I'm going to cover that, then start doing in-depth profiles and interviews with the skaters." I glanced around the table for some sign of response, but expressions ranged from blank to dubious.

"Ice skating?" Alan said. I glared at him; after all, he's my friend.

"Cute costumes," Dewey Andersen said weakly.

"Oh, come on," I wheedled, "you *know* how much attention that sport gets. People love watching figure skating; it'll be a great distraction."

There was a thick silence around the table until Doll finally nodded. "You're right," he said soberly. "Figure skating is upbeat—it's exactly the kind of story we can use now."

Now that response was a *true* measure of the morale level around the station: Doll hates most sports, and only concedes to having a sports segment at all because of those ignoramuses out there—his words—who'd rather hear about Wayne Gretsky's latest salary negotiations than see pictures of babies bleeding in Bosnia. I fall between the two categories; I like to think of it as a harmonious blend. I certainly do want to know about Gretsky's contract, but I also have too much social conscience to not watch at least part of a report on children in danger. Doll tolerates me because he knows that these qualities coexist fairly peacefully in me and, I suspect, probably more to the point, because I can be counted on to work equally as hard on either kind of story.

"Oh, please," John Weidendecker moaned theatrically, resting his beefy forehead on his equally beefy hand. "Who cares about figure skating anyway? All that silly Broadway music and those stupid spangly costumes." He looked briefly and nastily up at me, his eyes glazed with their usual Monday morning patina of vascular rheumy redness. "No one in *my* audience is going to watch it," he assured me. "It's pansy stuff."

"A little too much of the single malt last night, John?" Alan interjected mildly.

Weidendecker is KSDG's full-time sportscaster, whose umbrage at my emergence as a part-time rival is equaled only by his not-so-secret happiness that he doesn't have to stay sober quite as much of the time as he used to. Windy, as he's called by the staff behind his massive back, can be counted on to consistently jumble up his statistics, make idiotic observations about sporting events and players, and head for happy hour at Pirelli's rather than do any of the above. No one's ever been able to figure out why the audience likes him so much, and, in fact, we've given up trying.

"You don't like figure skating? You've got to be kidding!" I just wanted to needle him. He's always an easy target, but when he's hung over, he's even easier.

"Of course I'm not kidding," John said sourly. "I never kid."

"Of course not," Alan whispered. "It takes a brain to have a sense of humor, doesn't it?"

I bit back a grin. "I really think you're wrong, John," I said firmly. "Even if you don't personally go for skating, it's big business. The Olympics women's long program draws more viewers than the Super Bowl!"

"Ridiculous!" John scoffed. "It's a sport for pansies."

"You already said that, John." Dewey Andersen looked fatigued.

"Well, it's true."

How do you argue with reasoning like that? "At any rate," I continued, still trying to create some enthusiasm, "I think the viewers—the *sports* viewers, that is—will love it. There are some top-level skaters who're going to be competing here—international stars."

"Sounds like a good idea to me." Max nodded.

"I like it, too," Tricia announced, as if that confirmed something. "It's so glamorous. Those skaters really know how to make themselves look beautiful." She turned her gaze thoughtfully on me, her eyes narrowed down. "I hope you're giving some serious thought to *your* appearance, Kit," she said.

I didn't bother to reply. I had originally been hired as an investigative reporter at the station and had been happily doing just that—and *only* that—for over a year before the night John Weidendecker had consumed that ninth or tenth bourbon and collapsed in the makeup chair. I'd been lobbed onto the set against my will and better judgment as an ad hoc replacement, simply because I happened to know something about sports. It had panned out from there and, much to my surprise, the new job unexpectedly won my heart. I wound up fighting to keep it—thus, the Tricia and John wars. "The two top medalists from the Olympics are competing," I told the table at large. "Joelle Kistler and Greta Braun—gold and silver respectively. They reversed at the World Championships: Braun got the gold, Kistler the silver. And there's the real potential for an upset, too," I barreled on, "from at least two of the other top-ranked contenders. Seriously, this could be great sports drama—you know, rags to riches, dark horses, upsets, things like that." I was getting excited just talking about it. I'm a sucker for figure skating—I cried when Midori Ito blew her short program.

"Do you think any of them are going to try the triple axel?" Alan asked.

"Absolutely," I nodded. "The top five or six women have to, to give themselves some edge. The men will, naturally—it's a standard jump for them now. Some of them are even doing quadruples."

"But the girls always fall on their butts," Weidendecker said petulantly, still firmly stuck on his point.

"Women," I said through gritted teeth, while Alan groaned softly.

Weidendecker didn't appear to notice. "Personally," he said in his most pompous tone of voice, "I don't think they should even try to do that sort of stuff—they're not correctly equipped."

Even Tricia had the grace to look appalled. Not that it would do any good. Weidendecker is far too convinced that his opinions are unimpeachable truths to let a little thing like a room full of coworkers' disgusted reactions have any effect on him.

Still, I couldn't just let it slide. "John," I said firmly, "of course they should try it. They're athletes. And, by the way, they're women."

"Now, there you go with that feministical stuff," said Weidendecker dismissively. "They're *not* women, they're too *young* to be women—that's why they're still *girls.*" He looked at me smugly, perfectly satisfied with this logic.

"Feministical?" the usually unflappable Max echoed in disbelief.

Doll sighed. "Why don't we just go on with the meeting," he suggested. "Max, how's the special on cancer coming?"

While they discussed medical issues—ethics, chemotherapy, breakthroughs, that sort of stuff—I allowed myself to drift off. Out of the newsroom, beyond the reach of Tricia or John, past the gloomy stories, far from uncomfortable thoughts about Nick Strummer. Instead of dwelling on suicide machines, broccoli as a cancer preventative, troubled romantic relationships, or professional rivalry, I pictured the graceful pas de deux and heart-stopping overhead spins of the pairs skaters and the triple and quadruple jumps of the singles competitors. I thought about the combination of balletic grace and sizzling power with which these elegant athletes made nearly impossible moves look magically easy.

This is going to be terrific, I thought, my spirits lifting along with those imagined leaps. A happy story for a change. Right.

JOE BUSTANADO and Tony Gaines and I loaded up the KSDG van and got out of the parking lot before anyone else could claim it for breaking disaster coverage. We hit the road, heading east on the 94, and the guys talked about their respective weekends while I stared out the window of the van, only marginally attending to the passing scenery, still thinking about lifts and leaps and spins. We passed out of the city proper, cut south past Rancho San Diego and, after traveling for another ten minutes, exited the freeway at Sweet Water Springs, where we found ourselves smack in the middle of a building boom that hadn't quite fulfilled its promise.

The state-of-the-art skating arena Bill Bethlehem had erected was located in a developing community with the sanguine name of Pleasant Valley. Large pseudo-Spanish tract homes, mock-Tudor condos, and antiseptic malls had sprung up here in the late eighties, but the upwardly mobile population had been somewhat stalled in its tracks by the economy, and signs of the soft market were everywhere. Half-finished houses, half-empty strip malls and For Sale signs gave the community the slightly eerie ambiance of an old *Twilight Zone* episode.

Still, it wasn't completely vacant or depressing. Lawns and gardens were nicely manicured, helmeted kids skateboarded and biked along the residential and business streets, and there were some cars in the lots in front of convenience stores and nail salons. Tricia Blaize would no doubt see the latter as an irrefutable sign of economic recovery.

"Where's the new plant?" Joe asked. "I haven't been out this way in ages."

"Down off Manzanita Road, about five miles from here," Tony replied, fiddling with the lens on his camera.

I was surprised. "How do you know?" I asked. The plant they referred to was Bill Bethlehem's newest business venture; it was a ray of hope for the area's out-of-work blue-collar workers, but it wasn't completed quite yet.

"My cousin is trying to get a foreman job there," Tony said. "He got laid off from the GM plant up in L.A., and he wants to come back to San Diego with his family."

I thought about Bethlehem's empire, which already included tobacco and cereals, and was now diversifying further. They had recently decided to locate the production of their new line of frozen gourmet health foods here in the Southland. Bethlehem had taken a medium-size family business and turned it into a megabusiness in the past twenty years. Building a new arena and bringing both jobs and a high-profile athletic competition to the area had made him a kind of local hero.

The pristine white dome of the arena loomed up in front of us, its marquee announcing the Bethlehem Pro-Am Invitational Skating Championships in glittering four-foot-high letters. We pulled into a parking lot that already held a gaggle of news vans—local and national. My pulse picked up. This was a major sports event, national, a first for me.

We grabbed our equipment quickly and walked in, flashing our press credentials at the single guard posted by the door. Inside the cavernous rink, the temperature dropped precipitously, and we headed quickly toward the grandstand, where a group of what had to be officials had gathered. Tarps had been laid down in front of the stand for the news crews and anyone else who didn't have blades attached to his shoes. I waved casually to a few of the sports reporters I knew as we found a good spot and set up.

All around us, the skaters were already on the ice practicing—gliding around, warming up, and doing the easier jumps and spins in preparation for the real stuff. I turned to watch them and was immediately struck by the pure athletic power of the sport. This was all without the benefit of the theatrics—there was no dramatic music to be swept up in, no sustained beginning poses for the audience, no flashing smiles. The skaters uniformly wore looks of intense concentration; this was deadly serious work, as rigorous as high-impact aerobics and as sweat producing as weight lifting. There were no fancy, glittering costumes or trailing organza scarves to be seen, no skillful makeup; lightweight sweats, arm and ankle weights, thick leggings, and T-shirts were the order of the day.

I spotted Greta Braun whirling rapidly around in a camel, making it look utterly effortless and airy. Her form was perfect, her opposite arm and leg extended in a graceful, continuous line. Her famous white blond hair was pulled back in a simple braid that hung nearly to her waist; and as she spun, the braid whipped out and around like a platinum plume, the black bow at the end making a swirling punctuation mark to the move.

"Wow, look at that!" Joe exclaimed as a tiny figure in red tights and a black sweater whipped across the ice and jumped straight up into the air, executing a perfect back flip. She landed solidly and raced back across the ice in a series of loops and jumps. It was a complete contrast to Greta's grace—this was a show of gymnastic energy, full of power and adrenaline.

"Shannon Ngao," I told Joe as the skater went into a dizzyingly rapid sit spin. "Very good and still young—I think she's only nineteen."

"She looks like she belongs on the parallel bars," Joe remarked.

"What's she doing, skipping the Olympics and going for the endorsements?" Tony asked, shooting footage of Ngao.

"Actually, she did compete in the last Olympics," I replied. "She came out ranked seventh. . . ."

"Wants to make some bucks?"

I shrugged. "She must—she's a heavy favorite in the next Games."

"But you can't do both, can you?" Joe asked.

I nodded. "You can now," I said. "That's why it's called Pro-Am. Skaters who've turned professional can reinstate for Olympic competition. Witt and Boitano did it—it caused some flap." I pointed to a tall young woman with mocha-colored skin who was gliding easily around, keeping a close watch on Braun and Ngao.

"Speaking of comebacks and reentries, that's Melinda Parsons—she hasn't skated in any competition for over three years."

"What's she been doing?" Joe asked, following Parsons's lithe figure with his eyes.

"Teaching skating in Portland," I said.

"Oh, come on!" Tony exclaimed in disbelief. "A teacher?" We watched Melinda Parson's willowy body arch backward in a layback spin.

I nodded. "Melinda was working her way up the ranks, and then her father was hospitalized with cancer. She tabled competition to stay with the family and to bring in some money. He pulled through, but it's been a couple of years since anyone's seen her skate—no one knows if she still has the kind of strength she had. It will be interesting to see—and it's a good story, too." We watched as Melinda Parsons effortlessly executed a series of toe loops. I knew she was still widely regarded as an unknown quantity, but people acknowledged her potential to upset the anticipated standings.

One of the pairs teams whirled by in matching electric blue sweats: Canada's Paul Cavanaugh and Susu Jenrette, a couple with a solid midlevel history of performing, one whose artistic merits hadn't ever quite matched up to their technical abilities, to their speed and strength. A groin pull had kept Paul out of the finals in the last Olympics, where they'd been counting heavily on a bronze.

Just then a young woman glided out onto the ice, and as if drawn by a magnet, all eyes turned toward her. Dressed in black leggings, a pink-and-black polka-dot skirt, and an off-the-shoulder purple sweatshirt, Joelle Kistler flashed her trademark shy half smile toward the onlookers and then began to warm up.

"Kistler?" Tony said, nudging me. I nodded. "She's cute," he said, training the Steadicam on her as she did a series of simple jumps and spins.

And she was. With her thick chestnut hair cut short, her expressive hazel eyes, and her solid but fluid body style, she had a kind of Dorothy Hamill charm—a likable all-American aura that seems so accessible and so pleasing to audiences. She was the personification of bubbly happiness, with the looks of a Breck girl and a healthy glow about her that never even hinted at the grueling hours and physical trauma behind the easy grace she exhibited on the ice.

Halfway up in the stands, I spotted her mother, the guiding force behind Joelle's career. The story went that Joelle had begged her parents for skating lessons when she was four years old, and from the first time she set blade to ice, it was obvious that she was a gifted athlete. In a stark contrast to Melinda Parsons's need to work for a living, Joelle had been given everything her indulgent, upper-middle-class parents could afford. Of course, other rumors alleged that Ellen Kistler was more than a guiding force—that she was a pushy skating mother who drove her daughter mercilessly toward a goal more hers than Joelle's. And that daddy, John Kistler, was a Milquetoast who sat on the sidelines and watched, while his money went for all it could buy.

There was another person watching Joelle carefully from the sidelines, a large-boned woman bundled up in a heavy wool jacket. I recognized Joelle's famous coach, Terese Steiner, who had come to the U.S. from East Germany after the fall of the Wall . . . bringing with her *her* most famous student, Greta Braun. But now Terese was coaching Joelle Kistler, and Greta was currently coached by Milo Vonderah, training out of Colorado Springs. As the bearlike Milo skated over to his charge, telling her something and pointing to the ice, I wondered what had caused the rift between Braun and Steiner, if indeed it had even been a rift. And how Greta Braun must feel now, seeing her old coach working with her most serious rival. Greta nodded impatiently at Milo's words; she was reputed to be temperamental.

"Ladies and gentlemen, could you get your crews in front here?" A man's voice summoned our attention back to the stands. The speaker was a florid, fortyish man with silver hair and a determinedly cheery smile. "Mr. Bethlehem would like to make some introductory statements to the press, then introduce you to these fabulous competitors. But first, I'd like to say a few words."

The speaker cleared his throat. "My name is Norman Sloan," he said, "and it has been my very great privilege to be in charge of putting this event together for Bethlehem Enterprises. As you probably all know," he continued, looking from one news crew to

15

the next, "this is the first time that a figure skating competition of this magnitude has been held here in San Diego." He paused for a smattering of applause. "I can't say that getting everything done has been easy, but it's often the real challenges in life which reap the greatest rewards."

"I'd say the rewards are more financial than anything else," I murmured. One of the reasons the Bethlehem—a newcomer to the Pro-Am circuit—had drawn such attention in the first place was the prizes it held out. Not just substantial dollar awards (over six figures for the top winners) but the chance of landing one of Bethlehem's own product endorsements as well.

"But we're here," Sloan continued happily, "and we believe that this competition is going to be a terrific one." He grinned a public relations grin—slick and planned. "Now, before I turn over the microphone to Bill Bethlehem, I'd like to say a few special thanks to some people from this community without whom this whole endeavor wouldn't have been possible. . . ."

"What'd he do, buy off the city planning commission?" Tony murmured.

I stifled a laugh and kicked his ankle, while Norman Sloan launched into a series of brief introductions to several people seated behind him; one by one, they stood to acknowledge the polite applause they received. It was the usual A-list of rich, civic-minded activists and rich local sports fanatics. I paid only minimal attention to Sloan's list; I was more engrossed in thinking about how I wanted to schedule my interviews with the athletes and coaches, what kind of human interest stories to do, and how the hell I was going to maneuver my way onto the ice for those on-the-spot quotes. Until one name intruded into my drifting thoughts like a sucker punch.

". . . Channing Strummer, who has not only donated generously of her time in pulling this new community together behind the Bethlehem Arena and the Bethlehem Plant, but who has proven herself an invaluable source of creative ideas . . ."

My eyes may not have widened to the size of platters, my jaw may not have fallen unbecomingly open, and I know I didn't drop my notes, but I was damned glad the camera wasn't trained on me at the moment, just in case. There she was, my sort-of-boyfriend's soon-to-be-ex-wife, big as life, rising graciously to acknowledge Sloan's compliments. And if I had harbored any secret hopes that if and when I ever came face-to-face with Channing Strummer, she would prove to be perhaps marginally less attractive than me, or at the very least, less *interesting* looking, well, I could kiss that wish good-bye.

Channing Strummer had wheat-colored hair that looked perfectly natural—thick, shiny, cut in a blunt bob that was both sophisticated and flattering to her face. And her face was, I had to admit, simply great. A perfect oval with just enough strength in cheekbone and jawline to make it interesting; wide, intense blue eyes; and a mouth that had that natural smile curve to it. In a deceptively simple cream-colored suit, she looked well toned, well kept, and put on earth with all the right equipment—along with all the money needed to keep it right. Jesus, I thought uncomfortably, my roots needed touching up and I hadn't jogged or done sit-ups for weeks. At least I was wearing a nicely cut black linen jacket over my basic sweater and jeans.

I had to force myself to stop staring at her as Sloan finally led the applause to greet Bill Bethlehem himself. After all, this was my job. I put my emotions on hold and studied Bill Bethlehem carefully; for your basic midfiftyish CEO type, he was a remarkably youthful and fit-looking man. The body under his beautifully tailored suit could have belonged to a man twenty years younger. His dark brown hair was still thick and wavy, just beginning to go flatteringly gray at the temples. His eyes were dark, deep set, and piercingly intelligent.

"I'd like to welcome you all to this informal opening of the Bethlehem Arena, and to thank you for coming down here today." His pleasantly melodious voice held just a hint of his North Carolina roots. "We at Bethlehem are thrilled to be behind this terrific competition, and equally thrilled to be expanding our growing business into this lovely area of the country.

"I know this isn't the time for elaborate speeches." Bethlehem gestured toward the skaters who—obviously according to plan— had stopped whirling and jumping, and who had gathered in front of the grandstand. Photo op coming up. "I just want to say one thing—that these wonderful young people you see here today are some of our most gifted athletes. They are proof positive that hard work and determination, and more than a little natural talent"—here he smiled broadly—"can get you anything you want in this great country of ours."

Was this guy planning to run for political office? And why was Channing Strummer still using Nick's last name? I had sensibly gotten rid of any official reminder of Terry Brody before the ink was dry on *my* divorce papers. . . .

There was a sudden flurry of activity somewhere in back of the arena, and I saw Bill Bethlehem's expression turn from happy to puzzled.

"Hey, you!" someone shouted. "You can't just burst in here like this!"

A startled murmur ran through the group of people on the grandstand, and the media swiveled automatically, as a group, to see who or what was creating the disturbance. The single guard who had been posted beside the door, the one who had shouted, was struggling awkwardly with a bizarre figure—someone dressed in full camouflage, wearing a gas mask. Then the figure broke away from the guard and positioned itself in the middle of the ice.

"Hey, Bethlehem!" The words were screamed, combative. "You make such nice speeches—full of uplifting sentiments, very smooth. But *I'd* like to hear how you justify using these great young athletes to sell lung cancer to the public! Any answer to *that*, Bethlehem?"

It was impossible to tell if the speaker was male or female; the strident voice was gender-muffled behind the gas mask. "Come on, Bethlehem," the figure goaded him, "tell the newspeople how you manage to peddle death to the public and make it seem like such fun!"

Bill Bethlehem forced himself to regain his composure immediately. "This is not the forum for this kind of discussion," he said loudly and firmly. "And I don't believe you have any press credentials, so if you will just leave quietly . . ."

But the words weren't even out of his mouth before the doors—now abandoned by the startled guard—banged open, and more angry demonstrators burst into the arena. Faces disguised by gas masks and surgical masks, they ran in and fanned out across the

18

ice. These people were well organized: they knew exactly where to position themselves for the maximum exposure to the cameras, which were now trained on them and the signs they carried.

Some of the protesters brandished placards with graphic pictures of lungs riddled with cancer and emphysema, others waved drawings of gravestones on them; still other signs bore nasty, colorful skulls and crossbones.

One protester was actually dressed as death—black robe, white face, sickle, the whole bit; he or she carried a red-lettered placard that read, "I'm behind Bill Bethlehem all the way."

"Call security!" I heard someone on the grandstand yell.

Then the verbal accusations erupted, a violent chorus of indictments.

"There's blood on your hands, Bethlehem!" someone screamed. "Why don't you admit it?"

"Burn down the damned tobacco fields!"

"You're nothing but profiteering scum!"

"Jesus," Tony muttered, getting the chorus of anger on tape.

"You belong on death row, Billy boy—you're no better than Charlie Manson!"

"My mother died of lung cancer, you bastard—get the hell out of this town and take your poison-for-profit with you!"

The air was suddenly filled with objects sailing over our heads onto the grandstand. What looked like water balloons burst open as they landed, splattering something that resembled blood on the horrified honorees. One of these missiles smashed directly into Bill Bethlehem's shoulder, drenching his clothing and his face in dark red liquid.

"Ugh," I heard a rival station's sportscaster exclaim as he stared down at his feet.

I followed his disgusted gaze and saw, on the ice right in front of him, a sloppy brown lump of dark leaves that had landed short of its intended destination.

"Chewing tobacco?" I hazarded.

"*Pre*chewed, actually," said Tony, staring at the sticky pile.

Then it was over, as quickly as it had begun.

"Let's go!" someone shouted—it might have been the first protester, the one in camouflage. "It's time!"

At first I thought it was someone with good ears—good enough, at any rate, to discern the sound of approaching sirens, even over the pandemonium inside the arena. But I couldn't hear a thing, and I quickly revised my assessment: someone in the group of protesters was savvy enough to have timed just how long it would take the police to respond to this kind of call.

"Should we stay or follow them?" Tony yelled over the chaos and noise.

I glanced quickly from the retreating backs of the protesters to the shocked people in the stands, gauging our next move. Bill Bethlehem hadn't even tried to get out of range of his attackers; he remained standing, dazed and drenched. Ellen Kistler had raced down from the stands to Joelle, whose face was a mask of bewilderment, and had her arms wrapped protectively around her daughter; the other young athletes looked equally stunned and confused by what had just occurred. All, that is, except Greta Braun. Her fine-boned face wore an expression of pure disgust, undiluted by fright or confusion.

I was certain the protesters had already executed a quick getaway: there had been the air of a precisely planned surgical strike about the entire operation—in and out in minimum time, with maximum effect. I didn't think there was any real point in trying to follow them right now. We'd be seeing them again—these people had a point to make. There would be time later to piece it together, time to find out exactly who they were. This wasn't exactly starting out to be the enjoyable, upbeat little piece I'd so blithely promised my newsroom cohorts, but what could I do? My story, for the moment at least, was here inside the arena.

"Stay," I told Tony and Joe.

3

WE HEADED BACK to the rink early the following morning, grumpy fatigue providing a quiet respite in the van after I informed Tony that if he didn't turn off the A.M. shock jock assault on my senses, I just might resort to a nonverbal type of violence. The skaters kept to a grueling schedule that included four to five hours of practice every day, starting as early as 4:30 in the morning, and I wanted to catch a few impromptu interviews and shots that showed the athletes' dedication to their sport. It wouldn't all be on ice, either; there was weight training, running, ballet and jazz choreography to work on as well. It was all physical, all intense and rigorous and suited only, I thought, stifling a yawn and clutching a plastic cup of Kwik-Stop coffee, to the very young. No one else possessed that kind of stamina.

From the other angle, the emotional, psychological angle, I was curious about just what went into creating the kind of temperament that allowed someone so young to possess this kind of focus—a late teen who would, given a more normal disposition, be ping-ponging hormonally between resenting parental authority, resenting school authority, worrying about tickets to the next Poison concert, and wondering if she were or weren't going to a) have sex or b) show up positive on the early pregnancy test.

"Hey, check this out," Joe said as we pulled to a stop in the nearly deserted parking lot.

I followed his line of vision and was surprised to see a few people milling around the front entrance to the arena. I squinted and could just make out a few of the words on the picket signs they carried. "Jesus," I said, "tobacco protesters?" There were no outlandish outfits this time around, no skeletons. Just ordinary-looking folks with placards and a message. "At eight in the morning?"

Tony shrugged as we piled sloppily out of the van. "A good cause is a good cause," he said. And off my look, he shrugged again. "My dad died of lung cancer."

"I didn't know," I said. "I'm sorry."

"Three packs a day," Tony said tersely. "That'll do it."

Joe nodded toward the picketers. "Want to get some footage?"

I shook my head reluctantly. "Maybe later—let's get the sports stuff first, or we'll be stuck listening to Tricia whining about how hard news isn't my territory for the next week." I had no doubt Tricia would seize on the protesters as a story she, premiere anchorwoman, should be covering. It would become an *issue*. It would take up time at meetings. It would piss me off.

Just outside the back entrance to the rink, guarded only half attentively by an elderly man in an ill-fitting uniform, we passed Joelle Kistler talking to a fan in the cool morning air. At least, that's what I assumed he was until I got a quick, closer look at him. Lean, strongly built, he might have been in his late thirties or early forties, but it was hard to tell: he had the furtive, hardened look of someone used to encountering trouble on a regular basis. Thinning brown hair was slicked greasily back off a high forehead over dark glasses, and he wore an oddly out-of-date blue polyester jacket with faded, baggy slacks. He didn't look like any skating fan I'd ever seen, but Joelle, although preoccupied, didn't appear to be frightened or threatened in any way, so I kept going.

"Boy," Joe remarked sotto voce, with a nod toward the strange duo, as we entered the arena, "the weirdos are all out early today."

Inside, the rink was bustling with skaters, trainers, choreographers, even a few die-hard onlookers willing to get up at the crack of dawn to watch their favorites practice the same loops and jumps and spins again and again. Paul Cavanaugh and Susu Jenrette, finishing up a series of well-executed side-by-side jumps, waved at us with friendly smiles, signaling their eagerness for some press coverage.

I waved back, and they skated obligingly over to where we stood. They were a little older than most of their competitors, and I knew they had to be feeling the pressure of hitting the top spot once and for all. If they were planning to retire from competition as was rumored, winning here could certainly help their bargaining position when it came to a contract with one of the traveling ice shows. Susu, like Shannon Ngao, was also going to be competing in the women's singles; there, too, she had only managed to rise to middle ranking, and there, too, she would have to shine.

Paul Cavanaugh was a big, stocky twenty-eight-year-old whose main asset on the ice was his strength; Susu, with her golden ponytail, pug nose, and sprinkling of freckles, looked like the athletic girl next door, Quebec-style. She spoke bouncily, with a barely discernible accent, Paul with none at all.

"I'm here with Canada's reigning pairs skaters," I told the camera, and we proceeded to launch into an impromptu interview.

Cavanaugh and Jenrette, with years of experience behind them, didn't miss a cue or fluff an opportunity to connect with the camera or with me. Susu cheerfully admitted that this was their last duo performance; after this, they would go their separate ways. They seemed very much at ease but very competitive. Susu readily acknowledged that this was one contest in which the unexpected could probably be expected; but that, she said with a grin, would be working in her favor. She had been working hard on her artistic interpretation, the area in which she invariably scored lower than technical performance.

"I'm in top form," she assured me. "Better than ever." Self-doubt didn't seem to be a problem.

Ari Kotzloff skated up to Shannon Ngao, and I moved toward them, filling Joe and Tony in on his background as we went. Ari had been born in Russia, had immigrated to Israel with his family when he was nine, and had eventually wound up in the U.S. in order to skate. Ari and Shannon were both skating in the individual categories, and together in pairs.

They were beautifully suited to pairs skating—Ari had just

enough height and strength to handle tiny Shannon with a seem-ingly effortless ease. I'd seen a recent clip from one of their compe-titions, and he'd been able to toss her high enough over his head for the acrobatic Shannon to twist twice in midair before he caught and balanced her on one hand overhead. They were the kind of Mutt and Jeff physical match that would look awkward, if not downright comical, anywhere but on the ice. On ice, however, it could be magic.

Ari's accent was a curious combination of Russian, Hebrew, and American street slang; his speech was alternately amusing and difficult to understand. Shannon spoke excellent English, how-ever, having spent most of her life in the U.S., and she seemed to take a shy delight in interpreting for Ari. Ari happily lifted Shan-non over his head after Tony complained that the foot-and-a-half height difference was making for some strange camera angles. Then the tall, slender young man twirled rapidly around, while Shannon contorted herself into an impossible-looking arch that made the word *chiropractor* spring immediately to my mind.

"We win," Ari assured me when they stopped spinning, "the pairs and the singles."

I thought this odd couple would be an appealing interview. We agreed to a more in-depth report and set up a time in studio for the following day.

"Good luck," I said cheerfully, moving on to Greta Braun.

"News?" she inquired in a clipped voice. "Which one, please?" Large light green eyes stared challengingly at me. Her platinum hair was braided again, pulled tautly off her oval, doll-like face.

"Local, KSDG," I replied equably.

Greta rolled her eyes. "I must warm up before I talk to any-one," she said. The Ice Queen, I thought, coming right from the Brothers Grimm to you out there in television land.

"What a friendly girl," Joe remarked. "Direct descendant of Attila, perhaps?"

"Could be," I agreed. As Greta skated off toward Milo Von-derah, who waited on the other side of the rink, I wondered idly if all those tight, well-developed thigh muscles might possibly turn into plain old fat in another few years.

24

"Let's go see if we can find Melinda Parsons," I said. "She'll probably be happy to get some coverage."

Parsons wasn't on the ice, so we trekked down the tunnel that led from the rink to backstage and its maze of workout rooms, locker rooms, and storage spaces.

"Ms. Parsons?" I called out as I spotted her in a cavernous dance studio. She had one long slender leg resting easily on the bar while she mopped her forehead with a towel. "Kit Powell from KSDG. Is this a good time for a quick chat?"

Melinda Parsons smiled and nodded. "Sure," she said. "I just finished up here." She removed her leg from the bar and strode over to us with a walk of singular grace. Parsons was a little taller than the other skaters, about my height, but small boned. Her face was finely chiseled, her skin a pale mocha color, and her long, coppery, curly hair tied back casually with a ribbon. "Nice to meet you."

The young woman had a guarded quality, but she still projected a natural warmth that was in stark contrast to Greta Braun's chilly demeanor. It must be difficult both physically and emotionally, I thought, to come back into this kind of competition at twenty-four, battling all these younger women who'd spent their entire lives with the spotlight on them.

I said as much.

Melinda Parsons shook her head. "No," she said seriously. "It's not hard at all. This is something I've dreamed about all my life. I just had to put it off a little longer than most people do." She shrugged. "The age thing is no big deal—Susu Jenrette is a couple of years older than I am."

"So when did you decide that you'd compete again?" I asked.

"As soon as my father was strong enough to tell me he didn't want me hanging around anymore," Melinda said with a surprisingly impish smile. "This is a dream my family has for me, too. They didn't even want me to stop competing when Dad got sick, but it was something I felt I had to do."

"No regrets?" I ventured.

"Not one," Melinda told me firmly.

Melinda Parsons made her choices sound very direct, very simple, but I knew it couldn't have been that easy. News-wise, she was the perfect underdog for this contest, a heartwarming focal point for my kind of sports color spots: lovely, talented, hampered—but ultimately undeterred—by some rough twists of fate. And now, against the odds, she was here. My mind was already racing ahead to the kind of story I would put together on her.

"Can we get some shots of you on the ice?"

Parsons nodded obligingly. "Sure," she said. "Let me just stop by my locker and get my stuff and I'll meet you—"

"Can we follow you?" I interrupted. "Shoot this in a sort of documentary style? Then I can edit it together for the most effect."

She hesitated for a fraction of a second, but then she nodded again. "Of course."

Melinda picked up her extra ankle weights and towels, and the four of us made our way through the corridors and into the women's locker room, after Melinda had made sure that there was no one in the middle of dressing or undressing there. Joelle Kistler was on her way out as we entered, and although she nodded at us and at Parsons, her usual flashing smile was absent; she looked preoccupied and serious. Well, well, I thought a little cynically, perhaps that smile is all PR, just a part of the Kistler persona developed to look good on cereal boxes—which was exactly where she was hoping to be after the Bethlehem Invitational. Of course, that's exactly where Melinda Parsons and at least three other young women were hoping they would be as well.

The lockers were full-length storage spaces, with built-in combination dials. Melinda juggled her armful of weights and paraphernalia while she spun the numbers to open the metal door. Shelves and hooks were arranged to maximize the space inside; everything except the precious exhibition costumes would be stored in here, close at hand. Those would be kept guarded and unwrinkled right up until the last moment.

Melinda stuffed the towels she was carrying into a laundry bag and reached for her skates. "Not very glamorous, is it?" she joked, indicating the interior of the locker. "Dirty laundry and sports equipment." Her smile seemed more relaxed than it had a few minutes ago.

Then, as she pulled a sweatshirt from the top shelf of the locker, a small object tumbled out from behind it and fell to the floor.

My eyes widened in shock as Melinda moved to block my view. "What's that . . . ," I began.

Melinda quickly reached to swoop it up.

"Nothing," she said quickly, tossing the thing back in the locker and slamming the door shut. She turned and headed for the door at a race-walking pace, Joe, Tony, and I hastening behind.

"Melinda, wait . . ."

But she kept going and didn't say another word until we reached the rink.

Then she turned to me—and the camera—with a carefully composed expression. "I'd love to arrange a more in-depth interview later," she said, her voice controlled. "After you get this practice on tape, that is."

She was clearly cutting off any questions I might want to ask, and I knew I couldn't push it. I had seen what she had so hastily pushed back into her locker. "I'd like that, too," I assured her. Then I handed her my card. "Why don't you call me at the station later today?" I suggested. "We can work out the best time."

Melinda Parsons shoved the card into her sweatshirt pocket, smiled tightly, and skated out to the center of the ice, where she proceeded to begin her warm-up with small, careful circles. She stared unwaveringly down at her feet; it might have been to make sure that her technical form was perfect, but somehow I didn't think so.

"What happened?" Tony asked me.

I shook my head. "Let's see if we can get a couple of words with Joelle," I said. She had arrived on the ice and was now practicing a series of jumps in front of her watchful coach.

As we made our way carefully around the ice, I thought bleakly about what I'd caught a glimpse of before Melinda Parsons slammed her locker door shut: a black Barbie doll in a pink sequined skating outfit, with a rope around its neck. The image was a vicious one, a gift with a clearly nasty intent. I wondered how it had gotten into a locked locker. I also wondered if it was the first time something like this had happened in the African American skater's experience. There had been that hesitation about us filming her opening her locker; or had it been my imagination? There was a sick twist in the pit of my stomach as I tried to think of something I could do or say, some way I could help. But Melinda Parsons had seemed intent on guarding her secret, and I was at a loss. For the time being, I back-burnered my concern and turned my attention to the next competitor.

"Darn it," I heard Joelle exclaim as we came close, camera focused on her.

"Try it again," Terese Steiner said patiently. "Pull to the left and complete the rotation."

Joelle tried her double toe loop again; it was an easy jump for a skater of her status and experience, but she came down wrong, wobbling and off balance, barely able to hang on to the landing. It was the kind of thing that could shave precious fractions of points off a skater's score, and it was out of character for a technically meticulous skater like Joelle. She skated adamantly off toward the edge of the rink, preparing to pick up speed before her next attempt.

"Ms. Steiner, I'm Kit Powell, from KSDG. Could we get some footage of Joelle this morning?"

Terese Steiner turned to greet us. She was a no-nonsense woman, her short dark blond hair held off her broad face by a plastic headband, her nose red from the cold of the rink. She was bundled up in a quilted down coat and heavy wool scarf.

"Yes, of course," she nodded. "I'm so sorry to look like this," she apologized, "but I have the congestion." Her accent was similar to Greta's, a little less pronounced. Then she sneezed. "But of course, it is not me," she continued, "it is Joelle you want on the camera anyway, not her old coach."

"Her old coach" was hardly how I would classify this consummate professional, the woman who coached the East German team to success after success, who had brought the seemingly unbeatable Greta Braun to the States, who had then left one champion for her most obvious rival. And, I suspected, made quite a nice little nest egg for herself in the process.

"That's all right," I assured her. "We can get you on tape later, when you feel better."

She sneezed again, her light blue eyes watering.

"You should be in bed," I added, "with a hot-water bottle and chicken soup."

"With a hot toddy, I think," she joked. Then she cast a worried eye toward Joelle, who had gone into a very easy flying camel, camera conscious. "But this is not the time," she added somewhat cryptically.

As if to belie any worries her coach might have, Joelle came out of the spin easily, landing with perfect grace. Terese waved her over, and as the young skater approached, I thought she, too, looked a little distracted. Her eyes darted around the rink before landing on us.

I introduced myself. "Are your parents here this morning?" I asked Joelle, who had been touted throughout the Olympics as the all-American girl, the perfect product of that rarest of all circumstances, a happy family. According to the talk shows, at least. And Joelle usually looked the part, with her open, pretty face, her well-cared-for hair and skin, her bouncy attitude.

But the attitude was off this morning. Joelle shrugged, her dark brown eyes flickering for an instant. "I'm sure my mother will be," she said in a neutral voice. "She always is."

"Joelle . . ." Terese Steiner's voice held a subtle note of warning.

"I just meant that she's always been wonderful!" Joelle exclaimed defensively. "So supportive and, you know, active."

Active, in this case, possibly translating into pushy, aggressive, tunnel-visioned. I sensed a distinct turmoil beneath that seemingly well-adjusted all-American exterior of Joelle's, and I wondered what was causing it.

"Yes," Terese said firmly, "she has been."

Joelle's expression shifted abruptly from neutral to vivaciously enthusiastic. "Would you like to see a little bit from my long program?" she asked me.

"Of course," I replied.

Terese and Joelle turned away for a moment, as Terese talked quietly to her pupil about a certain approach to a jump. Joelle listened obediently, then seemed to visibly back away, impatient and distracted again.

"I know," she said flatly as she skated back toward the center of the ice. "Stop worrying."

Terese Steiner blew her nose and looked anything but unworried. And she had reason: Joelle not only skated roughly and unevenly, but her second jump was a complete miss. She overrotated and went sprawling on the ice, spinning to a stop in a sitting position. Falling on her butt, as John Weidendecker would have so graciously phrased it.

"Do me a favor," she called out to me. "Don't use that on the news, okay?"

"No problem," I called back. Of course I wouldn't. I wanted viewers to see how glamorous, how exciting, how graceful the sport was. Even how tough. But definitely not what day-to-day drudgery it could be. Not how Joelle Kistler could fall on her ass, or how Greta Braun could be snottily dismissive, certainly not how Melinda Parsons apparently had much more to worry about than just her scores.

"Shoot around the stands, get some shots of the judges' box, the celebrity boxes, that kind of stuff," I murmured to Tony. "Let her relax for a minute."

"Uh-huh," he nodded.

I glanced up into the stands and saw a man watching Joelle intently. It was the same man I'd seen her talking to outside the arena.

Joelle got up and began the routine all over again, and this time she executed the jumps well enough, technically speaking. But there seemed to be something missing in her performance, some passion that the best skaters bring to the ice with them, even during practice sessions—a passion Joelle Kistler had amply demonstrated in her previous performances.

"Let's try it again," Terese said hoarsely.

A look passed between Joelle and Terese Steiner, but I couldn't read it.

Joelle nodded and started over. From across the rink, I saw Greta Braun pause and focus intently on Joelle's performance.

During this pass-through, Joelle's form was perfect, her face set in concentration.

"Better," Terese wheezed.

"We've got enough," I told Joe and Tony after we got a shot around the entire rink, catching lively tape of the various skaters warming up, leaping, circling, moving in tandem with their partners or their coaches. This would be plenty to work with for a short segment on the early evening news—flashing glimpses of the players, introductions to the personalities, the kind of things that gets viewers hooked in. The kind of thing that makes them want to tune in again to see what happened to that little brunette from Orange County or that cute Asian kid.

When I turned to say good-bye to Terese Steiner, I found that she had moved about ten yards away and was talking to a forty-something couple whom I recognized as the Kistlers. I didn't want to interrupt what appeared to be a serious conversation, and as I glanced back at the ice, I saw that Joelle had come to a complete stop and was staring obliquely at the three adults.

"Miss Steiner, telephone. Terese Steiner, phone call." The words came over the PA system, and Terese Steiner excused herself and moved away from the Kistlers. They turned their attention on their only daughter, who now wore the look of a serious athlete working on inner focus, completely detached from her physical surroundings. Joelle spun into a series of whirls and jumps, her expression remote.

Outside the rink, the number of protesters had grown, but I still didn't want to cover the action in the parking lot—not without checking with Doll first. At any rate, I was more curious about what was going on inside that ice palace, which seemed fraught with even more tension than I had expected to find. I knew what was motivating the protesters, but the skaters—aside from the obvious competitive desire to win—were a different story. Granted, there was a lot at stake for these young athletes. But beneath the surface, it felt like rippling waves of anger and stress were undulating, more than the usual high-tension competitive atmosphere that was to be expected. And it was, metaphorically speaking, making my nose twitch. I wanted to know more.

                                  * * *

I HAD JUST FINISHED applying my lipstick and was ready to
perch behind the glass bricks of our "news desk" during a com-
mercial break when the call came through.

"Powell, it's Stan Mardigian."

"Hi," I said, puzzled. Mardigian is Nick Strummer's partner in
Homicide. He's a glum sort who favors polyester and has an affin-
ity for my cat, Dancer, a fat, nasty feline who generally doesn't get
along with anyone other than my ex-husband. It certainly hadn't
been love at first sight between Stan and me, but we'd managed to
come to a grudging acceptance of each other in Nick's life and,
well, I won't go so far as to say mutual respect, although I certainly
respect what *Stan* does for a living. "What's up?"

"You're covering that ice-skating thing, aren't you?" Stan
asked.

I glanced at the set—I had about forty-five seconds to get out
there. "Yes."

"Thought so. We just turned up someone connected to that
contest, thought you might want to know."

"What do you mean by turned up?" I asked.

"A body. A coach. Uh . . ." I heard some papers being shuffled.
"Terese Steiner?"

"What?" My exclamation brought looks from the newsroom.
"Terese Steiner is dead? Are you sure it's *her?*"

"Uh-huh," Stan replied laconically. "Just got a . . . uh, Mr.
Vonderah to ID the body."

"Holy shit. Where? Hey, hang on a second." I called out to
Doll, "Hey, bump me back behind weather, okay? This is a breaking story."

He nodded. "Okay, Stan," I said, "tell it to me. What happened?"

"This is kind of weird," he said. "Some street people found her
at a freeway underpass."

"What?" I exclaimed again. "A freeway underpass? What the
hell was Terese Steiner doing at a freeway underpass in a strange
city?"

"I told you it was weird. I don't have a clue. But it's the same
spot the last transient body was found."

"Jesus!" I filed that fact away for further probing, recovered my newshound sensibility, and went for the facts. "How'd she die?"

"Shot."

I winced. "My God."

"Three times. That's all we know, so far. Thought you might want to be the one to break the scoop, or whatever you call it." He gave me the location so we could send a crew out.

"Thanks, Stan," I said. "I owe you."

"Huh," Mardigian replied as he hung up the phone.

"What's up?" asked Max Flores as I slipped into place and adjusted my collar.

"Murder," I said. Then, off Tricia's arched eyebrow, I amended the statement. "A *sports* murder."

"That's real news!" Tricia hissed. "I should be the one . . .

"Shut up, Tricia," Doll told her. "There's no time, let Kit go with it. And four and three and . . ."

4

As SOON AS the five o'clock broadcast—which featured my necessarily brief "breaking story" exclusive on Terese Steiner's death—had ended, I told Doll exactly what Stan Mardigian had told me. It wasn't very much information, and Doll called for a crew to go to the crime scene to get more details, do some live on-the-spot coverage.

I insisted on tagging along with them, despite Tricia's vocal objections. "I got the call," I reminded her firmly. "My source, not yours. Me, not you. Remember? It wasn't that long ago."

"Oh, please! What difference does that make? Might I point out that you do sports color, and barely that?" Tricia snapped. "This is a *real* story."

"I got the call." Sometimes deadpan, monotonous repetition was the only thing that would have an impact on Tricia's brain. I decided to forego asking what the phrase "and barely that" meant, but I filed the insult away as another black mark on Tricia's ever darkening record.

"Oh, for Christ's sake, Tricia," Doll finally said. "Kit's right—she took the call and she's got the right to go with you to the scene."

"That's right," I said smugly.

"Although I don't know why anyone wants to see dead bodies if they don't have to," Doll muttered. He stared at Tricia. "Don't worry, it will be your story—"

"But Kit broke it," Tricia said, "and the audience will think that she's the one . . ."

"Enough!" Doll snapped. "No more whining or the goddamn figure skating coach can get up from the dead and report it herself!" He shook his head. "Christ, sometimes I feel like I'm officiating at the Miss America Pageant."

"Hah!" Tricia said, tossing her hair.

Doll continued to grumble along in the same vein. "An East German skating coach bites it at a freeway underpass. . . . Let's just try to make sense of this one." He looked disgusted, but whether it was the squabbling in the newsroom or the fact that this was just more bad news where there wasn't supposed to be bad news was unclear to me.

"Okay, Kit can come," Tricia said finally, even though Doll had already walked out of earshot, "but she's got to stay out of the way." Which meant off camera. Tricia stared stubbornly at me.

"Ready to roll, sunshine?" I asked.

The look she shot me probably could have done Terese Steiner in.

Of course, most of my flippancy with Tricia was a cover for a bad case of nerves: I was on the way to see a body, the body of a woman I'd met briefly, a woman I had spoken to. It hadn't qualified as anything more than very fleeting acquaintance, but Doll was right about seeing bodies. When the Sharks case had been unraveling all around me, I'd been forced into contact with the first and only two corpses I'd ever seen—and both had been people I had known just a little better than Terese Steiner. My stomach lurched at the memory of gunshot wounds.

Still, I was going. This was my story, if not Terese Steiner's murder itself, then certainly what it might mean to the Bethlehem Invitational. Would this tragedy cast an irreversible pall over the competition? How could it not? What effect would this have on Joelle Kistler's chances to win? Would she even compete? The simple, upbeat news story I'd been planning on, the one that would distract our glum audience from the realities of everyday life, was taking on wrinkles that were darker and nastier than anyone could have expected. Tricia or no Tricia, I'd follow it. I got into the van.

The crime scene was a grungy speck of no-man's-land not far from our own downtown building or the police station, and it was still bustling with uniforms, detectives, and the people from the medical examiner's office when we arrived. Milo Vonderah was gone, and Terese Steiner's body had already been bagged and loaded into an ambulance. I took a deep, thankful breath at the reprieve, then began to look carefully around.

The place where the bodies of the East German coach and the unidentified transient had been found was lit up by floods. They cast bright, unsparing light on the dark triangle of steeply angled land beneath a freeway underpass, mostly asphalt, its widening cracks sprouting with tangled ivy and thorny, forbidding brush. Never intended to be used by humans for anything at all, it nevertheless showed that it had been occupied, at least temporarily: there were the charred traces of small fires where hands had been warmed and cans heated, and there was litter—scraps of cloth, broken bottles, rusted needles. A stained old mattress, shredded practically beyond recognition, was half hidden in the bushes. It was the kind of place that you could imagine any terrible thing happening. And it had, I thought, it had.

I wandered around the areas that weren't cordoned off. How had Terese Steiner wound up in this place? It just didn't compute. Had she gotten lost or been lured here? Had she been killed somewhere else and dumped here? My mind skipped across the possibilities.

Tricia had grilled me on the coach, on Joelle, on the competition, during our ride down here, and she launched right into an on-the-spot report that sounded as though she had had the facts and figures and personalities involved committed to memory for the past five years. I was once again forced to grudgingly admit to myself that she was capable of sounding articulate, intelligent, and knowledgeable, which just went to prove that you could fool most of the people most of the time. I watched her for a few moments, then looked away, staring somberly into the dirty mist but not really seeing anything.

"Hello, Kit."

In the middle of this grim, dark scene, detective Nick Strummer appeared calm and removed, his even features relaxed, his expression steady. But I knew that look, knew it didn't necessarily mean anything about how he really felt.

"When did you get back into town?" I asked. Why bother with preliminaries?

"About twenty minutes ago." His light gray eyes were clear and cool behind his glasses. "Stan called you?"

I nodded, scuffling the dirt with the toe of my boot, digging a line between us. "I'm covering the Bethlehem Invitational."

"I know."

The way we spoke to each other, it was as if we'd only just met, as if we were exchanging tentative civilities and halting information for the first time. Not as though we'd ever shared anything as important as a murder investigation. Or a bed.

"Well," I said, my voice sounding flat and forced to me, "this is certainly the last thing I'd have expected to happen. . . . and this place . . ." I gestured around, shuddered.

"She probably got lost." Nick's voice was just as flat as mine.

"Probably," I agreed, pro forma. Nick's investigative abilities and his curiosity are at least on a par with mine; surely he'd considered that there might be more to this than a simple case of getting lost. "Either that, or we're about to give Miami a run for its money in tourist bashing," I said, baiting him.

Nick shrugged, refusing to take it. "That's the last thing this town needs," he said neutrally.

Just then, as we were either about to run completely out of small talk or launch into something far more potentially dangerous, Stan Mardigian appeared out of the fog and the lights, a plump apparition in a plaid sports jacket and a florid, unmatching tie. "Powell," he said, nodding pleasantly at me.

"Thanks for the call, Stan," I said.

"No problem." His eyes swiveled from me to Nick, and I wondered suddenly if this was actually some sort of attempt on his part to force the two of us to talk to each other. That, of course, presupposed that Nick actually confided in Mardigian about his personal life; stranger things have happened, but I'm not sure what. "If she was wearing jewelry, it's gone," Stan told Nick. "And so are the

37

credit cards and cash." His eyebrows met, wrinkling over puzzled hound eyes. "It looks like a robbery gone wrong, just someone in the wrong place at the wrong time, but I don't know. . . ."

"Because of the transient?" I asked.

Some silent communication passed between the partners, and Mardigian shrugged. "It's just a feeling," he said evasively.

"I'll call you later," Nick said abruptly to me, his eyes blank behind wire-rimmed glasses. Then he turned and walked away.

Stan Mardigian stood there awkwardly as I muttered, "You do that." I put a hand impulsively on his arm. "I meant it, Stan, thanks. Not that I get the story, but the station can always use the jump."

Stan jerked his head toward Tricia and the camera, just as she finished her spiel. "Too bad you can't report it," he said, "instead of the Kewpie doll."

I was grateful for his effort to make me feel better. "And thanks for that, too. I gotta go."

Tricia did a good job with her coverage, Doll was happy that we'd gotten to the crime scene faster than any other news crew, and the atmosphere at the station was generally self-satisfied. It's a peculiar thing how normal tragedies get transformed into items, lead-ins . . . ratings.

The whole scene had left me uneasy and off balance. Not just the murder itself, although that would certainly have been enough to shake me up. It was the place, the seemingly accidental, random nature of the act, more unwanted evidence that there are people who really do think a human life is worth nothing. Or not much, at any rate—just some jewelry and cash.

I drove home on autopilot and fed Dancer, who only hissed three or four times before hunkering down over his bowl. After a long, hot shower, I settled into bed by myself in my quiet little cottage on quiet little Coronado, tucked safely away from the outside world. But I didn't sleep well. I couldn't stop thinking about Joelle Kistler and what this would do to her; thinking about Melinda Parsons and that nasty doll; thinking about Terese, who'd outlived the Berlin Wall only to die in a strange, hostile place with a bad head cold; thinking about Nick, who hadn't, after all, called.

* * *

THE ATMOSPHERE at the station was utterly ordinary, business as usual, when I arrived at work the following morning. Not, I told myself, that there was any reason for it not to be; after all, one more inexplicable killing wasn't necessarily big news. Not these days, not here. The staff joked and squabbled, ate jelly doughnuts and bagels while we discussed stories, muttered about assignments.

But there was a certain difference in attitude, a moment of recognition that *something* had happened, when Ari Kotzloff and Shannon Ngao arrived for my interview with them. It was a subtle ripple of perception that ran through the newsroom staff, a reaction, I thought, that probably had more to do with the fact that these two young athletes had been touched more by violent death than with the killing itself. The glamorous reflection of violence, I thought. Soon to be mutated into a movie of the week, no doubt.

I had planned to talk to them off camera for a few minutes before taping. I had a feeling that the two skaters might need a break-in period—verbally, that is; they were used to expressing themselves through leaps and strength and grace, not generally through words. And since English wasn't the first language for either of them, I thought that no matter how much they wanted to shine in an interview, there would be stumbling blocks.

I always try to put people at ease for interviews, and with athletes, that's not generally a difficult task. They tend to be happiest in the spotlight and eager to let their audience know just how well they're doing at whatever they do best. I had sensed that same quality—competitive and fiercely proud—definitely coming from Ari Kotzloff. But the tiny Shannon seemed more bashful, reticent, less likely to self-promote.

We got ourselves seated, coffee for Ari and me, mineral water for Shannon, and it quickly became apparent that the warm-up period had been a good call on my part: today, even the normally outgoing Ari was subdued. I plunged in and broached the subject of Terese Steiner's death—there was no way to avoid it, and if that's what was going to be the biggest conversation stopper, I thought the sooner we got it aired between us and out of the way, the better it would be.

It was Shannon who replied first, her small face looking equally bewildered and distressed. "This kind of killing, it happens here so much," she said softly. "I don't understand why. . . ."

"It's senseless," I agreed.

"This is such a violent country," she continued. "And I come . . . from a violent country." Her eyes filled suddenly with tears, and I wondered what kind of horror stories Shannon had heard from her parents, who had immigrated to the United States in one of the roughest ways known to mankind: they had been what were called boat people. Shannon had been very young at the time, too young, I would have thought, to remember whatever those brutal experiences might have been. But then again, maybe not. Kids retain all kinds of things, unpredictable things, both good and bad. Perhaps figure skating—the ultimate sport of fiction, the one that acts out fairy tales and fantasies—was her way of putting that kind of reality behind her. Until it intruded again, in the form of a murdered coach.

"Shannon and I, we are very distressed," Ari said somberly, "by this terrible, terrible thing that has happened." His eyes were a deep, intense blue, and his curly dark hair tumbled raggedly over a bony, interesting face. It was a face, I thought, too severely dramatic for someone his age. But he was going to be an intriguing-looking man some day. "Poor Miss Steiner," he said mournfully, "and poor Joelle, too." He shot a worried glance at his partner. "But we will not let this thing stop us from doing our best."

I sensed that his words were directed more at Shannon than at me; it was as though he were sending her an urgent subtextual message: Don't let this get to you, it read. Don't break down.

I glanced over at Shannon, who was wringing her hands together in her lap. Her bottom lip was quivering dangerously.

"If you'd like to reschedule this interview for a later time," I said gently, "that would be fine, Shannon. Really."

She looked up at me, her eyes starting to spill over, then at Ari. "No . . . ," she whispered, "I, that is, we want very much to talk. . . ." The words trailed off.

I was in an awkward position. Shannon was clearly not in condition to go in front of the cameras; just as clearly, she and Ari were determined to do precisely that. I didn't want to blow them off, insult these young stars and get myself declared persona non grata at the rink, but I also didn't want a teary, inarticulate segment airing on the news.

"Are you certain . . . ?" I began.

"It is difficult, I think, to be different in this country," Ari said unexpectedly.

"What . . . what exactly do you mean?" I asked him, bewildered.

"Different." Shannon nodded in agreement. "There is so much hatred for those who are different here."

"Like Miss Steiner," Ari said, "look at what happened to her. . . ."

I was confused by the direction they were was taking. How was Terese Steiner different? Because she was foreign? Like Ari, like Shannon?

"But . . . Terese Steiner's death was a fluke," I said. "I mean, it was one of those terrible, senseless murders. Surely you're not saying she was killed because she was . . . *German.*"

Shannon glanced uncomfortably at Ari, then stared down at her lap.

Ari's mouth was set in a grim line. I had struck a chord.

"Has something happened to make you think . . . ?" My words trailed off as I glanced quickly from one of them to the other, abruptly recalling the graphic image of the lynched Barbie doll that had come tumbling out of Melinda Parsons's locker. The connection clicked into place. "What happened to you?" I stared intently into Ari's troubled blue eyes. "Did you get something—did you receive a threat?"

Ari seemed to take my measure for a moment, then he nodded. He fished around in his shirt pocket and came up with a shiny little object, which he handed to me. It was a brass swastika.

"It is in my dresser drawer," he told me as I turned the object over in my hand in disbelief. "When I am back at my hotel room from practice yesterday. And Shannon, she got a, how you say, a . . . jar?"

Shannon shook her head. "A plastic container."

"Yes," Ari said, "a container of rice filled with . . ." He shook his head impatiently. "Damn!"

"Maggots," Shannon said softly. "It is rice with maggots and broken pieces of bamboo chopsticks in it."

"Jesus!" I exclaimed before I could stop myself. "Have you told the police?" I asked, trying to quell the physical revulsion that the image had evoked.

"The police . . . they have their hands full with murders," Ari said impatiently. "You think they have time for bad jokes?"

I hardly considered these nasty little gifts in the category of bad jokes. I said as much.

"Neither do we," Shannon said, "not really. But it all seems so . . . strange, why would the police believe us?"

"I don't understand," I said. "Why *wouldn't* they believe you? You've got the . . ." I indicated the ugly little swastika.

"But the connection, I don't think they believe that, and we don't want to cause . . ." He glanced helplessly at Shannon.

"Ripples," she said firmly, recovering her poise. "With the competition. But we are worried because we think that Miss Steiner's death is no coincidence."

I shook my head, mystified. "These are two separate crimes," I told them. "A hate crime and a murder—probably a random killing."

"No," Ari said stubbornly. "I think Miss Steiner's murder is also a hate crime."

"Who hates East Germans?" I asked in amazement. "That doesn't make sense."

"Miss Steiner was a Jew," Ari told me.

I stared blankly at Ari. "Are you sure?"

"I am sure," he said firmly. "She told me. And she also got one of these." He held up the brass symbol of hatred.

I sank back in my chair, assimilating this information, trying to make some sense of it. "I think you should tell the police," I said finally.

Shannon shook her head vehemently. "No!" Her eyes were huge, pleading. "You do not know how much hurt this would bring to my family. It is, it would be a . . . terrible disgrace to us."

"What has happened *to* you is the disgrace," I told her. "Not the other way around."

"No!" She shook her head again. "You do not understand what this would do to them. . . . I cannot tell them!" She blinked her tears resolutely back. "We will just go on, all right?" She glanced at Ari for confirmation, and he nodded.

Together, Ari and Shannon proved to be an implacable and resilient young force. Their admission to me had apparently provided some sort of emotional catharsis for them; and now that they had gotten it off their chests, they seemed relieved, ready to continue with the interview, absolutely unwilling to consider divulging the information to the authorities. So I made my own decision—for the moment—based on their attitude: I'd follow their lead, do the happy story, show the pretty skaters. We went ahead and taped.

But later that day, after the segment had aired, I flipped through my Rolodex and found the number I wanted. Maybe the young athletes could shake off the ugliness that had targeted them, but I couldn't. There was too much ugliness all the way around here, and it begged examination.

I wanted to know who was behind this kind of racist attack on Melinda, Ari, Shannon. I wanted to know if other skaters had been targeted. And, as far-fetched as it seemed, I wanted to know if Terese Steiner's death could possibly be connected in any way to that threat—to the fact that she was Jewish, or to the swastika that Ari claimed she, too, had received.

According to Max Flores, there were rumors floating around that the murders of the homeless men had been committed by a white supremacist group; these creepy messages smacked of the same mentality. Could there be a thread that linked them? Then again, perhaps the tobacco protesters might just be fanatic enough about their cause to want to disrupt the event any way they could. I punched a number on the phone.

"Council for Ethical Observation," said the polite woman at the other end of the line.

I identified myself. "I'd like to set up an appointment to speak to Arthur Gold as soon as it's convenient for him," I said.

"Mr. Gold retired two months ago," the woman informed me.

"But if you'd like, I could put you in with Sandy Harrow, Mr. Gold's replacement."

"That would be great," I said, relieved.

CEO was a national watchdog organization that monitored things like the rise in hate crimes, the efforts of religious extremists to infiltrate school boards, any and all possible infringements on civil liberties. Arthur Gold had run the local branch office for years and had been a reliable source of information in the past whenever I was investigating stories that touched on those kinds of topics.

If anyone would know about the local fringe groups who might be engaged in this particular insidious kind of activity, these not so subtle threats, it would be the people at CEO. And, of course, I reminded myself, the cops. But I had promised Shannon and Ari that I wouldn't betray their confidence, that I wouldn't go to the authorities. And that was just as well, I thought ruefully, since at the moment, my connection to my so-called connection at the police department was, to put it mildly, in a state of uncertainty. I set up an appointment to meet with Arthur Gold's replacement late the following afternoon. Then I snagged Alan McGill as he hurried by me.

"Hey, you're doing the background digging-up for Tricia on the tobacco protesters, aren't you?" I asked.

"Yup."

"Anything odd you've turned up?"

Alan's ears pricked up. "Odd like what?"

I told him about the lynched doll in Melinda Parsons's locker, then what Ari and Shannon had just revealed to me.

"Holy Jesus," Alan said, wrinkling his face in disgust.

"Do you think anyone connected with the protesters could be that extremist?" I asked.

"I'm going to have to go digging just a little deeper to find out," Alan said. "And I'm happy to do it," he said grimly. Bigotry is high on his hate list; publicly exposing those involved would be right up his alley. "Even," he added just a little sadly, "if it makes a better story for Tricia."

5

ANOTHER STORM came pile-driving into the area the next day, guaranteeing a whole lot of weather-related problems and a proportionate number of headline stories for KSDG. We could count on more disaster slide coverage of those precariously perched cliff houses; on more potentially fatal freeway pileups and daring rescues—the Jaws of Life always plays well on the six o'clock broadcast; on more dire warnings of flash floods in areas where children play; and on canyon roads closed because of mud and boulders, creating excellent opportunities for on-camera interview spots with unhappy locals who couldn't get home. All this and the unsolved murder of Terese Steiner, too—never mind the transient murders investigation, there was barely enough time in the broadcast to fit in all the up-to-the-minute bad news. The newsroom is always an intense place, and that can be energizing for the people who work there, keeping us manically upbeat even when the news is grim. But this storm seemed to be getting seriously under people's skins.

Tricia was in a bad mood because she doesn't like to go out in the rain to cover disasters. John Weidendecker was in a bad mood because he was hung over or because he didn't relish the idea of getting wet crossing the street to Pirelli's for happy hour. Or both. Alan was snarly and tired—his new puppy had kept him up all night whining to go out instead of using the newspaper he'd put down for her. Even Max, who is generally a port of rational calm and equanimity in most KSDG storms, was antsy and rightfully worried: the backyard pool at his hillside house was threatening to become a tiny freshwater addition to the Pacific Ocean. After a sour morning meeting, Doll locked himself in his office, and occasionally I could hear swearing emanating from it.

Dewey Andersen seemed to be the only person in the entire newsroom who was actually in a good mood. Despite all those satellite maps and fancy equipment, weathermen are wrong so often that when one of their predictions—and I use that word and all its crystal-gazing, palm-reading connotations on purpose—comes true, they tend to be relieved. Who can blame them? Dewey comes in for a lot of pissed-off looks and comments—in person from the newsroom staff and over the phone from irate viewers—when his rain forecasts send people scurrying to put that plastic over the unvarnished new back door or drag in all the lawn furniture, and then it's a sunny and temperate seventy-five degrees the next day, no cloud in sight.

Actually, I wasn't in such a bad mood, either. I don't own my own home, and my sturdily built old rented cottage was holding up perfectly well against all weather assaults. Traffic coming across the bridge had been lousy, but I'd expected that and had sat calmly through the slowdowns and stops letting the suitably moody jazz tape I'd selected play me along.

After the snarly morning meeting, I flipped on my computer and went to work, trying my best to stay out of the line of fire and concentrating on a construction graft story I was helping Max put together. The screen helped create my own personal cocoon, and I focused on the work at hand, although occasionally thoughts about the trouble lapping around the skating competition intruded. I forced myself to put them on hold until I could devote full attention to them and tried not to notice when the scent of Joy, Tricia's signature perfume, stopped wafting and landed at my desk.

"Wasn't that your boyfriend at the murder scene?" Tricia chirped loudly, perching uninvited on my desk. Naturally she didn't care if she was disrupting my train of thought: she knew I wasn't working on a story of hers. "I could have sworn you said he was out of town."

I glanced briefly up into her eyes—today's contact lenses were an intense violet color, but she didn't look anything like La Taylor.

"He's not my boyfriend and he was out of town," I said tersely.

"Goodness," Tricia said, widening her eyes, "*that* was certainly a quick romantic interlude!"

"I'm working, Tricia. Was there something you wanted?"

"Actually, I was hoping you could put me in touch with him— what's his name?" Tricia looked quizzically at me. "Strummer, isn't it?"

"Yes," I said through gritted teeth. I knew she knew Nick's name, and I had a sinking feeling about what was coming, since Tricia keeps up on all local social gossip.

Tricia snapped her fingers as if she'd just remembered something. "He isn't . . . the homicide detective who was married to Channing Philton, is he? Wasn't that her married name, Strummer?"

I was right. "That's him," I agreed blandly.

"How perfectly fascinating," Tricia mused, playing with the heavy gold links of her necklace. "From Channing Philton to *you*. Well, I guess he must have wanted a change of pace. What's that phrase? Interim relationship, right? Something like that, anyway. Well, no *wonder* it didn't last long."

I kept quiet, counted to eight, and refused to be baited into a catfight. The plain truth is that Tricia is an anchorwoman with the heavy leverage of widespread popular recognition, locally at least. I'm a part-time sportscaster and nearly full-time investigative reporter; the two jobs don't add up to the clout that she has, and I don't want to lose my job. Sometimes it's just a better idea to keep quiet; I still manage to get enough nasty jabs in to keep my self-respect.

"Well, can you put me in touch with him?" she asked again.

I reached into my desk and retrieved one of Nick's business cards. "Put yourself in touch with him," I told her.

She took the card and slid off the desk, brushing imaginary dust off her size 2 skirt. "I will. But first I feel I simply must say something to you, Kit." Her phony colored eyes took on a phony sincerity. "We are a team at KSDG. And I certainly hope for the sake of the team you've managed to maintain a cordial working relationship with Detective Strummer."

"Don't lose any sleep over it," I said.

Tricia sailed on. "Because I'd hate to see a perfectly good police source for the station dry up just because of someone's inability to manage her personal life."

I forced myself to turn my attention back to graft and shoddy construction, a relatively pleasant diversion, all things considered. I didn't want to think about Nick and what had happened. Or what hadn't happened. I certainly didn't want to think about Tricia Blaize meeting with him somewhere up close and cozy, although I was certain Tricia wasn't Nick's type. Then again, her words about Channing Philton Strummer echoed in my head. Nick's estranged wife was a country-club blonde with a sleek, manicured look that read "spa." I'm a brunette gone auburn with intelligent hazel eyes and a passably pretty face. I don't look like I play tennis and I've never spent a day in my life being pampered at the Golden Door or anywhere else. So what *was* Nick's type?

Our relationship had begun when, in my new capacity as KSDG sports color commentator, I got tangled with the football murder investigation Nick was handling. It had been particularly bad timing: Nick was right at the point of splitting up with Channing, who turned out to be not his first but his second wife. I had been divorced for a couple of years, but the wounds were still tender, and I'd recently made the colossal mistake of a one-night encounter with my ex-husband. Neither of us was exactly a prime candidate for true love. But an unmistakable electricity jumped and flared the minute I met Nick. The attraction between us was as strong as anything I'd ever experienced, and anything he'd ever experienced, apparently, as well; and we tumbled headlong into the kind of immediate intimacy that burns up the road and feels like it should either lead somewhere conclusive or just implode. True to the unpredictable nature of human relationships, it did neither.

We'd spent several intense months in each other's company, work schedules permitting—which automatically put a lot of restrictions on our time together. It was frustrating, but it kept the excitement level jacked way up between us. We didn't talk about the future or commitment or even the "relationship." And then it stopped. Nick's schedule got more demanding with the leaping number of murders in our happy little county, and he'd cooled down, backed off . . . withdrawn. I was too self-defensive to press the issue: if he wanted to disappear, I told myself, let him disappear.

My mood became as dark as the newsroom, and I had to force myself to think only about the story I was working on. I had no segment that evening, so at six o'clock on the dot, I packed up and headed for my appointment at CEO.

The storm had let up, and the rain was now medium light but falling steadily. Traffic was predictably clogged and slow, but the lakelike water levels that plague the streets during heavy downpours had receded to normal runoff state. I saw lots of tow trucks and a few abandoned cars and minor accidents on the way to my appointment, but nothing too awful. All in all, things seemed to be letting up.

I managed to find a parking space right in front of the small, unobtrusive brick office building near the renovated Gaslamp district downtown that houses the Council for Ethical Observation. There were decorative black wrought-iron bars on the downstairs windows, and I had to buzz to be let in, since it was after hours. The center can't afford a full-time guard, but they're constantly receiving threats, and a few precautions—like a locked front door—are in order. The place has been evacuated with bomb threats so often that the word is workers come out with their Danish and cups of coffee now, resigned to waiting it out in some amount of comfort.

After identifying myself, I was buzzed in. I signed the register on the table in the empty lobby and climbed the narrow stairway to the small outer office at the top of the stairs.

Mona, the efficient gray-haired woman whom I remembered as Arthur Gold's secretary, was filing. Her reception area was neat as a pin.

She smiled pleasantly at me. "Good evening, Ms. Powell, you can go right in." She motioned to the half-closed door that opened off to the right of her office. Then she nodded toward a credenza that held a tray with a coffee pot and cups. "Help yourself to a cup of coffee if you'd like."

"Thanks," I said. I poured some into a ceramic mug with a picture of dolphins on it and added a little cold water.

I knocked lightly just to be polite and stood in the doorway. Sandy Harrow had the phone cradled on his shoulder, but he waved me all the way into the crowded office and pointed at the chair across from his desk. I sat, and while he wound up his conversation, I checked him out.

It was strange to see someone so young, relatively speaking, occupying what I still thought of as Arthur Gold's chair. Gold had been in his late sixties when I had known him, and Mona in the outer office was probably not far from that age herself. I suppose that a few years of contact with the two of them had left me with the impression that anyone working for the Center for Ethical Observation must automatically be older—sort of a second career consisting of good works rather than financial reward.

But in spite of the premature salt-and-pepper mix in his thick, unruly hair and a few deep character creases on his narrow face, Harrow didn't look like he was out of his thirties yet. He was half hidden by the big walnut desk, but he looked lanky and tall, and his jacket was draped casually over the back of his chair; he wore a blue oxford shirt with no tie. I noticed that Arthur Gold's honorary awards, plaques, and pictures with the likes of Golda Meir and Pope John had been replaced with plaques and pictures of Sandy Harrow with Bono and Mother Teresa. A new day had dawned.

"Miss Powell," he said as he hung up the phone and reached across the desk to shake my hand. His eyes were bright blue and he had a sharp, energetic demeanor. "Nice to meet you. I'm a fan when I've got the time."

"Thank you," I said.

"So"—Harrow leaned back in his chair, his hands clasped behind his head—"what's a sports reporter doing at CEO?"

Right to the point. I thought about how busy Arthur Gold had always been; clearly, not everything at CEO changed with a change of leader.

"I'm not exactly here in my capacity as a sports reporter," I told him, "although this certainly does connect." I proceeded to lay it out for him, piece by piece. Harrow never looked surprised, not once. Not when I talked about the swastikas or the maggoty rice. Not when I told him that Ari Kotzloff claimed that Terese Steiner was Jewish and had received a swastika, too. Not when I told him about the lynched black Barbie in Melinda's locker. He simply listened and nodded occasionally, his expression unreadable.

When I got to the part about the transient murders, he nodded. "I know about the theory," he told me.

His response wasn't really surprising. "I assume you've got your own sources," I said.

He nodded neutrally.

"Official?" I asked.

"Whatever," he said.

"So . . . you think it's true?" I asked. "Skinheads or some other Aryan group?"

He shrugged. "It'll certainly fly for me unless something better comes along."

"Meaning . . ."

His blue eyes darkened. "Meaning that unfortunately there's no reason not to believe it. Hate crimes of all kinds are on the rise all over the country—you know that, don't you?"

"Yes, of course." In a sour economy, hate crimes always jumped statistically.

"This particular kind of action—maiming, killing the mentally ill and the helpless—is quite a long-standing tradition with the younger supremacists." His expression flickered with momentary disgust. "A sort of rite of passage, it's been theorized."

I grimaced. "Rite of passage sounds about right to me," I said. "It smacks of the warped school-yard bully mentality." I thought about it for a moment. "Do you honestly think this could be just some unaffiliated skinheads? Some kids?"

Harrow shrugged. "It's possible, I suppose—it's certainly happened in other cities. But this is so well planned, so neat, that it reads more like adults, organized adults to me. With the power that comes in numbers and secrecy and a complete conviction that you're God's true messenger."

"White makes right?" I said.

Sandy Harrow nodded. "That's the thinking," he said. "So, back to the beginning—what's this about for you? Are you actually going to do a story on this kind of harassment in the middle of the competition?"

"Hell, no." I almost laughed. "I'd get canned in a second if I tried to weave this one into sports news—this isn't exactly a Marge Schott kind of scandal." I shook my head. "No, I work in two different capacities at the station, and this is more in the line of investigative reporting—it's the kind of story that I do the legwork on and that I eventually have to hand over to someone else at the station. An anchorperson."

Harrow's expression was curious. "But I'm still not certain . . . what exactly is it that you are investigating?" he persisted. "And where exactly does CEO come in?"

"Terese Steiner, the East German coach I mentioned? She was murdered last night."

"That was . . . the woman they found at the freeway underpass, right?" I nodded, and Sandy Harrow frowned. "And you what—think there could be some kind of connection between the threats to the skaters and her death?"

I figured he had heard more bizarre suppositions in his time, so I plunged in. "Actually, I do," I told him. "I know it sounds like I'm stretching it, but think about it. First, the skaters get these racist threats, and according to Ari Kotzloff, Terese Steiner gets one, too. Next, Terese Steiner's body is found at a freeway underpass, which, by itself, appears to be a bizarre, spontaneous incident—a robbery, maybe, the poor woman was just at the wrong place at the wrong time, that kind of thing. Although," I added, "I haven't been able to confirm whether or not she was actually killed there or somewhere else."

Sandy Harrow nodded, his eyes attentive.

"But wherever she really died, *this* particular freeway underpass has a history—it's where the last transient body was found."

"Okay," Harrow said slowly. "And?"

"And the transient killings are rumored to be the acts of a bunch of skinhead thugs." I looked at him. "Don't you think there's some kind of thread that's running through this?"

His frown deepened as he mulled over what I had said. He had an interesting, angular face filled with character; in some ways, it was not unlike the face Ari Kotzloff would have when he grew up.

I stared speculatively at him, suddenly aware of how attractive he was in an offbeat sort of way, and a little surprised by my even noticing the fact. Sandy Harrow whistled tunelessly for a few moments, turned inward. Then he looked hard at me, his blue eyes sharp and assessing. "This is mostly . . . instinct on your part, isn't it?"

"I suppose it is," I admitted reluctantly.

"And am I correct in thinking that instinct is what makes you good at your job?"

"It's one of the things," I agreed with alacrity. This wasn't the time for a display of false modesty. I wanted him to believe me. I wanted him on my side. I wanted his help.

Another moment passed and then he shrugged. "Instinct is often as good as any other impulse," he said thoughtfully. "Actually, it's often better. It's saved lives more times than we can count. But what does CEO have to do with all this?"

"I'd like your help," I told him.

His brows knit. "Why us? What about the police? What do they think?"

"I don't know," I confessed. "I got the call about Terese Steiner, but I don't have any idea if they're working on the angle that the killings could be connected. Besides, they don't know about what's been happening to the skaters."

"What do you mean?" he asked sharply.

"I promised Ari and Shannon I wouldn't go to the police with what they told me," I admitted.

He raised one salt-and-pepper eyebrow.

I shrugged. "I know it's problematic."

"Problematic?" Sandy Harrow's smile was wry. "Interesting choice of words. I understand your promise to the skaters, but this is a fine line you're walking here—legally, that is."

"I know," I said. It wasn't the first time it had happened, either. "But there's no proof that these things are all tied together."

"And you want to be the one to tie it up?"

I shrugged, then nodded. "I suppose so." I knew so. Equal parts ambition and curiosity were driving me.

Harrow's eyes had narrowed in suspicion. "What is it you want from me, Miss Powell?"

It was time to come out into the open. "I need to make contact with these people," I said bluntly. "And I figured you must have someone . . ."

Sandy Harrow stared blankly at me for a moment. Then his expression turned to one of amazement. "To the neo-Nazi groups? People like Eagle Road Church or White Nation? You want to make contact with them?"

I nodded. "You get your information somewhere," I said. "And from what I hear, it's extremely accurate information most of the time."

"And you want me to just hand over the name of someone who will talk to you? A source of mine?"

"Yes."

"So that you can infiltrate?" he asked in disbelief.

I hadn't planned that far in advance, but I nodded. "Yes," I repeated.

Sandy Harrow looked stunned. "I'm sorry, Ms. Powell, I don't think I can be of any assistance to you."

"I'll protect the source," I assured him. "No one will ever know. . . ."

"I don't think you have the slightest idea what you're asking." His voice was chilly. "I think this is all film noir fiction to you—spies and neo-Nazis and bullyboys. You haven't got a clue about these people you're asking me to put you in contact with, or what they're capable of." He stared almost angrily at me. "If you did, you couldn't possibly believe that you could just go waltzing into one of these enclaves and then waltz out again."

I was stung by his attitude, but I understood it—I must have appeared to be an overeager cub reporter with something to prove. "And you're underestimating me," I replied quietly. "I'm not that naive. I was almost killed investigating a *football* story, for God's sake—that hardly has the social implications of this kind of story. This is important." I stared at him.

He registered the information but shook his head. "No," he said. "I won't do it."

"Listen to me, Mr. Harrow," I said. "Someone is doing something horrible to these kids, and someone killed Terese Steiner. And I believe it's connected to the same people you're trying to expose. Anything that works to bring them into the open is worth the effort. Please help me."

"It's too dangerous. . . ."

"I'll be careful."

"And I don't like the fact that information is being withheld from the police. . . ."

"I'll tell them about the swastika Terese Steiner got," I said promptly. "That way I won't betray my promise to Ari and Shannon, but the police will have the pertinent information." I didn't say *when* I would tell them.

Harrow hesitated, staring into my eyes as if he could tell by looking how I'd handle myself in a threatening situation. Then he shook his head again. "I don't know, Miss Powell. I have to think about it."

That was clearly as far as he was willing to go. "Okay," I said. I scribbled my home number on the back of my business card and got up to leave. "Just in case."

Sandy Harrow's blue eyes were somber as he took it. "Just in case," he echoed.

I DIDN'T REALLY KNOW what to expect from the skaters when I arrived at the Bethlehem rink the following afternoon for the series of photo-op interviews I'd set up prior to Terese Steiner's murder. Terese's body had just been released by the medical examiner and was being flown to Germany, where she still had family, for burial. There was so much media attention focused on the tragic turn of events that how the skaters would deal with it was anybody's guess.

Outside the rink, the lot was empty except for parked cars; whether it was respect for the tragedy that had struck the competition or simply a prearranged lull in their well-planned assaults on Bill Bethlehem, the tobacco protesters were nowhere to be seen. Inside the arena the skaters were hard at work, leaping and spinning, concentrating ferociously on their movements. But there was no spark of normal excitement or competitive tension in the air; the atmosphere was so dampened and subdued that a feeling of overwhelming depression seemed to permeate the entire ice dome. That might have been my imagination, but I didn't think so.

I spotted Greta Braun, darkly clad and off in a corner of the arena, and I decided to try to get her on camera first. While Joelle Kistler was always cheerfully available for the media, this other one of the two reigning ice princesses was much more difficult to pin down. But I'd been persistent—everyone wanted to see Greta. And Braun had finally, after much sighing and emphasis on the scarcity of her time—and the demands made on it by much more important interviewers, i.e., the national press—agreed to a short taped interview. I had the feeling that Greta did these obligatory local news interviews just to keep in practice for the really big one that would accompany her *Time* cover story, the really big one she no doubt had her eye on.

I caught her attention as she came out of a graceful spiral spin, waving and gesturing at my crew. I expected a wait, but to my surprise, she promptly stopped what she was doing and came skating over to us, stopping only to retrieve a large black nylon knapsack from the judges' stand.

"Good afternoon, Miss Powell," she said in her husky, heavily accented voice. To my even greater surprise, she nodded courteously at Tony and Joe; technicians were generally beneath notice. Greta was dressed in a deep forest green turtlenecked sweater that hit her at midthigh over thick black tights and black skates; the dark severity of the practice clothing set off her exceptionally fair coloring and hair. It was one of her trademarks, this dark and dramatic clothing, even during practice sessions—never any pastels or whites for Greta. But despite the conscious attention she had paid to her image, it was obvious that she had been crying. There were dark circles under her light green eyes, and the tip of her slender nose was red.

I'd never seen Greta Braun exhibit much emotion at all before; even when she won at the giant events, her smile—practiced and set and always the same—seemed to be turned on for the close-up cameras and turned off again just as quickly as they stopped focusing on her. "Are you all right?" I asked impulsively.

Her pale eyes met mine and I saw the fatigue and tension as well as deep grief in them. She shook her head. "Not really," she said quietly. "Not at all." She sighed. "It has been a terrible night with almost no sleep, thinking about what has happened. I could please put on a little lipstick before we tape, yes?" She pointed to the black knapsack.

"Of course."

Greta took out a small makeup bag and quickly sketched some brownish plum color on her mouth and added a little blush to her cheeks. "Enough," she said wearily after a cursory glance into a compact mirror. "It is the best I can do. Nothing is really going to help today, I think." She looked candidly at me. "If you could use the long shots, perhaps, later we go back and film the closer ones of me talking to you. It is just . . . I don't want to look dead for the camera, yes?" As her own phrasing registered, her expression changed from controlled to bleak. "Oh my God, I didn't mean to say that . . . dead." She closed her eyes, her face a mask of pain.

Tony lifted an eyebrow in inquiry. I nodded, and he and Joe faded into the background.

"Why don't we sit down here and just talk off the record for a few minutes?" I suggested to Greta, and she nodded with obvious relief.

One person I'd never have expected to need a warm-up period before an interview was the consummately cool and professional Greta Braun, but Terese Steiner's death had clearly shaken the skater to her core, and she wasn't making any effort to hide it. Greta and I sat down together in the front row of the bleachers.

"I'm so sorry about Miss Steiner," I said to her. "I know this must be terribly difficult for you."

Greta nodded, anger mixing with deep sadness in her expression. "It is such a terrible waste, this thing," she said, her voice hoarse. "After all that has happened back home for her to die like this in America, so much the . . . innocent victim. So unfair, I think."

We specialize in innocent victims over here, I thought grimly. "Were you two still close?" I ventured. "After your split, that is?"

Greta shrugged, a noncommittal gesture. "Not close, no, not to talk all the time and share every little thing, if that is what you mean. Not the way we were when I was young, when Terese was my coach." She looked quizzically at me. "But what you are really asking is if we had the rift, right? The big rumor that always people want to ask me about?"

It was my turn to shrug. Of course I was dying to know, but I knew it would be tacky to press the subject right now when Greta was vulnerable. Then again, nagged my less ethically stringent newshound inner voice, this could be a golden opportunity; Greta was so rarely revealing about anything. "Well, this can all be kept strictly off the record," I reminded her tactfully. "But naturally, it's up to you."

"We didn't part so badly or have the knock-down-drag-up," Greta told me firmly if not quite correctly. "And you can put that *in* the record. We just went . . . the separate ways when we came to the States. And when the rumors started, we just . . . let people think what they want." She shrugged, a rueful half smile hovering tentatively on her lips for just a moment.

"For the publicity?" I ventured.

Greta nodded. "Yes," she admitted frankly, "for that reason. It is almost always a good thing to have, you see, even if it's not so good." Her green eyes met mine.

I nodded. "There's a pretty famous saying to that effect," I murmured.

Greta didn't catch the reference. "It is not so unusual, you know, for a skater to outgrow a coach," she told me.

"Outgrow?"

"Yes . . . no." A frown creased her pale forehead. "It is not what it sounds, it is not a bad thing to happen, it is quite natural. And it is, how do you say . . . mutual, yes? When a skater has gone so far as she can with only one person, no matter how good that person is. It becomes the . . . beneficial action for the skater to make a change, you understand?"

I nodded. "Yes, I think I do."

"It forces you to grow and make things . . . different. And for a skater in competition, you must be a . . . what is the word? You must provide the drama and the changes, or you fall behind."

A consistent chameleon, I thought. Someone utterly predictable in technical skills but varying in artistic interpretation. Greta Braun was nothing if not technically excellent all the time and dramatically mutable in her presentation, veering in her music choices from Bizet to Charlie Parker to Jerry Lee Lewis. "So it was your decision to leave Miss Steiner and go with Milo Vonderah?"

Greta nodded. "Yes, I had been thinking about making the change for over one year, and when Terese took Kistler on, that was what made up my mind to really go." She shrugged. "I did not want to be one of two stars, only one of one."

Her English could have been a little better, but her point was perfectly clear.

"And you think it's been the right thing to do, obviously," I said, coaxing her to run with her own train of thought. "Training with Vonderah has given you that fresh approach?"

Braun nodded slowly. "Yes, of course, look just at my record. But now, for this terrible thing to happen to her . . ." Her voice shook a little. "It makes me wonder if I hadn't left Terese when I did, if things had not changed, perhaps this might have never happened." She tugged nervously on a chain around her neck, glancing down at the the heavy gold cross she pulled from beneath her sweater. She fingered it, as if the talisman could bring back the luck and the life that had run out for Terese Steiner.

"Don't do that to yourself," I said a little more sharply than I intended.

"Don't do what?" she asked, clearly surprised at the intensity of my tone.

"Don't second-guess what might have been or what might not have happened," I said. I was in the unfortunate position to know what I was talking about: I had spent far too much time agonizing over the question of whether I could have saved the life of a singer named Jenny Blue if I had arrived at her apartment ten minutes earlier than I had, when I found her bullet-riddled body sprawled on the floor of her luxurious bathroom. Even now, the memory made me queasy and sad and angry. "The 'ifs' will get you," I continued. "You can 'if' yourself to Nevada and back, but it won't change anything. It can't. Believe me, hindsight doesn't count."

"You honestly think not?" she asked curiously.

"I know not," I replied. After all, as Nick Strummer had reminded me more than a few times during soul-racking guiltfests of my own, there was a damned good chance that the only thing that might have changed had I arrived at Jenny's earlier was that I might have been a second corpse on the floor, instead of the person still alive to call the police.

Greta stared at me, then down at her shiny cross again. "Perhaps you are right," she said finally. "There is a time and a reason for everything, and perhaps what has happened to Terese, as terrible as it is, is only God's will."

I was startled by this swift, seemingly religious turnaround on Greta's part. I've never been quite able to make that apparently comforting connection between violent death and God's wishes, but then again, the concept of organized sports has always made far more fundamental sense to me than the concept of organized religion. "Well, maybe," I agreed dubiously.

"After all," Greta said matter-of-factly, "you have to look at the big picture. God brought Germany back together in his wisdom; who knows but that he wanted Terese with him."

For what? I wondered. To help him govern? This was a leap of logic—or perhaps it was a leap of faith—that defied instant analysis, so I played for time by changing the subject. Sort of. "That's a beautiful cross," I remarked, picking it up and studying it closely. It was a large, ornately engraved piece of jewelry set with diamonds and rubies. I supposed they were there to distract from the discomfort of the man with the nails in his extremities.

"It is a gift from Milo," Greta said. "We are both very devout."

"How nice," I said, for lack of anything better to say. "Did you know that Terese was Jewish?" It just popped out.

Greta turned light, pained eyes on me. "We didn't talk about religion," she said. "I knew she would not embrace our savior."

Yikes, I thought. "Greta, was there ever any . . . trouble about Terese? I mean, about her being Jewish? Or you being German?" I wasn't sure exactly where I was heading with this, but she'd provided an opening for me to start prying, and I wasn't going to let the opportunity pass.

Greta frowned. "About Terese, there were a few little"—she made a noncommittal hand gesture—"nasty comments. Back in Berlin, a long time ago. Oh, and in Prague, yes. But she ignored those people, they are just the, how do you say, fanatics?"

"That's how you say," I agreed. "And you?"

Greta wrinkled her nose. "For me, well, not really. I have been called a Nazi by other skaters—it is just silly. You know"—she shrugged—"when they lose they are angry. Is that what you mean?"

The question didn't seem to faze her any more than those silly Nazi comments had. Either she hadn't received the same kinds of nasty little missives as the other competitors, or she was a very good actress. "Yes," I said, "that's what I mean."

"But why do you ask?"

I shrugged. "No reason, really—just curious."

I didn't think she believed me, but it didn't seem to matter to her. She had regained her equilibrium and was focused on herself again, ready to skate for the cameras and talk for the cameras, so we proceeded to do what we'd come to the rink to do. We got some wonderful footage of Greta managing a very difficult double triple—a triple salchow followed by a triple toe loop.

"I guess she's recovered," Joe remarked.

I shrugged and nodded in agreement, but I didn't think she was quite as tough as I had before. "She's a pro," I reminded him.

Melinda Parsons had recovered as well. She was shocked and saddened by the murder of Terese Steiner, but it wasn't a personal loss to her. She said she saw it as just another example of rising urban crime in America, and another reason to work to push gun control legislation through. In this usually nonpolitical venue, I was certainly getting a lot of opinions about God and country this afternoon, I thought. We got a little footage of Melinda, her long-limbed grace notable, even in warm-ups; then she said she had to hurry off to a jazz dance lesson with her dance coach and choreographer.

"Melinda, I did an up close and personal with Ari and Shannon, and I've scheduled Greta, and the Canadian pairs—can you fit it in? The public is going to want to know about you."

She flashed a sardonic smile at me. "You bet!" she said. "I told you before, Miss Powell . . ."

"Kit."

"Okay, Kit, this is my one big shot—I'm going to grab every chance for publicity I can while I'm here. You want to interview me discussing philosophy with the dolphins at Sea World, I'm going to go for it. That's off the record, okay?"

I laughed—it seemed like the first time all day. "Okay," I agreed. We set a time for her to come to the station the following afternoon, and as she picked up her gym bag to head to the locker room, I said impulsively, "Listen, Melinda, I know what . . . that is . . ." I was stumbling uncomfortably over my words, and she looked quizzically at me. "I saw what was in your locker the other day," I told her.

Melinda Parsons's hazel eyes were suddenly wide and startled. She seemed to be at a loss for words.

"If there's anything I can do—"

"I don't want to talk about it," she said brusquely, and turned to go.

"Wait a second, Melinda, please," I called after her, and she turned reluctantly back. "Listen, I just want to help."

She stared blankly at me. "And how on earth do you think you can help?" she asked.

"By finding out who's behind it," I said firmly. "Have there been any more incidents like that?"

"I told you, I don't want to talk about it," she said, and walked rapidly away.

I jogged after her and caught her arm. "Listen to me," I said. "This isn't an isolated thing. You aren't the only one."

"What!" This information appeared to shock her even more than the revelation that I knew about the doll to begin with.

"Other skaters have been targeted, too," I told her.

"Really?" she said dubiously.

I didn't want to betray Ari and Shannon, but if I was going to assemble the pieces of the vague puzzle I sensed, I had to start digging and prying somewhere. "Really," I assured her. "Has this kind of thing ever happened before?"

She chewed on her lower lip for a moment, then appeared to make up her mind. "I got a letter right before I flew down here," she said, "warning me to stay away from the competition." She shrugged angrily. "You know, black skaters aren't exactly the norm, and we—well, we tend to stick out, I suppose."

"What did you do with the letter?" I asked. "Did you keep it?"

"I burned it," she said flatly. She glanced at her watch. "Listen, I really am running late."

"I'm sorry," I said. "I'll see you at the station tomorrow."

I waved Tony and Joe over from their vantage point at the empty judges' stand.

"Wow," Tony said, gesturing to Shannon Ngao, "I can't believe how high she jumps."

Joe nodded toward Susu Jenrette. "And I can't believe how cute she is."

"Can we chill the fan club?" I asked mildly. They were making me feel like I was at a high school pep rally and my boyfriend was drooling over the cheerleaders. "Never mind." I reversed myself promptly as I caught sight of Joelle Kistler's parents huddled with Bill Bethlehem in conference. "I'm going to see about Joelle," I told them. "You guys just keep on gazing wistfully at your lost youth."

"Bite it, Powell," Tony said genially. "You're the one who was a jockette—it's *your* misspent youth we're looking at."

I grimaced at the truth beneath the words. Not that I'd trade my adult status—and brains—for the teenage me, but I'd gladly have been able to perform some of those long-gone athletic feats. Volleyball, surfing, softball; now if I jogged on the beach or rode my stationary bike more than twice a week without getting achy afterward, I congratulated myself.

I caught Bill Bethlehem on his way down the stairs. He was polite but harried as I introduced myself. No wonder. Between the unexpected protesters and the shocking death of a coach, this no doubt wasn't how he had envisioned the grand opening of his arena, his business, his presence in the community.

"I don't have even a minute right now," he told me. "But you'll be at the Bethlehem Bash tomorrow night, won't you?"

I nodded; I wouldn't miss the gala opening of the rink and the flashy introduction of the skaters for anything.

"How about if I give you a few minutes on camera then?"

"That would be great," I said. He spoke to an assistant who jotted something down in a notebook, then rushed off.

I just managed to flag down the Kistlers as they, too, were about to leave the arena.

"How's Joelle?" I asked them sympathetically. Her parents exchanged glances. They were well dressed, a sandy-haired matched pair, but it was Ellen Kistler who was clearly in charge.

"I don't want to make any statements to the press," she said flatly. That was a first: Ellen Kistler usually couldn't get enough press coverage for her daughter.

"Don't worry," I assured her, "this is just me asking—my

crew's down there, and this is off the record." As was nearly every conversation I'd managed to have this afternoon.

Ellen Kistler seemed to gauge my sincerity, then shook her head. The worry lines on her Doris Day face seemed out of place. "She's not in the best shape," she finally admitted. "She hasn't come out of her suite for two days, and we can't get her to talk about it. She was talking about going to Germany with the body, but I . . . we persuaded her not to."

John Kistler looked just as worried as his wife. "Joelle is such a strong person," he told me. "I've never seen her react to anything like this."

She might be strong, I thought, but she was only nineteen, and nothing like this had ever happened to her before. A big part of her world had just been blown away. I wondered if these parents—rumored to be so supportive and well meaning—weren't discounting their daughter's chronological age just a little.

"Do you think she'll skate?" I asked.

They exchanged glances again.

"Of course she will," Ellen Kistler said firmly. A true skating mother, I thought, with a pang of sympathy for Joelle. It's a variation—and not a big one—on that better-known species of stage mother. Women living their dreams through their kids.

"First we have to work on getting her out of bed," John Kistler said quietly.

I gave them my card. "Please let me know if there's anything I can do," I said. "If Joelle decides she wants to make a statement—a tribute to Terese Steiner, whatever—I'd be happy to set it up."

I motioned for Tony and Joe to meet me at the door to the arena, and we emerged into the late afternoon sunshine and a mob scene.

Outside, the protesters had converged in force and were chanting and marching. There were already a couple of news crews filming.

"Want to get this?" Tony enquired.

I spotted another KSDG van and then saw Tricia, her blond hair glinting in the light.

"Too late," I said.

"Too bad," Joe said.

I shrugged and waved genially in her direction—maybe it would be distracting enough to make her blow a line—as we headed for our van. I was mulling over the various truncated conversations that had just taken place in the rink as we drove slowly around the milling protesters and headed out onto the road. An old beater of a car, something big and Bondoed, from the mid-seventies, swerved past us and sped up, barely missing scraping the side of the van.

"Asshole," Tony yelled.

I did a double take. The man driving the dented old car had slicked-back brown hair and dark glasses. But it was his passenger who caught my interest. Even with her eyes hidden behind large sunglasses, there was still no mistaking the auburn hair and Breck-girl profile of Joelle Kistler—the grief-stricken skater who hadn't, according to her parents, been out of bed, let alone out of her hotel suite, for the past two days.

7

I SPENT THE REST OF THE AFTERNOON editing a piece on the skaters. I tried to keep it upbeat, but since Terese Steiner's murder was still very much the lead-in hard-news story, there was no way to skirt the effect it was having on the competition. Right before he went on air, Max Flores asked me if I'd found anything out from my sources.

"No," I said. "My sources aren't talking."

"There's a lot of clamor about this one, Kit," Max said. "You know, the 'Are we the new Florida?' editorials, stuff like that? It would be really impressive if we could get the jump on any new facts that might emerge."

I frowned. "I know," I said. "I'm trying my best, Max."

"I know you are," he said.

I put in a call to Stan Mardigian, hoping I'd get some crumb of information I could pass on to Max, but Mardigian wasn't in. I left the station just a little after seven o'clock. It was raining again.

As I got into my car, I realized that I was feeling antsy, verging on irritable, the way I always do when there's too much information swirling around inside my head in a way that doesn't completely add up. And I knew I couldn't make it work yet; I'd just be worrying the fragments like a surly terrier if I kept at it. I needed a break, if only for a little while.

I'd been sort of neglecting my family recently—not that my various siblings can't take care of themselves or go for weeks on end with no communication, and not that my parents don't have enough to keep them busy. But when petty familial squabbles and differences are put aside, we get along pretty well, and contact with them does keep me grounded in some way. Even though I knew I'd be forced to face some gentle but annoying probing into my personal life, I decided a quick stop at my dad's bar in Linda Vista would let some fresh air into my head and do me good. I viewed it as a kind of reentry: my father's personal questions would be a lot less intrusive than my mother's, so this was a way of diving back into the family without getting the bends.

"Jesus," I muttered to myself, "listen to what you just thought." It figured: homilies and homespun wisdom abound among the Powells, but the metaphors sometimes get mixed along the way.

I headed for the Ringside, my father's pride and joy, the sports bar he's owned since the sixties when he dropped out of his real business-world job as a sales representative. I practically grew up at the Ringside, being naturally inclined toward an interest in sports myself and happy to be hanging out someplace where I wasn't expected to look like a Barbie doll—fat chance—or behave like a perky Mouseketeer. The bartender, Ernie, and the regulars were an extension of our family.

And it wasn't as if my mother, Betty, could ever really object to my hanging around there; after all, it's the family business. Never mind that my presence at the Ringside instead of at home pretty much precluded her steering me toward ruffled dresses and neatly combed hair. Betty shrugged it off fairly good-naturedly—after all, my sister, Janet, was everything a normal mother could hope for in a normal daughter. One out of two wasn't bad. And my brothers didn't count: they were *expected* to be interested in what went on at the Ringside. I was an aberration, but a tolerable one.

The blue neon sign of a boxer throwing the same punch again and again winked cheerily at me through the rain as I turned up the slickened street, and I could feel myself crank down a notch just looking at it. I pulled into the lot next to the bar and hurried through a minidownpour toward the heavy front door. Inside, the familiar smoky atmosphere greeted me like a comfortable bathrobe, and Ernie looked up briefly from the glass he was polishing and smiled, a horizontal crease in his wizened face. He didn't say anything, but he rarely does. As a bartender, he once explained to me, his main professional function in life was to listen to people; he'd taken that job requirement seriously enough to expand it to normal social intercourse, too. Once in a while an opinion would pop out, but not for want of his trying to hold it in.

"Hey, honey!" My grizzled, cheerful dad appeared next to me and gave me a bear hug that nearly knocked me off balance. Mike is aging, but he's still a big guy. It served him well when he first took over the Ringside, whose clientele back then was a mixture of bikers and rowdy sailors looking to blow off steam. He had turned it into more of what he terms a nice neighborhood saloon, and that conversion had occasionally required a bouncerlike approach to unwanted customers. "Where have you been keeping yourself?"

"Work," I said, throwing my purse onto the bar and hopping up on a stool. "Been jammed." I smiled at Ernie. "Can I have a glass of chardonnay?"

He made a face.

"Okay, a draft."

"I saw your piece on the Bethlehem Pro-Am," Mike said. "So what's the deal? Are you going to milk that one?" He winked at me, his hazel eyes—older, lined versions of my own—bright and knowing.

"Oh, give me a break!" I laughed. "It's not called milking it when it's an ongoing story, it's called following up. And there's plenty of stuff to follow with this one. The competition hasn't even started and look how much publicity it's already generating."

"I think it's great that he built that arena," Mike said.

"I think it's great that he's bringing jobs to the area," said Stu Palliser, a newcomer—relatively speaking—to the regular circuit. Stu hadn't found his way to the Ringside more than ten years ago, which made him a neophyte at this bar.

"Have they found out anything about the death of that coach?" my dad asked.

I shook my head. "Not that I know of."

Mike's eyes turned suddenly speculative and I braced myself. "Hasn't Nick mentioned anything to you about the investigation?"

"No." I smiled blandly. I'd made the now-apparent mistake of bringing Nick Strummer to a family picnic a few months back. He had actually seemed to enjoy it, but I couldn't say the same for me: I'd spent the entire afternoon keeping an eagle eye on my mother, who kept staring at Nick as though he were the final piece in the jigsaw puzzle of her children's lives, just waiting to be popped into place so that Betty could relax and stop worrying that her recalcitrant younger daughter might spend the rest of her life as a divorcée.

"Really?" my father prodded.

Luckily for me, cranky Artie Malone unwittingly interceded on what threatened to become a more personal inquiry.

"Personally, I think it's ridiculous how much attention this skating nonsense is getting," Artie called over from his regular seat at the end of the curved red-vinyl bar. "I can remember a time when nobody in their right mind paid any attention to figure skating and all those sissy sports."

Myrna, a lady of indeterminate age and tough constitution, looked up from her shot at the billiard table. "Don't be such an old-fashioned fart," she said crossly to Artie. "You can probably remember when Shoeless Joe was in knee pants, too."

I stifled a laugh. Mike and I had secretly speculated that the Myrna and Artie had—or had once had—something going.

Right on cue, Artie shot Myrna a very sour look and sent a hefty plume of cigar smoke in her direction. You wouldn't find tobacco protesters at the Ringside. "What do you know?" he muttered.

"I'd watch it if I were you, Artie," I said genially. "You sounded just like John Weidendecker when you called skating a sissy sport."

Artie had the grace to look horrified. Windy was the last person on earth any serious sports devotee who hung around the Ringside ever wanted to be likened to. "Well," he amended grudgingly, "I guess these days it could be called a real sport. Sort of."

"That's the spirit of conciliation, Artie," Mel Boudreaux piped up. He was in his usual spot, too, directly in front of the big screen, which tonight, for some unfathomable reason, actually had college wrestling on it. "Keep up with the times."

Artie grumbled and shot both Mel and Myrna a dirty look. Love triangle? I wondered hopefully.

"So what's been going on, Pop?" I asked my dad as I took a sip of my beer.

"Well . . ." Mike stretched the moment for effect, then broke into a big grin. "I've got some good news. Your mother and I are going to be grandparents."

I couldn't figure out why he was so excited: he and my mother are already grandparents, seven times over. "Don't tell me Janet's pregnant *again,*" I groaned. My sister had sworn to me that after the birth of her fourth child she was through breeding forever. I have no idea how she does it, any of it—personally, I get exhausted just trying to keep track of the birthdays of her four and my oldest brother Pete's three. Never mind Christmas, which is a nightmare.

"No, it's not Janet." Mike shook his head looking like the proverbial canary-swallowing cat. "It's Mason and Felice."

My mouth dropped open. Mason, my closest sibling—literally and figuratively—had shocked everyone a year ago by marrying Felice Bruckner, a petite, savvy woman a little older than he and definitely not Mason's historical choice, the brainless cream-puff beach-bunny type. Dark, sophisticated, smart as a whip, Felice was of that certain age which demands biological reproduction now or never. And I had a feeling that the word *never* wasn't a major part of her vocabulary.

"That's great!" I exclaimed. I guiltily remembered two unanswered recent phone messages from Mason. I knew they'd been trying to have a kid, but things hadn't been happening according to plan. They had spent a small fortune on various fertility drugs and procedures I didn't really want to hear the details about. "That is really terrific. Finally. So when's Felice due?"

Mike shook his head. "They gave up, they're adopting," he informed me.

"You're kidding," I said.

"Uh-uh." Mike shook his head again. "It's one of those private things."

Warning bells went off in my head. I'd done some of the research on that very topic for a heartwarming Tricia Blaize piece on adoption that had aired about eight months ago, something she had insisted on calling "Boomers Go Bust on Baby Making," and I knew that the process was incredibly expensive and not always strictly aboveboard. "Really?" I said dubiously. "They're going to go that route?"

"It's going to cost them a bundle," Mike continued cheerfully, "but at least they know they're getting a healthy baby."

Don't bet on it, I thought. Given all the horror stories splashed across front pages about custody battles and women who never intended to give their babies up, what guarantees were there really? Of course, you could always go to Haiti or South America and find an unwanted baby, or you could fly off to Romania in hopes of finding a perfect blond infant and take your chances with their nightmarish paperwork systems and hinky prenatal care.

"So . . . do they have a prospective mom already?" I hazarded.

"Sure do," Mike nodded happily. "A little gal from Palm Desert—they contacted her through a private adoption lawyer."

Uh-oh, I thought.

"That's . . . great," I said. "I'll call Mase when I get home and get all the details from him."

"Yeah," Mike said, "he's real happy. So's Felice."

"I'll bet."

"Your mother . . . ," he began.

"Well," I said, picking up my purse before he could remind me that Betty wouldn't be truly happy until all her children had replicated. "I'd better be shoving off."

Mike gave me a look that said, I know exactly what you're doing. But all he said out loud was, "Don't forget Kelly's birthday party Sunday afternoon."

"Huh?"

"Kit!" Mike looked shocked. "Kelly is your godchild as well as your niece. You'd better be there or we'll never hear the end of it from Janet." He fixed me with his sternest glare. "Pinky's Pizza Party Heaven, one o'clock sharp."

"Oh yeah. Well, I'll try to make it," I said evasively.

"You'd better do more than try. And in case you haven't thought about it, she wants new Rollerblades."

I kissed Mike on the cheek, waved good-bye to the regulars and Ernie, and made my escape, suddenly tired. Maybe it was just the thought of Pinky's Pizza Party Heaven and all the bells and whistles and kid confusion it portended, but I wanted badly to be home in my quiet little haven.

I drove across the bridge and pulled gratefully into the overgrown driveway by my clapboard bungalow. Dancer was waiting by the door, his tabby fur ruffled and pumpkin colored, his amber eyes slitted down. He doesn't like me all that much, but true to feline nature, he resents the hell out of it when I'm not around to pay him what passes for the requisite amount of attention in his little kitty brain. He meowed, then swatted at my ankle to race through the door first. I let him; Dancer usually wins in these little ego contests.

My mail was pure junk except for a postcard from my friend Lori, who was vacationing on Majorca with a fellow lawyer. I read the card with a pang of envy for sunny beaches and a sunny love life, tossed the rest, then fed Dancer, who was hunkered down by his bowl, looking mean if not lean.

I had just shucked my work clothes sloppily, thinking about a trip to the dry cleaners, and pulled on jeans and a sweatshirt when there was a knock at the front door. I glanced at the clock and frowned: it was past nine, and I don't encourage people to just show up at my door at night unannounced. Maybe it was Woody, I thought, my across-the-street ex-marine neighbor—a sort of one-man neighborhood watch—with the latest in burglarproof window locks he wanted to install. I padded to the door and looked through the peephole, then pulled it open.

"Hello," I said calmly to Nick Strummer.

"Can I come in?" He stood on the front porch, his pale blond hair glinting silver in the lamplight, his eyes the same shade behind wire-rims, his trench coat beaded.

I hesitated. "Sure."

Inside the little front hallway, Nick shrugged out of his coat and hung it familiarly on a brass hook behind the door. Well, why shouldn't he? He'd spent enough time here.

"Drink?" I said. It seemed to be the easiest course: keeping my verbalization level to monosyllables, at least until I knew why he was here. The sight of him had begun to produce the predictable internal reaction in me: attraction combined with anger and sadness.

"Sure, Jack . . . ," he began, then shut his mouth. As if I didn't know.

I poured the Jack Daniels for him and a glass of chardonnay for myself, and sat politely in the overstuffed green plush chair across from him in the living room. I wanted to keep space between us, even if it was just to demonstrate that I could: Nick had been doing a pretty good job of that himself lately. I had told myself that it didn't matter, that I didn't miss him. But here he was, sitting on my couch just as he had a hundred times before, all khaki-blond-silver, all bland exterior over a tough, edgy inside. And I felt my throat constrict a little as I waited for him to speak.

His first words were unexpectedly wimpy. "So . . . what's new?" he asked.

I stared at him for a beat. "You mean, like what's new at the office?" I asked sweetly. "Well, let's see. There's this icky murder of a skating coach that I'm very curious about, but . . ." I shrugged. "I just can't seem to get anyone from the police to talk to me about it."

"Kit, it's an open investigation," he began.

"My sources seem to have just dried up. Imagine that."

Nick shrugged wearily. "What do you want to know?" he asked.

I might as well get something useful out of this, I thought. "Was Terese Steiner killed at that freeway underpass?"

"We don't know yet."

"Did she get any suspicious calls? Any threats?"

"Not that we've turned up," he said shortly.

"Where's the car she was driving?"

Nick's face got grimmer. "We haven't found it yet."

I wasn't in the mood to be nice. "Doing a bang-up job, aren't you?" I sniped. "It's only the biggest story in town."

He looked straight at me. "I know this isn't about Steiner, Kit. I really fucked up, didn't I?" He took off his glasses and massaged the crease between his eyes.

"Oh, I don't know," I said coolly. "Murders do get solved after the trail has grown cold. Some murders, anyway."

He looked at me quizzically. "You aren't going to make this easy for me, are you?" he asked.

I thought about games and evasions and pretense. Then I shook my head. "No," I said evenly.

He nodded, accepting the truncated honesty of my reply. "You know," he said, "I don't want to stop seeing you."

"How would I know that?" I countered, feeling a cold anger beginning to rise.

"Because you know me," he said simply.

I felt my anger become tempered with unwanted compassion: I'd been through a divorce, I know about the turmoil involved. About the desire to run to someplace safe—to someone; about the equally strong desire to pull in and protect yourself. But I wasn't about to offer that up to Nick as a salve, and so I just looked at him, waiting to hear what would come next.

He took a sip of his drink. "I know I've been remote, I know I've been avoiding you . . . us." His gray eyes went deep and troubled. "I just can't . . . I have two busted-up marriages behind me, Kit. I don't know what the hell I'm doing getting involved with someone else before I know why I've never been able to make it work before."

"Maybe you should have thought of that earlier."

Nick sighed. "I guess I wasn't thinking at all. And we just started so *fast*. . . ."

"Yes," I said neutrally. "We did." A sudden, vivid memory of one wonderfully intimate, relaxed weekend we'd spent up in Ojai jabbed at me with a visceral immediacy. Wheeler Hot Springs hadn't generated the only steam then. I shoved the memory down, away.

He looked ruefully at me. "Are you playing shrink here?" he asked. "Are you just going to nod and say 'mm-hmm,' and ask me how did I feel about that?"

"I'm not going to ask you how you feel about anything, Nick," I snapped.

"Are you going to talk to me at all?" he asked mildly.

I stared at him without blinking. "Apparently you want a sounding board this evening, and that's what I'm obligingly providing. That and a drink. Anything else is smoke." I tried to control the fury that was beginning to run through my veins.

"You aren't being fair, Kit. I want to work things out, I want to be able to see you. . . ."

"At your convenience?"

"I didn't mean it that way."

I shook my head in amazement. "You really think this is your call, Nick?"

He had the gall to look surprised. "You're furious, aren't you?" What insight. "I'll get over it," I said coldly.

"I didn't mean to hurt you. . . ."

That did it. Condescension makes me go ballistic. "Listen, if this visit is just your way of relieving a guilty conscience for your shoddy behavior . . ." The words began to pour out.

"I'm sorry—" Nick made an effort, but it was like trying to stop a steamroller.

". . . for your shoddy, shitty, disrespectful behavior . . ."

"Kit! Damnit, listen to me—"

". . . then consider it done. Consider it *all* done! You can tell yourself you gave it your best shot, Nick, for what that's worth. Now get the fuck out of my house!"

There was no mistaking my sincerity. Nick had seen me angry before—everyone who's close to me has. But this was different; even when we'd quarreled before, this kind of intensity and simmering rage hadn't been present. Neither had so much willingness to just walk away from whatever it was we had begun. Nick Strummer is a very smart man with instincts like a bloodhound's, when it comes to investigation, at least. He must have known that in trying to make amends the way he did, he'd made a real mistake with me—pushed every wrong button it was possible to push in such a short time. And as the door shut behind him, I wondered for the first time if Nick's two ex-wives hadn't known exactly what they were doing when they had said adios, muchacho, to him.

I was pouring myself another glass of wine when the phone rang. I snatched it up, ready to bite the head off any unsuspecting caller.

"Is this Miss Powell?" asked an unfamiliar male voice. "Kit Powell?"

I hesitated—I didn't need any more surprises this evening.

"Yes," I finally said.

"My name is Donny," the man told me. "I heard from a mutual acquaintance that you'd like some information about . . . certain kinds of gatherings."

It took me a moment to register what I was hearing. Then I realized that Sandy Harrow had rethought his position after all. I felt a little thrill of anxiety and satisfaction. "Are you from Eagle Road?" I asked.

"Not them."

"White Nation?"

There was a pause. "Yes," said Donny.

All right, I thought triumphantly. "I would definitely like to talk to you," I said. "Is it possible for us to meet somewhere?"

"I could come to your place."

"No!" I said hastily. "That is, my husband wouldn't, well . . ."

"I get the picture," the man named Donny said. "But I'm kind of choosy myself when it comes to being seen, if you catch my drift."

"Um . . . how about the zoo?" I ventured. The weather had been so rotten I figured it was a good call: there wouldn't be many people there, but it was still wide open and public, a safe place.

"That's okay," he agreed. "Tomorrow at two, at the big-cat compound."

"Fine," I said. "How will I know you?"

"Oh, don't worry," Donny assured me. "I know who you are."

It was a little creepy to hear that, but I am on television a couple of times a week. "Okay," I said. "Two o'clock."

"Miss Powell, the information isn't free."

"Oh! Of course not," I said hastily. "How much exactly does information cost these days?"

"One-fifty," he said.

I winced. Explaining this to Doll in order to ransack petty cash was going to be some task. "Fine," I said.

"Cash."

What did he think I was going to bring, a personal check? "I'll see you tomorrow," I said, and hung up.

I got myself to bed quickly before anything else unsettling or infuriating could happen. I spent a very restless night.

I CAN'T SAY that Doll's reaction came as a complete surprise.

"I absolutely cannot authorize giving you that much money out of petty cash without an explanation," he said to me. He shook his head emphatically, his tiny little china blue eyes glinting with suspicion.

"Oh, come on, Doll, it's not very much money," I countered. "We spend more than that on sweet rolls for the staff every month."

Doll's lips compressed. "You're right," he admitted. "So let me amend that statement, Powell. I can do any damned thing I please; what I really meant to say was that I *won't* give you that much cash without some sort of an explanation."

"Just trust me," I said equally emphatically. "I really need it. This could turn out to be a big story, Doll, a very big story—the kind that could make you a happy guy."

Doll laced his hands behind his neck and tilted his desk chair back. It was a dangerous angle that lifted his stubby little legs completely off the floor, and I knew it was all for show. He gazed up at the ceiling in phony contemplation, then came back to earth and stared cynically at me. "Oh, I trust you, Powell," he said. "What I trust you to do is always go sticking your nose in places where it doesn't necessarily belong, which right now, if I'm not mistaken—and the last time I looked I was still the station manager and pretty well aware of what everyone was working on around here—is a series of puff pieces on a figure skating competition." The cynical look turned to a glare. "So what exactly are we talking about here as far as this sudden need for cash?"

This was going to take some tactical tap dancing, I could see. But I like to play things a little close to the vest: maybe a full explanation could be avoided if I handled it right. "I am working on the figure skating pieces," I said sincerely. "And this is, well, it's *related* to skating," I added vaguely, making a drifty gesture with my hand.

Doll snorted. "Uh-huh. Sure, it is. So what do you need the cash for, brand-new blades?" Evasive tactics didn't appear to be working.

I stared stubbornly at Doll, but he wasn't backing down.

"Come on, Kit," he said. "You're going to have to tell me what this is all about." Sudden comprehension lit up his blue eyes. "Does this have something to do with these tobacco protesters?" he demanded. "Is that what this is? Because you know damned well that HRH Blaize has co-opted that story for herself and if you step on her toes, she's not going to be happy." He snorted. "To put it mildly."

"No, no—it's not that at all." I shook my head. I realized I had to come at least marginally clean; this pleading business was going to go nowhere if I didn't. "Doll, listen." I leaned forward earnestly and gripped the front edge of his desk—it was about the only clear spot on it. "I really need this. I have the chance to buy some information about something I think may connect to the murder of Terese Steiner."

His brow furrowed. "The skating coach?"

I nodded. "Yes."

"What the hell are you talking about? You have an . . . informant?" he asked me in disbelief.

"Well," I hedged. "Sort of."

"About a murder?" The decibel level in Doll's little office began to soar. "Good Christ, Kit, you're a sports reporter!"

"I'm also still an investigative reporter," I reminded him sharply. "Remember? Twice the work at not much more pay, Doll." Considering that the marginal pay scale at an independent like KSDG wasn't exactly going to buy me a mansion in La Jolla anytime soon, even working double duty, I'm certainly not above reminding Doll of that fact when the occasion calls for it, i.e., when guilt is required as the motivating factor in any professional negotiation. "Besides," I reminded him, "this is a lead story, and no one has turned up zip on it so far."

Doll took a measured sip of his coffee as he considered my words. "You know," he said, stroking his chin thoughtfully, "I seem to remember that the last time we had a conversation like this you were heading down to the docks to meet with a mobster on his boat."

"Yacht," I corrected him automatically.

"Alone," Doll continued. "A suspected killer. To have a nice little chat, just the two of you, and see what you could dig up. About a murder. Am I right?" It was a rhetorical question; Doll has a knack for remembering details. "Also, if I recall correctly, it was raining then, too." He smiled grimly at me. I knew that smile: it meant that either I really talked, gave him everything I knew or thought I knew, or the cash for the mysterious Donny was coming out of my own pocket.

"Okay." I threw my hands up in a gesture of resignation. I wasn't about to spring for a payoff, and besides, I reminded myself, it wouldn't hurt to have someone aware of what I was doing. Someone who had more of a vested interest in wondering about my safety than Sandy Harrow did. At least this way Doll would know if I went missing. "Here's the deal." I launched into a rapid explanation of what I had discovered, what I suspected, and how I believed it all could be tenuously tied together. I admitted that the connection between Steiner's murder and those of the transients had nothing in common except location, but I pointed out the thread of racial hatred that seemed to run through all these events—the killings and the messages to the skaters. As I talked, Doll's expression went from skeptical disbelief to merely dubious to, at last, genuinely interested.

"Well?" I demanded when I had finished. "What do you think?"

He shook his head slowly. "What I think is you may be taking a dive into a real quagmire on a pretty slim premise."

"But?"

"But go ahead and dive, if that's really what you want to do."

I nodded with satisfaction. "So you think there's a connection, too, don't you?"

Doll gazed up toward the ceiling for a moment, then directly at me, his eyes deadly serious now. "I think that whether or not there's any kind of connection that you can prove, you're about to ruffle some feathers in a big way. And these are not easygoing folks."

"It could be a big story," I reminded him again. "Think about it, Doll."

Of course, that's exactly what he was thinking about.

"Do I get the money?" I persisted.

"You get the money." He reached into his drawer for a voucher. "Promise me you'll be careful with this, Kit."

"I will," I agreed, taking the voucher. He wasn't talking about money. "I promise. Thanks." I got up to leave.

"Powell?"

"Yes?"

"So what does your cop friend think about all this?"

At least he had the grace not to assume Nick was still my significant other. Or the sensitivity not to phrase it that way, given that Tricia had no doubt already broadcast all around the station the fact that I had denied Nick was my boyfriend any longer. I hated the idea that I was fodder for gossip, but there wasn't much I could do about it. Alan McGill, of course, in his status as my closest friend at work, already knew; but he achieved that status by being able to keep his mouth shut. "I haven't exactly talked to him about it," I dodged. "Not in detail, anyway."

"Uh-huh," Doll said, nodding sagely. "I see. Well, considering where this might be heading, maybe you should."

I shrugged and pretended to think it over. "Maybe I will."

I got out of Doll's office and headed over to my own desk, brooding about his last words of advice. Like hell I'd discuss this with Nick Strummer, I thought as I gathered my things. I'd spent a basically sleepless night, but it had more to do with anxiety about today's meeting than it did with Nick. Like most of my alleged adventures with members of the opposite sex, I thought ruefully, this one had all the earmarks of a colossal misadventure, but

I wasn't about to let it throw me off my stride. Been there, done that, as they say.

I ignored John Weidendecker, who was wearing an expression I'd seen before and knew all too well: those furrowed red creases around his eyes indicated that he was sober enough to suspect that I just might be on to something he wanted for himself, and that he was probably going to make trouble. Fat chance, Porky, I thought grimly, and gave him a patently phony grin and cheerful wave as I left the newsroom. No way he was getting his meaty hands on any of this stuff.

I knew Doll might throw Windy a bone and allow double coverage of the opening of the Bethlehem Arena, since it was a big local event, but he certainly wouldn't let him near the figure skaters. Weidendecker, with his proudly Neanderthal attitude, was all but guaranteed to make a huge gaffe with them, and Doll knew it. As for the rest of it, well, I'd just have to hoard my sources and hide my suspicions in order to keep Weidendecker—and Tricia Blaize by association and general nastiness of intent—off the track. I could feel that old familiar creature called competition raise its sharp-toothed little head inside me as I cashed the voucher at the cashier's office. I stashed the money in the inside pocket of my trench coat and went out into the rain to meet Sandy Harrow's snitch.

The rain had slowed to a light drizzle as I paid my admission and entered the huge zoo. I'd been right about the choice; the inclement weather made it undesirable for throngs of the usual tourists. A few die-hard grade-school teachers were leading scraggling lines of small children along the paths and pointing out various species. The kids looked like ducklings in their little slickers and boots. They gabbled and exclaimed, pointed and skipped around; the weather didn't seem to faze them a bit. Maybe in a couple of years, I mused, Felice and Mason would have one of those of their own. I made a mental note to call them, since plans to do so had been completely blown out of the water last night, and wondered what Mason, who still seemed like a kid to me, would do with a child of his own. Probably go skateboarding with it, I thought, hang out in virtual-reality arcades together. If Felice would let them.

I arrived at the big-cat compound exactly on time but saw no one waiting for me, so I contented myself looking at the tigers snoozing the gray daylight hours away on the flat rocks under a sheltering ledge.

"Hello, Miss Powell."

I turned and came face-to-face with the tall, pale man who had moved silently up beside me. He had thinning straw-colored hair and paper-white skin with a few pockmarks. His eyes were a hidden behind very dark glasses, and his jean jacket hung loosely on his frame.

"Hello . . ."

"Call me Donny." A crooked smile revealed decent teeth.

"Donny," I nodded, but I couldn't bring myself to smile in response.

He removed the glasses to reveal pale blue eyes with large dark smudges of fatigue beneath them. His pupils were tiny pinpricks, even in the darkened afternoon. Great, I thought, a junkie. They make such reliable informants.

Washed-out eyes surveyed me up and down. "You look different than you do on television," he remarked neutrally. Then he put his glasses back on.

Lack of makeup, mousse, and spray will do that to you, but I wasn't here to engage in personal chatter. Still, I supposed we had to break the ice somehow. I shrugged. "Well, the cameras make a big difference. . . ." I ran out of small talk and plunged in. "So, the reason I wanted to see you is that Sandy Harrow thought you might be able to help me out with some—"

Donny rubbed his hands together nervously. "Money talks first."

"Yes. Of course." I reached hastily into my coat pocket, retrieved the envelope, and handed it to him.

He stuck it into his own jacket pocket. I must have looked surprised. "Don't worry, I trust you," he told me with a smirk. "Come on, let's walk."

We took off from the big cats down a windy, wet pathway;

leaves dripped from the foliage around and above us. I decided to let him begin.

He was restless, jittery. Watchful. "Known Sandy very long?" he asked.

"Not long," I replied. "How about you?"

The crooked smile appeared and disappeared again. "We've been doing some business together for a while," he told me. "He pays good and he always comes through, but I don't know what a guy like that's doin' working for that kike organization."

I kept my expression resolutely unresponsive but was tempted to suggest a detour into the reptile house. Donny was moving fast and I had to skip a step every now and then just to keep up with him. He seemed to be a man who spent a lot of time looking over his shoulder.

"So what is it that Harrow thought I could do for you?" he asked as we passed the hyena cage.

Cut to the chase, I thought. "I'd like to find out something about the White Nation," I replied. "And he thought you might be able to help me."

He stopped and swiveled, fixing on me a vague, curious look. "Why? You wanna join up?"

I hesitated for just a second. It was too early to reveal what I really wanted to know, whether this organization had anything to do with the transient murders. Or with Terese Steiner's death. "No, it's for . . . work."

His face showed no flicker of anything. He was still testing the waters. "What does White Nation have to do with sports?"

"Oh . . . it's not for my regular job," I lied promptly. "This is for an article I'm working on—it has nothing to do with the station."

He paused, thinking that over. "Then what do you want?"

"I'm trying to, well, break into serious journalism, maybe get a job with one of the big newsmagazines, get out of San Diego. And the competition's stiff—I need something different to stand out."

"Why White Nation?" he persisted.

"Because it's a hot topic," I replied evenly. Which was the truth. "Everyone wants to know more about what's going on inside organizations like White Nation. *Really* going on, I mean. The problems have been all over the news. . . ."

"Problems?" he echoed sharply. "What problems are you talking about?"

I had the idea that I had somehow offended him by implying that perhaps White Nation wasn't an adjunct of the Boy Scouts, so I hastily backtracked. "Problems in the cities, all the gangs and urban war zones and, um, racial tensions. The statistics, well—*you* know that violence is on the rise all over the country and that a lot of people think it all falls along color lines."

"What I know and what White Nation knows is that white people didn't start the shit that's going down in the cities, that we're being stomped on and our rights and our jobs are bein' taken away, and we have a right to defend ourselves against the enemy," he said sharply.

"Well, that's it, that's exactly what I mean," I told him with as much sincerity as I could muster, and I'm not a bad actress.

"You mean you agree with us?" he said, curiosity mixed with doubt.

The man, whatever else he was, wasn't stupid. And he was really listening to what I said. I'd have to be very careful. "I think both sides of every story need to be explored and presented with objectivity," I said calmly. "That's what real journalism always sets out to do."

"I thought all of you reporters were bleeding-heart liberals." Donny took a pack of Camels from his jacket pocket and lit one. He offered me the pack; I shook my head.

"The point is," I said, "that personal beliefs have nothing to do with journalism. You can't let them get in the way of being objective. It doesn't matter if I'm a liberal or a conservative personally, what matters is getting the story and getting it right."

Smoke streamed out through his nostrils. "You mean you'd be willing to just report the truth?" he said.

"Yes."

He nodded and scratched his arm, rubbing hard against the thick denim material. Then he hurried on ahead again, jittery and fast. I kept up. The rain began to come down harder and the zoo seemed utterly deserted and kind of sad.

"Hey, Donny, I'm getting soaked," I said, tugging at his sleeve. "Come on, let's sit down and I'll buy you a cup of coffee."

He checked out the surroundings as if he expected to see the Mossad come popping out of the bushes. Then he nodded okay, and we got out of the rain and sat down under a metal umbrella with two steaming plastic cups in front of us. Donny loaded his down with five packets of sugar and lit another cigarette with a shaky hand. I didn't know how long I could keep him sitting in one place.

"So what exactly is your connection with White Nation?" I asked him, trying to make conversation and keep him in one place.

He shrugged evasively. "I go to the meetings sometimes," he said. "I . . . believe in what they say."

"But you aren't an . . . official?" I probed.

Donny shook his head. "I don't much like groups of people on a regular basis," he said. "I'm more of a loner type." He glanced sharply at me, as if he'd revealed something he was worried about. "You aren't gonna write about me, are you?" he demanded. "I mean, if I help you with this?"

"Not unless you give me permission," I told him.

He shook his head emphatically. "Uh-uh, no way," he said. "I need the bread, that's all. That's why I tell Sandy what's goin' on when he wants to know. But no way I want my name connected to any story. These people are my friends."

"No problem," I said crisply. "You just get me into a meeting, and I promise, I'll look right through you if you're there. We never even met, okay?"

His eyes washed over me as he considered the proposition. I held my breath. The consideration phase went on a little too long, and I caught on. "There's more money in it," I offered.

Finally he nodded. "Okay, you're gonna have to get in with me, you want to go to a meeting, but it's gonna have to be like I just met you at . . . uh . . ." He seemed to be at a loss. Where did your average racist junkie develop his social relationships? I wondered.

"Coffee shop." I filled in the blank. "I'm a waitress at a place up in Linda Vista, and we got to talking about all the problems my kid's having at his school with the gangs. . . ."

"With the niggers and the greasers," Donny added promptly. "They're always causing trouble for white kids. Yeah, so we got to talking and I was telling you there's a lotta people just like you out there, and you said you wanted to meet them." He was getting into it, a spy at heart. "Yeah, that's good." He scratched his arm again.

I cringed inwardly but nodded placidly. "Okay, so that will work," I said.

"But you gotta do something about the way you look." Donny was staring at me speculatively. "You know, a lotta people know who you are—cause it's so weird to see a chick doing sports, guys like to watch. . . ."

I nodded hastily. "Really, that's no problem," I said just to stop him from talking. There are times when I don't even want to think about my audience—I've had more than enough suggestive phone calls and letters sent to the station to make me shy away from picturing who's out there watching. "A wig or something, I can look like a whole other person. So when does this happen?"

He paused. "Meetings aren't always regular," he said evasively, "but there's supposed to be one on Thursday night."

"Where?"

"Don't worry about it," he said. "I'll take you there."

Oh, terrific, I thought. "Fine," I said.

"I'll call you Thursday afternoon to let you know if we're on or not." He drained the last sugar-loaded drop of coffee and rose. "What kind of money were you thinking about paying for this, Kit?" he asked.

It made me queasy, hearing him use my first name that way. And I had no idea what to offer him. I squashed the sudden feeling that I was getting in way over my head. "A hundred?" I ventured.

He shook his head, the smirk back in place momentarily. "Actually, you know, I was thinking the figures should be moving up."

Doll was going to hit the roof. "I can't go more than that," I told him. "This is coming out of my pocket and—"

"And you TV people get paid plenty." His voice was harder now.

"Not really," I countered weakly.

He jiggled around for a few seconds, then shrugged. "Forget it," he said, and turned to leave.

"Donny, wait!" I called out.

He turned back, a stick figure against a gray green backdrop.

"Two hundred."

He stared up at the sky, then nodded. "I'll call you Thursday afternoon," he said.

And he was gone, vanishing into the gloomy afternoon like acid rain, money in his pocket, looking to get fixed. I shuddered and then read myself the riot act about being so reactive. After all, where I was planning to go on Thursday was bound to be a lot more bizarre than a quiet afternoon at the zoo with Donny.

I HELD MY TEMPER IN CHECK as the crew and I showed our press credentials and made our way into the arena for the Bethlehem Opening Celebration. I was still highly suspicious that, despite his denials, Doll had been happy to assign triple coverage of the media-loaded event just to keep me in my place: low person on the KSDG on-camera totem pole. He most definitely *hadn't* been happy to hear that all his hundred and fifty bucks of petty had bought him was some unverifiable information that White Nation might be holding a meeting this week, and that I might be able to get into it if I did a good enough job of disguising myself as a waitress and if a junkie informant came through on a promised bribe. I wouldn't have taken a bet on it myself, and Doll is no fool.

Alan McGill, the true oddsmaker in the newsroom, hadn't yet been apprised of that particular situation, but he had ambushed me on my way into the station for my spot on Wednesday evening and pulled me into a corner. Friend that he is, Alan gave me the news before I had to hear it from either of my two favorite coworkers: Tricia Blaize would be covering the Bethlehem event because the tobacco protesters had promised to show up in full force, and that was a potentially big story.

"Big deal," I shrugged. "I already have my hands full."

Alan shook his head. "That's not all, Kit," he said quietly. Then he told me the really bad news: John Weidendecker had somehow managed to co-opt the interview with Bill Bethlehem for himself.

It took me a minute to assimilate the information. "You're kidding," I said, stunned. "How the hell did he manage to . . . ?" I forced myself to regroup. I still have the skaters, I reminded myself, and that was important: finding out if anything else had happened to any of them was a crucial part of the story I was working on. Having Bethlehem taken away wasn't. But the more I thought about it, the angrier I got.

Alan could see it in my face, my posture. "Now, calm down before you kick Doll's door in," Alan warned me. "He's in a shitty mood."

"So am I!" I retorted.

I knocked and pushed Doll's door open before he could ask me to. "What the hell is going on?" I asked, glaring. "How did Windy get the Bill Bethlehem interview?"

"Bethlehem's press secretary requested him," Doll replied calmly.

"What?" I sank into a chair in disbelief. Bill Bethlehem had promised that interview to me. I said as much to Doll. "*Why?*"

Doll shrugged. "Don't know, Kit, but that's just what happened. I caught the call, and what was I supposed to say?"

I stared blankly at him. He was right, it wasn't an offer he could have refused.

"And as for Tricia," he continued, "who I'm certain is next on your list of complaints for me . . ."

"No," I shook my head. "I know why she's covering it. It's the tobacco protest thing, and that's hard news."

"That's exactly right," Doll replied. "Problem with that?"

"Not at all," I said coolly.

Doll eyed me suspiciously. It isn't like me to be so easily amenable. To anything.

"Honest," I said.

"Well, then," Doll shrugged. "That's all. And Kit?"

"Hmm?"

"Just stick to your assignment, okay?"

I glared at him. "I won't step on any important toes, Doll; you've got my word on it."

Right before I walked onto the set I pulled Alan aside for another hasty conference. "Do me a favor—see what you can find out about a call to Doll from Bill Bethlehem's office, okay?"

Alan grinned, eager to comply. *"No problema,"* he said breezily. He was hooked into the underground information system at the station better than anyone else, and there was little he liked to do more than figure out the intrigues that went on behind the scenes.

I delivered my profile of Ari Kotzloff and Shannon Ngao on the early edition of the news that evening, and it went off without a hitch. My presentation was calm and professional, despite sidelong, off-camera smirks from Windy and Tricia, who were clearly hoping I would break down on the set or something after getting the bad news from Doll. Instead, I glided through my segment like one of the ice dancers.

As I left the set, Max Flores whispered, "Nice job," and gave my arm a friendly squeeze. I was touched. Max never participates in the internecine catfighting at the station—he's genuinely a cut above that crap. But he always knows what's going on, and it was his tacit way of acknowledging his support. I smiled gratefully and thought I'd show Windy and Tricia that I, too, was genuinely a cut above that crap. At least until we got down into the trenches.

I reminded myself of that lofty aspiration as Tony, Joe, and I maneuvered our way into the Bethlehem Arena and surveyed the decked-out hall. Advertising banners circled the floor, all of them displaying the Bethlehem empire's most famous food products. The cigarette ads were just a little smaller and less prominent, but they were there, reminding me that just outside the door loomed Tricia Blaize. Tricia Blaize or the tobacco protesters—it was a toss-up, I mused, just who could create more havoc. Intertwined wreaths of gold and silver balloons arched across the arena, and gold and silver streamers waved gaily in an artificial breeze. Or maybe it was just the drift of the cool air that floated up from the ice.

The festivities were located on the concourse above the rink, and dressed-to-the-nines guests were already crowded in; the noise level was rising noticeably as the flesh pressers struggled to make themselves heard over the strains of a thirty-piece big band, which was in the middle of an even more than usually perky rendition of "In the Mood" that perpetual figure skating favorite. It was an upbeat, festive atmosphere despite the problems that loomed over the event, and I scanned the crowd, pointing my crew this way and that to get footage of important personages, politicians, athletes, and movers and shakers. I got a brief quote from Her Honor the Mayor, who was not unpredictably pleased as Punch to welcome Bethlehem Enterprises to the area.

The skaters were mingling, too, relaxed and self-promoting. Tonight would only feature a short bit of flashy exhibition skating; the rest was purely publicity and celebration. I was a little surprised to see Joelle Kistler in attendance. Looking pale but pretty in a short, flared black velvet skating skirt and leotard, she smiled halfheartedly at a little girl who presented her shyly with a long-stemmed red rose. "Did you get that?" I asked Tony.

He nodded.

I took Joelle's presence to mean that despite Terese Steiner's death, she was planning to compete. I was getting increasingly curious about the unpredictable Miss Kistler and her activities. We continued to circle the arena slowly, taking in the upscale glad-handing, the buzz of excitement, the aura of importance.

Then I spotted Bill Bethlehem up on the raised dais, next to the ice, with Weidendecker.

"How'd that happen?" Joe nudged me, looking in the same direction.

"Your guess is as good as mine," I told him.

"He'll screw it up, you know," Tony said supportively.

"I certainly hope so," I said fervently. Usually I restrain myself from wishing bad luck on others—it's karmically dangerous—but for Weidendecker, I made an exception.

"Miss Powell!" Ari Kotzloff hurried up to me. "I . . . we saw the piece on the show last night—it was terrific!" The big, gangly skater seemed fully recovered from the shock of the swastika, and in high spirits.

"Glad you liked it," I replied. "Where's Shannon?"

Ari scanned the crowd—with his height, it was a simple matter. "She should be here," he said, then shrugged. "Perhaps she is still getting on her makeup."

"Miss Powell!" It was Susu Jenrette, blond ponytail circled by a shocking pink ribbon that matched her dress. "Hi! Hello, Ari," she added.

Ari nodded brusquely and hurried off without a word. Susu looked at me and shrugged. "I'm just trying to be civil," she said. "You know, these younger skaters sometimes just don't have it down yet—there's more to life than competition, and it never hurts to be polite."

"And how are *you* feeling about Friday?" I asked Susu, while Tony trained the Steadicam on her.

She flashed a smile and looked confident. "Great," she confirmed. "Paul and I have never skated better together, and I feel as though my singles program has gotten stronger over the past two months, too."

"And you're going with the Ice Fantastic Show?"

Susu shrugged. "I think so," she said evasively. "I haven't made a final decision yet."

Which meant it depended on how much she could get from them as opposed to the Ice Capades or Ice Follies. Which in turn depended on how she skated in this competition.

"Paul's waving," Susu told me. "I'd better get backstage and get my skating gear on—after the exhibition the real party begins!"

I saw the skaters disappear from the crowd, filtering through well-wishers and autograph seekers, and I thought I should also head for the dressing rooms to get some footage. But as I turned toward the stairs, I felt a hand on my arm.

"Miss Powell." Sandy Harrow grinned down at me.

He was even taller than I had thought he was when I'd seen him sitting behind the desk at CEO. Six-three, at least, I thought, and lanky as a cowboy. His salt-and-pepper hair was thick and rumpled, his dark blue eyes friendly. A well-cut pin-striped suit and a maroon bow tie looked good on him. I grinned back.

"Mr. Harrow," I said. "What are you doing here?"

"I never turn down an invitation to an important event," he said with a mocking smile. "I can't afford to. You never know when you're going to stumble onto a potential contributor to the cause."

"Don't look at me," I cautioned him. "My sympathies are with you, but KSDG doesn't pay me enough to contribute to my own cause, let alone anyone else's."

Sandy took my arm and turned me away from Tony and Joe, who were trying not to look too overtly interested in what was going on.

"Did Donny get in touch with you?" he asked quietly.

I nodded. "Thank you—I wasn't certain you would do it."

Sandy nodded thoughtfully. "Neither was I. I guess you convinced me. What happened?"

"I met with him."

"And?" His blue eyes were very direct, inquisitive.

"He's going to take me to a meeting of the White Nation," I told him. "At least, if he comes through."

Harrow's angular face got even more creased. "He's not the most reliable—"

"I know," I cut him off. "He's a junkie."

Sandy Harrow stared at me, then did the unexpected. He laughed. "You're a lot faster than I am, Miss Powell. It took me four or five months to figure that out."

I shrugged. "It's not exactly a gift," I said.

"Could I . . ."

But Sandy Harrow didn't get to finish his question.

"Sandy!"

Sandy turned at the sound of his name and I turned with him. We both stared into Channing Philton Strummer's pretty face. And the second our eyes met I knew that she knew exactly who I was.

"Chan, darling!" He hugged her and gave her a friendly kiss. "Do you know Kit Powell?" he asked ingenuously. Behind him, I tried not to make eye contact with Tony, who was openly gaping. "Channing Strummer, Kit Powell."

"Nice to meet you, Miss Powell," Channing said without a bit of irony in her well-modulated voice. She held out a perfectly manicured hand and we shook politely. Channing Strummer was wearing a diamond the size of a stoplight on one finger. Not her ring finger. And not a piece of jewelry bought on a cop's salary, either. Her handshake was firm and her expression collected, and

I tried not to be too obvious as I studied her—natural light blond hair, thick and shiny, a lithe figure beneath a raw silk dress the color of the Caribbean, and perfect posture.

"How do you do?" I said, grateful this time that I'd put a fresh auburn rinse on my hair, that I'd taken some care with my minimal makeup, that I was looking professionally good in a chic khaki gabardine suit and heels high enough to show off my legs.

"Of course I know who she is, silly!" she chided Sandy. "She's a local celebrity."

"Not really . . . ," I demurred. For once in my life, I was actually at a loss for words.

"And Channing is one of CEO's staunchest supporters," Sandy told me.

More surprises. Channing Strummer of solid gold La Jolla background, product of private schools, yacht clubs, and cotillions, was a liberal? I saw the faintest trace of laughter in her round blue Dutch-doll eyes as she watched me digest this information. There was no rancor in her look, just a finely honed intelligence and amused understanding.

"Darling," Channing said to Sandy, "Listen. I came with Arnie Greist tonight, and he has tons of money he's looking to do something useful with—why don't you go talk to him?" She pointed to a well-built balding man in a dinner jacket.

Sandy shrugged and smiled at me. "I'll catch up with you later, Kit," he said. "I'm going to work the venue before everyone gets too smashed to think about good causes."

After he'd gone, Channing looked frankly at me. "I don't see any point in the two of us pretending we don't each know who the other is, do you?"

"No," I replied warily.

Channing Strummer's expression held something akin to sympathy in it. "Let me be frank and just get this out of the way. Nick is a very difficult man to deal with, and I hope you have better luck with him than I did."

I was taken aback by her open attitude. Whatever was or wasn't going on with their divorce or our relationship, I simply didn't want to stand around discussing it with Nick's ex-wife. It was too fantastically civilized. Too unreal. "I don't want to talk about Nick," I said bluntly.

Channing nodded in agreement. "Neither do I," she said. "I just wanted to clear the air and let you know that we don't have to play any games. Okay?"

"Okay," I said, relieved.

"Good," said Channing briskly. "Now, why don't you let me tell you about my involvement with the Youth Athletic Leagues and how having the arena is going to benefit underprivileged kids in the area."

As Channing talked about her part in the organization, a new project geared toward getting young kids off the streets before they could be recruited into gangs, I felt a reluctant admiration for her start to grow. She could be a little overwhelming; she seemed to be the kind of person with so much energy and multiple direction that just keeping up with the flow of information was a task. But she was impressive in her endeavors, no merely decorative Junior League wimp at all. She'd been actively involved in luring Bill Bethlehem to the area, and she was intent on improving the quality of life in San Diego.

"I don't want to press you if you feel uneasy with me, Kit, but I'd appreciate the opportunity to publicize our efforts." Channing was direct.

"You mean . . . on the sports segment?" I asked.

She shrugged, her movements fluid under the expensive silk. "Why not?" she asked.

"Wouldn't you be more comfortable with Tricia Blaize?" I asked curiously.

Channing shook her head. "I know Tricia from various charities, and I don't think she's the one for this kind of coverage. She'd turn it into a heartstrings story with no follow-up. We want to reach people who are already interested in sports and make them see it as a way to make a real contribution—you know, to get down there and coach in their spare time or donate equipment, that sort of thing."

I bit my lip, but a smile surfaced.

"What?" Channing asked.

"I know I just said I didn't want to talk about him, but I was just wondering," I mused, "how Nick could have gotten himself involved with two women who have an interest in sports when he's so uninterested himself."

Channing shook her head. "Nick only cares about one thing," she said. "Catching the bad guys." She laughed a little, but beneath the laugh I thought I could detect some bitterness. "But speaking of Tricia Blaize," she said, reversing the direction of the conversation, "why was she so adamant about getting Bill to talk to John Weidendecker?"

"What?" I said sharply.

"She called me early this morning and said that Weidendecker was dying to do the up-close coverage on Bill, and you had your hands full with the skaters. So I called Bill. . . ." She stared at me, comprehension dawning. "You didn't know, did you?"

I shook my head. "It doesn't matter," I lied. I'd throttle Tricia, I thought.

The big band blared out an earsplitting finale and pointed the trumpet section toward the dais.

Bill Bethlehem held up his arms and the crowd quieted. "Ladies and gentlemen," he said, "this is it." His smile was broad. "The official launch of the Bethlehem Arena, and the start of a new industrial and entertainment complex for southern California." There was an outburst of enthusiastic applause.

I turned to Channing. "Look," I said quietly, "I have to get down to the rink—he's going to announce the exhibition skating in a couple of minutes, and I need to get footage of the skaters."

She nodded. "I'll see you at the competitions, right?"

"Of course, and we'll set up that interview after the meet is over, okay?"

"Great," Channing said.

I'd do that interview with her, all right, I thought. And even if it took a surreptitious phone call to Stan Mardigian, I'd make damned sure that Nick Strummer had his set turned on for that particular sports spot.

Channing Strummer turned her attention back to Bill Bethlehem, while Tony, Joe, and I maneuvered our way down the stairs and into the brightly lit passageway that led to and from the ice.

"Ah . . . Kit?" Tony ventured.

"Hmm?" I said, gently nudging my way through a small knot of people mesmerized by Bethlehem, who was throwing phrases like "the future of our country" and "the bright light of youth" around.

"Was that . . . uh . . . ?"

"Yes," I said. "It was."

Tony and Joe exchanged looks.

In the hallway that led to the dressing rooms, a few of the skaters were already present. Even though tonight was to be strictly exhibition, I didn't want to disturb them as they worked up their concentration level. I just wanted to get some footage as they streamed out, get the feeling of the tension and energy. . . .

There was a loud exclamation from the women's dressing room as the double doors banged noisily open and Joelle Kistler stomped out, followed by her mother.

"Sweetheart, you don't have to . . . ," Ellen Kistler was saying, grabbing at Joelle's arm.

Joelle turned, her pretty face filled with an ugly fury. "Get your hands off me and don't tell me what I should or shouldn't do!"

Her father, concern written on his bland features, hurried over. "What's the problem?"

Other skaters and coaches were staring. Susu Jenrette and Melinda Parsons had stopped on their way down the hallway, their eyes riveted on the young star. Paul Cavanaugh was positively wide-eyed as he stared at Joelle. Shannon Ngao stared down at the floor, embarrassed. Even Greta Braun made no effort to hide her interest in Joelle's display of temper.

"The problem is you!" Joelle exclaimed, glaring at her parents. "Both of you!" Color had risen on her cheeks, and she seemed to be forcing tears back. "From now on, I make my own decisions. By myself. *Alone.*" The last word was almost spit at the bewildered Kistlers. Then Joelle whirled and ran away from them.

In the shocked silence that followed the outburst, we could hear Bill Bethlehem wind up his speech with the announcement that the crowd would be thrilled and delighted by what they were about to see: the best young skaters in the country.

The skaters recovered their equilibrium beautifully, making a

99

spectacular, racing entrance onto the ice. All dazzling smiles and acrobatic leaps, whirling and waving to the wildly enthusiastic audience. And the most dazzling smile of them all was on Joelle Kistler's face as she spun into the lights.

10

DONNY'S BEAT-UP RANCHERO smelled of years of cigarette smoke and other less immediately recognizable things I didn't want to know about. As we headed out of town, northeast on the 163 to the 15, past the city and into a dull, undulating series of brownish hills and unremarkable terrain, I did my best to remain relaxed and observant. I wanted to be able to full pay attention to my surroundings, to be able to recall everything I saw and heard; and if I was nervous, I knew I would miss things. I would also run the risk of drawing attention to myself at the White Nation rally, which was the last thing I wanted to do. I took deep, quiet breaths and watched the hills flatten down, then rise again. Eventually, we entered a broad canyon in the northernmost part of the county. The area was sparsely populated with small ranches and unfamiliar to me. I glanced sideways at Donny's profile. In the inky night, his eyes were still hidden behind those dark glasses, and I figured there was no point in asking where we were going.

He hadn't given me much time to get ready, which was no doubt his intent: he'd called me at the station just before five and told me to be waiting on E Street between Seventh and Eighth at seven o'clock, leaving me scrambling to get home across the bridge and back again, in my new persona. I thought I had done a pretty good job of turning myself into a faded nonentity. Temporary blond color, the kind used on Halloween, was sprayed over my own auburn hair, which was now scraped back into a tight, flimsy ponytail; the roots that showed probably lent authenticity to the look. No makeup except a slight cosmetic reddening of the tip of my nose and the rims of my eyes gave me a washed-out rabbity look, and large plastic pink-rimmed glasses added to the pallid appearance. Over old jeans and two T-shirts I wore a dark, bulky Orlon sweater from Goodwill and a quilted down jacket in a dull green. I looked tired, shapeless, and—I hoped—invisible.

As I had waited in front of the post office for Donny to show, the simultaneous absurdity and danger of my situation had made me want to turn tail and run. But just as I was actually considering it, Donny had pulled up in the dark and parked, motor running. When I approached, he looked me over sharply, then motioned me into the Ranchero. He nodded his approval as he pulled away from the curb. "You did a good job; you don't look nothin' like you do on TV," he'd commented. Of course, he'd said pretty much the same thing at the zoo. Then we'd driven in scratchy silence, Donny chain-smoking, me wondering what the hell I was doing.

"Don't say much when we get there, okay?" he asked abruptly after twenty-five minutes, turning three-quarters toward me in the dark.

"I wasn't planning to," I assured him.

"You're not carrying a hidden tape recorder or anything like that, are you?"

"No."

"Sure?"

I glanced over at him. "I'm sure," I said. "I don't even have a notebook with me."

He chewed on his lower lip for a bit. "Then how're you gonna remember what happens, so you can be—what'd you say?— objective, in your article."

"I'm trained to remember accurately," I told him. "That's what journalists do." The truth was even though I do have a good memory, I'd have given my right arm for a hidden aid of some sort—camera, tape recorder, whatever—but I was too scared to risk it. What if they frisked newcomers at these little gatherings? I glanced around in the darkness, thinking how isolated this country was, even a half hour out of the city. It was the perfect spot for a disappearance. I forced the thought out of my mind. After all, I reminded myself, Doll knew I was going. But, of course, he had no more idea exactly where I was headed than I did. All he could do was notify the right people if I didn't show up for work the next day. Big comfort.

A few miles into the canyon, Donny made an arcing right turn into a dirt drive that seemed to come out of nowhere and seemed to lead to the same place. I could just make out split-rail fencing in disrepair and weedy pastures to both sides of me.

"Is this someone's ranch?" I finally ventured as we bumped over rutted, muddy dirt.

"Mm-hmm," Donny replied.

So much for probing questions. I tightened inwardly, and as a large open area packed with cars came into view, I tried to compose my expression to one of meek forgettability. Donny pulled the Ranchero to a stop between a Dodge van and newer pickup and turned off the engine. He lit another cigarette. "Don't forget our story," he said to me.

I nodded. "My name is Ilene Beechum, I'm a waitress at the Jolly Roger and the mother of one miserable adolescent brat, I know, I know."

Donny stared at me; I wondered what he could see from behind those dark glasses at night. "You gotta sound like you mean it," he told me with an edge to his voice.

Flippancy is a defense, and Donny had heard it in my voice and gotten—rightfully—nervous. "I will," I assured him. "If anyone asks."

"Someone'll ask," Donny said as he swung his car door open.

I followed him around the side of a run-down ranch house and across a weedy backyard to a barn. Then we skirted the barn and arrived at an open area that had been set up with folding chairs and a makeshift dais. There were probably seventy-five people there already, some milling around and talking, some already sitting in the rows of folding chairs facing the stage. I saw a lot of men, a fair number of women, kids of every age, from toddlers to skinheaded teenagers. It could have been any kind of rural social gathering, except that the large purple banner draped above the platform was adorned with a gold swastika flanked by two crosses; the crosses were angled to intersect beneath it, forming a symbolic cup or holder for the infamous Nazi emblem. I thought about the swastika Ari had received and supressed a shudder. On one side of the banner the American flag was hung; on the other, the Confederate colors waved. No shortage of symbols, I thought grimly. Behind the dais, a huge bonfire blazed in the night.

Some casual greetings came Donny's way, and the few glances that were directed at me seemed only mildly curious, more dismissive. I felt a little relieved—the disguise appeared to be working. Now all I had to do was keep my mouth shut; that's normally difficult, but even a prying confrontational type like me has self-preservation instincts, and looking around, I knew this was the place for those instincts to go into high gear. There were all types of people there, in all types of clothing; but what was predominant was paramilitary attire and roughneck wear, and since this was no summer outing, the ready-for-battle look was unnerving.

"Hey, Donny, how're ya' doin?" The man who slapped Donny familiarly on the back had the look of a well-fed businessman, a Rotarian type in a cheesy off-the-rack suit—he was all smiles and handshakes and who-knew-what beneath the surface.

Donny introduced me to Harve by his first name only. Harve nodded congenially. "And what brings you here?" he asked, small, pale eyes more probing than the innocuous question.

"I met Ilene up at . . . ," Donny began.

"The coffee shop where I work in L.V.," I interrupted. The less specific the information, the better. "Donny was so sweet—he saw me having some trouble with these . . . boys."

A flicker of immediate recognition and disgust passed across Harve's face. He couldn't possibly know if my veiled reference was to black, Hispanic, Middle Eastern . . . boys, but clearly it didn't matter. There was us and there was them, and that was that.

I glanced meaningfully at Donny, who took the cue. "They were saying . . . suggestive stuff," he told Harve. "You know."

"And he told them to quit hassling me or they'd be sorry," I barreled on, "and then after they left, well, we got talking. . . ."

Harve grimaced. "Uppity bastards," he growled. "No decent white woman should have to put up with that."

I wondered if I'd actually ever heard someone say the word

"uppity" before. I felt like I was in a scene from *Gone with the Wind*. "And her kid, too," Donny interjected. "He's in one of those damned mixed schools, and he's been having some trouble."

Harve nodded angrily, his weak little chin set. "Goddamned aliens and goddamned busing," he muttered. "Pardon my French, Ilene. You've come to the right place. We're going to be changing some things in this country, things that have been going too damned wrong for too damned long."

"How?" I asked, doing my best to make the question sound like a wistful plea. "I mean, is it really possible to change?"

"Just listen to Gene," Harve told me. "He's got a recipe to cook down the stinking liberal bastards and take back what's meant to be ours." I nodded as though I knew what he meant. "This is my wife, Bonita," he said as a round-faced woman approached. "Honey, this is Ilene, and she's new."

Bonita smiled pleasantly at me and nodded.

"She's been having some trouble with her boy at school—you know," Harve said meaningfully.

Bonita's light eyes, as round as her plump, pale face, narrowed down. "Huh," she said. "How old is he?"

"Ryan's going on fourteen," I told her, trying to put maternal pride in my voice.

Bonita nodded again, knowingly this time. "That's such a tough age with them anyway," she said, "and what's happening in the schools just makes it that much worse. It's hard enough to try to keep them in line to begin with, but what with worrying if they're gonna come home with a broken nose or wind up in emergency with a bullet in their gut, well . . ."

I nodded rapidly in agreement. "Exactly! And I'm just so . . . scared."

"I know," she said sympathetically. "Listen, Gene's about ready to start the rally, you want to come sit with me and the wives?"

I hesitated and pretended to consider the option. "Um," I said, "I think I'd like to just stay with Donny," I told her. "But thanks anyway."

Donny and Harve had gotten into a conversation with two

other men, and Bonita took my arm and turned me aside. Behind us, the bonfire leaped and lit the night sky. "Do you know Donny real well?" she asked.

I shook my head. "Not really," I said. "We just met." Then I repeated the bogus story of Donny's chivalrous interference in my little problem at work, how one thing had led to another.

"Well, I suppose it can be a little intimidating to walk into one of these meetings without knowing anyone," Bonita said, "but we're always happy to see new faces here." She leaned toward me conspiratorially. "Listen, Ilene, Donny's a nice enough guy, but . . . well, he's got a few problems that maybe you should know about before you get real close."

"Oh?" I said, widening my eyes. "Like what?"

"Let's just say he's not the most reliable person," Bonita told me. "Not the best, well, role model for your boy."

I waited a beat, then nodded. "Well, I think I understand what you mean," I said. "Besides, I don't really think of him that way—he's more like a friend, you know?"

She smiled at me. "After Gene's through, we'll talk," she said, and returned to a group of women and children gathered toward the back of the crowd.

The crowd took their seats and quieted as a large, balding man in a three-piece suit, flanked by two equally large men, climbed the stairs to the platform. A strong burst of applause greeted him, and he nodded; his eyes, shadowed behind aviator glasses, swept the crowd. Donny and I sat.

"Good evening, good people," the man said in a booming voice that matched his powerful physique.

"Good evening, Gene," the crowd chorused.

"Eugene Ebberly," Donny murmured in my ear. "He's the leader of the group."

That's made for you and me? I wondered.

"Please rise for the Pledge of Allegiance."

We stood again and faced the flags and placed our hands over our hearts. The White Nation had enhanced the pledge with a few specifics of their own. Instead of "the United States of America," White Nation preferred, "the white United States of America." "Under God" became "under a Christian God," and "with liberty and justice for all" became "with liberty and justice for us." I felt a chill go through me. Tweaking the language even a little could make a very big difference in interpretation, especially for those who wanted to hear it.

Eugene Ebberly remained standing as the rest of us took our seats again, and then, without a preamble, he launched into what was more an impassioned blend of sermon and incitement to riot than a speech. Ebberly was a commanding figure, a charismatic speaker in the fundamentalist church manner; his phrasing was almost musically rhythmic, punctuated with emphatic repetition of key inflammatory words and phrases. I watched and listened, fascinated, as he recounted incident after incident that proved how decent white Christian folks in this country were losing their entire piece of the pie—which, according to Ebberly, should be the whole pie, no matter what the shifting ethnic statistics of the country showed.

He built a hate-filled case for justifiable outrage, filled with erroneous facts and figures aimed at hammering one point home, again and again: white Christian folks just struggling to keep their heads above water were being beaten down at every turn, and that was just plain wrong. He raged at what he called the left-wing courts that sided with minorities who didn't have any legal right to be here in the first place.

"They don't even take the time to learn our language," he hissed, leaning forward over the podium to look his audience in the eye. "And they're taking it all from us! This crazy upside-down system is giving filthy brown foreigners the breaks and jobs that should being going to folks like us!" There was a burst of applause, like gunfire.

This same system, he continued, was forcing our children to attend dangerous mixed schools where creationism was scoffed at and God mocked. He castigated an administration that served Satan; the Jewish moneylenders who financed the commies; the Hollywood power brokers who produced the on-screen garbage that promoted un-Christian values such as homosexuality, free love, and the killing of unborn babies; the radical feminists who wanted to castrate all men and practice witchcraft and baby burning.

He gripped the podium and his voice shook. "On every corner, we see them!" he said, a sweat breaking out on his forehead. "The welfare cheats and the scummy, lazy panhandlers who would rather beg and steal, break into our houses and rob us, than do a day's work for a day's wages." His eyes were fiery as he vilified the Italian and South American drug dealers who conspired to bring the country to its knees by addicting and enslaving our youth, turning them into zombies and prostitutes. Behind him, the bonfire crackled in the night with the promise of things to come, of apocalypse and anger.

It wasn't anything I hadn't heard before, but I had never heard it presented all at one time, all in one place, to a crowd of people who were true believers, people unquestionably accepting of all they were being told. Even when Eugene Ebberly slanted the facts and figures beyond the wildest fiction, even when he told blatantly outrageous lies, the nods and the murmurs of approval and belief didn't stop. It was like witnessing a mass hypnotism; not a doubt or a question was voiced. He fanned the frustration and fear of the people in the crowd into a vocal and active anger as he wound up to his fever-pitched finale.

"This symbol," he shouted, pointing emphatically at the swastika in the middle of the banner, "is not something to be despised! It is *not* something to be ashamed of believing in! It is the sign of the righteous and the good, of the best manifestation of God's plan. Good people, Adolf Hitler was a great man!"

A chorus of loud assent greeted him.

"He was a man with a vision! A man who saw with a clear and accurate eye what could happen if the dark forces were allowed to gain control over the light, if the evil disbelievers grabbed the scepter of power from those who have been entrusted by God to do his work!" He gestured again, this time to the crossed crosses. "And these, the symbols of God and purity and righteousness, these crosses are meant to defend the swastika, defend the holy, defend the good people of America—to defend us!"

"Right on, Eugene!" someone shouted.

"God bless you!"

Gene Ebberly raised his hands in the air. "We will take back this country of ours before it is too late," he shouted, "because we know that what they are doing far away in Bosnia is not wrong, it is right and it is righteous! Decent white Christians, just like you and me, engaged in the fight of their lives. The fight *for* their lives! Let the Jew bastard media call it ethnic cleansing, let them tremble before the power and try to lie to us, let them call it anything they want! Because we know the truth! *I* know and *you* know that God has called upon them to take back their country from the powers of darkness, and I know and you know that he has called upon us to do the very same thing, right here!"

The crowd roared and Eugene Ebberly shook his uplifted fists. "And together," he shouted, "we will do it! We will take back what is rightfully ours, no matter what means we have to use! We have been driven to desperation and outrage, and if we do not act now, and act with all the force the Lord has put at our disposal, then we will surely lose this battle. And we cannot—we *will* not— lose it! Stand with me and fight for what is right, what is just! And God bless America!"

The applause was thunderous as the crowd leaped to its feet, and a huge cross appeared in the bonfire, blazing and sparking into the night. Beside me, Donny clapping as loudly as anyone. I wanted to vomit.

"What happens now?" I asked him as Eugene Ebberly made his way off the platform.

"We break up into groups," Donny said. "Discussion and action groups." He glanced sideways at me. "They don't encourage newcomers to participate except in the discussion groups. Especially women."

I took the hint and made my way through the chattering crowd toward Bonita and the wives. It was clear that only a radical feminist baby-burning witch would wish to be included in any real action that might be taken: *Kinder, Kirche, Küche* mentality all the way. I nodded and smiled and tried to blend in as the ladies served punch and cookies and talked among themselves about the brilliance of Ebberly and how we were finally going to make the country safe again for the children, God bless them. I looked at the kids running around and wondered what hearing and seeing all of this did to them psychologically, safety aside. I lied with ease about my own precious teen Ryan and the problems he was having with those gang-banging, welfare-cheating un-Americans at that scummy interracial school. I threw myself into my role with all the feeling I could muster, and no one seemed to question me, although as a single woman I did garner a few suspicious looks from the happily married ones who knew their place . . . and how to keep a man. I felt frustrated and jittery: among the little women, no one was talking about action of any kind. No one mentioned the transients or clandestine activities, and I didn't dare bring the subjects up. I was a newcomer, and their ranks were tight.

I kept an eye on Donny, and eventually, after what appeared to be the hard-core inner circle of Ebberly's lieutenants had retreated into the house, Donny waved at me from the group of men he was talking with, and I walked over to him.

"Well, Ilene?" Harve beamed at me. "What do you think?"

I smiled wanly at him. "I swear, I don't think I've heard so much plain common sense in one place in all my life!" I exclaimed. "It made me feel . . . so much safer, just listening."

"Exactly right, Ilene," Harve nodded. "That's it exactly."

"We gotta be taking off, Harve," Donny said.

"Hope we'll be seeing you again, Ilene," Harve said to me.

"Oh, you will," I assured him. Just turn on the news sometime.

"And bring that boy of yours along, too."

And start the brainwashing young. I nodded. "I'll do that." I glanced at Donny, a signal to get moving, then nodded vaguely at the group we were standing with. Abruptly, my heart lurched into triple time. One of the men in the circle had greasy, slicked-back brown hair and a made-for-trouble face partially hidden behind dark glasses. I glanced quickly away and waved again to Bonita, then looked covertly back at him again. There was no doubt in my mind. I was certain this was the same man I'd seen talking to Joelle Kistler outside the Bethlehem Arena, the man who didn't look like any ordinary skating fan I'd ever seen. The same man who'd sideswiped the KSDG van and raced past us, with the allegedly grieving and shut-in-her-room Joelle sitting beside him. His cursory glance ran across me and passed without a flicker of recognition.

Donny and I trudged back across the fields, around the barn and the house, and got into his car in the muddy lot in silence. As we turned out of the long driveway and back onto the dark canyon road, I breathed a sigh of relief, even though the safe haven of San Diego proper was still a half hour away.

"So, what'd you think?" Donny asked finally.

"It was very interesting," I said noncommittally.

"Get what you needed?"

"There's a lot of area to be covered," I told him seriously. "I'd like to go to another meeting with you, if that would be okay."

Donny thought about it, then shrugged. "I was watching carefully, and nobody seemed to have any idea who you really were," he said. "So it's all right, I guess." He was silent for a moment. "But did you, like, understand what we're trying to do?" he asked.

How sweet, I thought grimly, there was more complexity to this man than I'd suspected. He wasn't just a junkie and an informant, he really did believe in the cause; he really did want to encourage converts—even among the cynical and satanic media. "Yes," I said. "I think so. But the angle that I think I'd like to pursue, well—I *was* a little surprised that it was so . . . religious."

"Why?" It was Donny's turn to be surprised. "We're talking about real Christianity here, Kit—it's exactly what the Lord says in the Bible, chapter for chapter and verse for verse. Not any of that watered down bullshit the Catholics try to pass off."

"I guess," I said vaguely, deciding that discussing religious philosophy with Donny had its limits. "Donny," I said, "do you know the name of the man who was in the group you were talking to when we left? The tallish guy with the dark brown hair; he wears it sort of slicked back—he had on a blue plaid flannel shirt?"

He glanced my way curiously in the dark car, then shook his head. "I've seen him around at meetings before, but I don't exactly know his name," he said. "Why?"

I shrugged. "I don't know, he looked kind of familiar to me, but I couldn't place him."

Donny reached for a cigarette. He was getting twitchy. "A lotta people tend to stay kinda . . . low profile under these circumstances, you know what I mean? There's a lot of first-name-only folks in the group, especially if they're maybe involved with some of the more aggressive actions the group's taking."

"What kind of aggressive actions?" I pounced.

"Oh, you know, defending our rights. . . ."

"Come on, Donny," I said, frustrated with the lack of information I'd managed to glean this evening, "can't you be a little more specific than that?"

His glance cut sideways at me in the dark. "What exactly are you after?" he asked softly.

I felt a sudden heightening sense of danger in the car. "I . . . well, there's a rumor that White Nation is involved in those transient murders," I said finally. After all, it was no secret.

"Oh yeah. I heard that," Donny said.

"Are they?" I ventured.

Donny shook his head. "I don't think you should be asking those kinds of questions," he said. "You could get into real trouble."

I looked around at the desolate mountainous terrain outside. "Okay, let's just drop it," I said. "But that guy I was asking about—just one more question. Is he involved in . . . action?"

Donny shrugged again. "Maybe. He knows some of the guys, I know that, and he looks like he's maybe originally from the Iron Chapter."

"What's that?" I asked.

"Iron, you know, like iron bars," Donny said impatiently.

"Do you mean someone who is recruited in prison?" I ventured.

"Recruited, huh!" Donny laughed scornfully. "That's a joke. Don't need to recruit in the joint, Kit. Guys there *dyin'* to get protection from the nigger rapists and murderers; they kill to get protection from White Nation behind bars."

Literally, I supposed; that made sense, given the context. The isolation, the insular thinking, the us-against-them closed-mindedness—they could be nurtured in the perverse hothouse setting of prison life. It could spring militantly committed supremacists with, in their minds, justifiable violent action to be taken, right into the arms of the Eugene Ebberlys of the world.

We rode the rest of the way into town in silence, and after Donny dropped me in front of the post office, with a promise to call me when the next rally was set, I drove home with more questions than I'd begun the evening with.

11

MOST OF THE WAY HOME, cruising easily with the light traffic in the city and across the bridge, I struggled to mesh the divergent images I'd seen, to make some sort of sense out of what seemed to be an increasingly complicated and messy puzzle; but I utterly failed to come up with a rational explanation for personal contact between a sheltered young athlete and a white supremacist who was probably also an ex-con. I jiggled and nagged and twisted at the problem, but no form emerged. Okay, I finally told myself, frustrated, let's back-burner this for the moment and think about the entire evening instead. Maybe a clearer picture will emerge if you approach it that way. So I turned my attention to everything I had seen and heard.

One of the things that had specifically struck me among all the rhetoric and hate mongering was Eugene Ebberly's invocation of the phrase "ethnic cleansing," and his linking it—by proximity in his speech—to the existence of panhandlers and "welfare cheats," his phrase. Given the distortions of the polemics here, the idea of ethnic cleansing could very easily be broadened out, generalized, and applied to the killing of any group that was considered undesirable—unfit to reap the benefits of the White Nation's closed society. Maybe I was reaching for connecting straws; maybe, I told myself, I just wanted to believe that any group spouting such hatred would act on its philosophy. But somehow I couldn't let go of the feeling that the White Nation was responsible for the transient deaths. Not some disenfranchised skinheads or sociopathic loner working on his own. I wanted to get this all down on paper and chew it over with Max, maybe with Doll and Alan, too, in the morning. As I exited the bridge and drove up the dark, quiet streets, I thought the first thing I'd do when I got home was shower and get the grime of both my disguise and that meeting off me. Then I'd flip on my computer and write down everything I remembered about the meeting.

I knew my plans were shot as soon as I turned up my block. Nick Strummer's sensible black Taurus was parked at a very insensible angle in my driveway, and the man himself was pacing on my doorstep. "Shit," I muttered as I climbed out of my car and he came striding toward me, a heated anger emanating off him in palpable waves, even at a distance.

He stopped on the sidewalk and glared at me, and I tried to just look quizzical and cool. I had a feeling it wouldn't work, and it didn't.

"It was you!" he exclaimed without bothering to greet me.

"How do," I said, trying for offhanded.

"Interesting outfit," he snapped as I brushed past him and unlocked my front door.

"Is this a fashion consultation?" I asked mildly. "Because if it is, you really didn't have to come all this way. . . ."

Dancer rushed by and hissed, ruining my entrance, but I managed to make it into my entryway without tripping. Nick was on my heels. He slammed the door shut behind us and grabbed my shoulders, twisting me to face him. There was real anger in his gray eyes. I felt the sinking sensation that you feel when you know you've been busted doing something you're not supposed to be doing. At the same time, I felt a twinge of satisfaction: Nick was worried.

"What the fuck were you doing at a White Nation rally?" he demanded.

"How did you know . . . ?" The words died in my throat as I realized there must have been an informant at the rally. And I'd been spotted.

"Are you out of your mind?" Nick rarely yells, but his voice was raised angrily now.

"Who saw me?" I countered, running mentally over the crowd.

I certainly hadn't spotted any undercover cops, but that, I supposed, was the whole point of undercover.

"It doesn't matter," Nick said, his voice rising a few decibels.

"It matters to me," I told him pointedly. "I thought I did a pretty good job of disguise."

He looked me up and down, gripping my shoulders harder than was comfortable. "You look like hell, all right, but it's not good enough."

There was no reply to that one. I shrugged out of his grip and turned away.

"I'm not leaving this house until I get an explanation," Nick said.

"What if I call the cops?" I snapped without looking back. "I don't recall inviting you in." I headed through the living room and toward the hallway.

Nick was right beside me, vibrating with fury. I looked coldly at him. "And stop acting like I owe you any kind of explanation for anything I do!" I turned and headed off down the hall.

"This is official business," Nick said through gritted teeth.

I whirled and faced him again. "Is it?"

Some enigmatic expression flitted over his face. Maybe it was honesty, because he finally shook his head. "No," he admitted. "Not really."

Somehow, the admission took the wind out of me. "Okay," I said grudgingly. "But I've got to clean up before anything. Why don't you go make yourself a drink, and I'll take a quick shower."

Nick clearly wanted an explanation right now, but I just as clearly had the upper hand. He nodded slowly and turned back toward the living room. "Want me to feed Dancer?" he asked.

"Thanks," I replied, and shut the bathroom door behind me. As the hot water sluiced down over my body, washing away the blond coloring and the real and imagined dirt, I quelled the feeling of sadness that threatened to overwhelm me. Nick was in the living room with a drink; he'd fed my cat, he was waiting for me to join him. It sounded just like the romance it had been but was no longer. It was the tweaked version, filled with leftover concern but not much else. The tattered remnants of temporal and fragile passion.

I towel-dried my hair, pulled on some faded leggings and a Padres sweatshirt, and sighed. Time to face the music. Nick had poured me a drink as well, and I settled into the overstuffed chair that is Dancer's favorite scratching post and my security nook.

Nick was on the couch, looking impatient. "From the beginning," he said. "Please," he added.

I told him only what I thought I needed to tell him, about the investigation of the story for the station; about the rumors of White Nation's connection to the transient deaths—something he, of course, already knew; about Sandy Harrow's association with Donny. I even touched on my suspicions of a connection between Terese Steiner's death and those of the transients, although I left out the threats to the skaters. It was eerily reminiscent of what had transpired between Nick and me when we first met, when I was looking into the Sharks football team jinx and suspected foul play in the death of their general manager. Then, too, I'd left out a piece of the puzzle, hoping to break the story. I should have known better, but old habits die hard, and ambition just gets the better of my common sense sometimes.

It's a quality of mine that Nick is perfectly aware of. When I'd finished, he nodded slowly, mentally adding up the pieces of my story. Then he said, "I know there's something you aren't telling me, Kit."

I stared blankly at him and said nothing.

Something flared behind those steel-rimmed glasses. "Damn it, I was scared to death when I heard where you were!"

Leftover concern. "Will you tell me who spotted me?" I asked him.

Nick shook his head impatiently. "You know I can't do that."

It was an impasse. Nick knew I wasn't going to tell him anything more, I knew he wasn't going to give up the identity of his informant.

"They're dangerous, Kit," he tried again.

"I know," I said.

Nick stared down into his drink. "If I give you something, will you promise not to pull a stunt like that again?" he asked quietly.

"It depends on what you give me," I countered.

Nick blinked first. "Okay," he said. "Terese Steiner was not killed where we found her."

"So . . . what are you saying? That it's a coincidence about the location? Or are the killings related?"

"We don't think Steiner's death had anything to do with white supremacists," Nick said. "This part it strictly off the record, Kit—we're not going anywhere with the investigation of her murder. But the transient killings, well, we're getting very close to being able to make an arrest."

"How close?"

"Close," he said firmly.

"Is it White Nation?"

"There were similar transient killings up in San Jose last year," he said. "Where White Nation is very active."

"But no proof?"

Nick's mouth was tight. "Not yet." His eyes were unrevealing. "I promise you that the minute we have anything definite, the minute I know we're going to be able to pick someone up, I'll tell you. You can scoop the whole fucking world."

"Really?" I said.

Nick put his glass down and stood up, an unexpectedly bitter smile on his lips. "I keep my promises," he told me.

I couldn't argue with that, since I had no data to base it on. We'd never made any promises to each other. "Okay," I said flatly. I stood, too, but made no move to go with him as he walked toward the door.

He turned, his hand on the knob. "So you don't need to go to any more White Nation meetings, Kit. Do you understand?"

I nodded. "I understand." But I didn't make any promises, either.

After I heard his car start in the driveway and pull away from the house, I went to the phone and called Max Flores. I told him what Nick had told me and promised him the story as soon as I got it. Then I summoned up what energy I had left, turned on the computer, and made my notes. Finally, I got ready for bed, wondering who at that meeting had been the snitch. It could have been Donny, I mused—after all, he was already selling information to Sandy Harrow and to me; what would stop him from making a buck off the police? I thought back about the people I'd seen and talked to. Could it have been the gregarious, friendly Harve? Or the woman named Sally who had prodded me just a little harder than the others about where I lived and what I did? Or . . . could it be the strange man in sunglasses, the one I'd seen with Joelle? I fell asleep still wondering, but I didn't wake up with an answer.

THE EARLY MORNING MEETING at KSDG was somewhat energized by the news that we would be getting an exclusive on the murders. Even Tricia, before retreating into a sulky but unnervingly thoughtful silence, had the grace to thank me. Sort of. "So I guess this means you've patched things up with your boyfriend, or whatever he is, doesn't it?" she said pointedly. "I'm glad to hear it—you know I was concerned that it might affect your work." Well, there were only about eight people at the table listening to her—why should I mind?

Alan grimaced at me. I'd promised to meet him and Jay, his significant other, for drinks at some point later in the week and spill the whole can of beans or worms, whatever it was, to them. I just shook my head in resignation. Tricia might be up to her usual ice-pick-in-the-back routine, but Max and Doll were genuinely pleased. Max breaking this kind of story would focus viewer attention on the little local station, and it was exactly what KSDG liked to see. And I got the credit. Happy, happy day. I met privately with Max and Doll in Max's office after the general meeting and filled them in on my attendance at the White Nation rally.

Max swiveled in his leatherette armchair to stare hard at Doll. "You approved this?" he inquired.

Doll nodded, then shrugged in my general direction. "Powell is pig stubborn, Max, you know that. What's the difference if I approve or don't?"

Max looked at me, frowning, his intelligent dark eyes speculative and a little concerned. "Kit, it's not that I don't appreciate you going all out for information, I really do—God knows I want the stories. But honestly, this kind of stuff makes me very nervous. It's just too damned dangerous."

I shrugged. "It didn't come to anything," I said. "I'm here, safe in one piece, unrecognized . . ." Well, except for an undercover cop or some other snitch, a fact I didn't bother to mention. Thankfully, no one had thought to question any of the details about how Nick Strummer had come to divulge the information to me; I assumed that they assumed—just like Tricia assumed— that the pillow talk scenario was back in place. Only Alan McGill would be privy to the whole truth, and he hadn't even heard the story yet.

"Thank goodness," Max said.

"And anyway, it's over," I mused aloud. "I mean, I suppose there's no real reason to go back. . . ."

Doll glanced sharply at me. "There certainly isn't. No repeat performances."

"But what about the skaters?" I persisted.

Max looked sharply at me. "What about them?"

I filled him in on the gifts. Max looked thoroughly disgusted. "Jesus, they're just kids."

"Forget about it," Doll told me. "We have a full plate of stories to cover right now, and I'd prefer to keep you breathing, purely for selfish reasons. And the threats to the skaters aren't even some-thing we're going to touch, not at this point, so no more playing dress-up for you." He grinned wickedly at me. "And that was not a feministical comment."

We wrapped up and returned to work. Early in the afternoon, Melinda Parsons came to the studio to tape her interview with me, and as I had thought she would, she proved to be a self-contained, personable, and very focused interviewee. It didn't hurt things any that she was an arresting-looking young woman, either—Tony ac-tually let out a very unprofessional wolf whistle when Melinda, wearing a pale green cat suit covered with geometric designs in primary colors, walked in. With her coppery hair pulled straight off a face with stunning bone structure, her large green gold eyes, and her lovely smile, she was an absolute knockout. The camera liked her as much as it liked Joelle or Greta, who were both very pretty, too; but Melinda had something else, an additional spark of real-life intelligence, a grounded sense of purpose beyond the fanatic tunnel vision of most of the other competitors.

And in comparison to the taut, emotionally laden interview with Ari and Shannon, this one was a breeze. Melinda was well prepared to promote herself without being obnoxious or overbearing about it; and her story was such a marked contrast to those of the other skaters that it stood alone.

"So, what happens after the Bethlehem?" I asked her. "Whatever your standing is?"

Melinda smiled. "Whatever my standing is, I'm going to keep competing," she said. "As often as finances will allow it. And I'm going to keep teaching. If I get my 'big break' here, or anywhere else, maybe I'll be lucky enough to land a spot with one of the ice shows."

And if anyone—scout or management—was watching from any of those shows, I was certain they were already drawing up the contracts.

"I'm getting married in the fall," Melinda continued. She faced the camera and waved. "Hi, Mark," she said gaily. Out of the corner of my eye, I could see that Tony was crestfallen. Melinda turned back to me. "We plan to start a family in a couple of years, but until then, wherever the ice takes me . . ." She shrugged and smiled again. "I'm just thrilled to be here."

We wrapped it up, and I shook her hand. "You are really a terrific interviewee," I told her as we took off our mikes.

"Thanks," Melinda said.

We sauntered through the studio toward the exit, Melinda stopping to autograph a few pieces of paper for staffers. "Is everything . . . all right now?" I finally asked when we were out of earshot of my coworkers.

Melinda nodded. "Nothing else has arrived, if that's what you mean," she said. "No more little surprises." Then she shivered. "But you said that some of the other skaters had also gotten . . . stuff?"

"Yes," I replied, "they did. And I've been investigating a white-supremacist group down here—I thought maybe they had something to do with it, but now"—I shrugged—"the story seems to have taken a different turn."

"It's probably just as well," Melinda said as she pushed open the door. "You don't really want to be messing with folks in sheets,

Kit. That's the genetic understanding on my part, anyway. You going to the preliminaries tonight?"

It was pairs and men's singles. "I wouldn't miss it," I assured her.

"I'll probably see you there," she said as she strode briskly off. Alan sprawled into the chair next to my desk and watched Melinda leave. "I've been digging and digging, but I can't find anything that ties the tobacco protesters into the kind of shit that happened to her." He shrugged. "Sorry, babe."

"Keep digging," I said.

John Weidendecker had graciously decided to allow me to cover the preliminaries alone. I figured he was smugly pleased to have scored the interview with Bill Bethlehem, and now that he'd accomplished that feat, he had reestablished himself (in his mind, at least) as the only real sportscaster at KSDG. So at 6:30 Tony, Joe, and I drove down to the Bethlehem Arena and positioned ourselves, along with several other crews, in the corner from which the skaters emerged onto the ice.

Despite Terese Steiner's death, there seemed to be a little less tension in the arena tonight, I thought, as I watched Paul Cavanaugh and the nine other male competitors perform their short programs. The skaters had settled down to business. This was the short, technical program that included specific required moves—it wasn't as glamorous as the long, artistic programs, but it was compelling from the purely athletic standpoint. Paul skated well and came in third behind newcomer Jared Bright and the predictable winner, Todd Allison, an Olympic silver medalist. Susu Jenrette was nearby as we taped, and she watched her partner closely, nodding in approval as he executed a perfect triple axel. "Nervous?" I asked her. The pairs short programs were next.

"Not really," she said.

Susu's confidence was confirmed, more or less. When it came to the pairs preliminaries, she and Paul skated strongly. They had clearly worked, as Susu had indicated, on their artistic impression; for once, their strength on the ice was balanced by a reasonably imaginative interpretation of an unimaginative Beatles medley. Their side-by-side skating was perfectly synchronized, their leaps were powerful, and when the evening ended, Susu and Paul were in second place. Ari and Shannon had skated brilliantly, and they were in first.

The tobacco protesters had settled down to a constant line of marchers outside, but no shenanigans worthy of their first appearance on the scene. I saw Channing Strummer sitting with Bill Bethlehem and the slate of local luminaries; we exchanged waves but never got close enough for conversation. Melinda was halfway up the stands, watching the pairs. Joelle was nowhere to be seen, nor was her creepy companion. The official standings were announced and the skaters left the ice to prepare for the next night's round of competition.

As we wrapped up to go back to the station, Sandy Harrow appeared in the corner and grinned down at me. "So when do I get to hear what happened?" he asked me. Tony and Joe were once again on the alert, I noticed. "Tonight?"

I glanced down at my watch. "How about night after tomorrow?" I countered. "I want to get some more work done this evening."

"Fine," Sandy said promptly. "No more excuses?"

"Not one," I assured him.

That disarming grin appeared again. "I'm going to take you for the best margarita the city has to offer and pry the entire story out of you."

"I happen to be a native," I told him. "I already know where all the best watering holes in the city are, and I hate margaritas. But I'll take you for the best martini you ever had."

"You're on," Sandy told me. "Someplace dark and smoky?"

"Naturally," I laughed. We were flirting, I realized with a start. Well, why not? He was smart, attractive, sexy in an offbeat way. And I was free and way over twenty-one.

Out of the corner of my eye, I saw someone frantically whispering into Bill Bethlehem's ear and pointing toward the outside. So much for the tobacco protesters not acting up, I thought, and grabbed Tony and Joe. Maybe I could get something that would make Tricia Blaize fume even more; it was a pleasant thought. "Come on," I said, "let's go see what's going on outside. I'll see you later," I called to Sandy as we raced away.

"Count on it," said Sandy Harrow.

Outside the arena, tobacco protesters were milling around the parking lot. But their placards had been abandoned and the commotion and confusion was coming from something else. "Is there a doctor here?" I heard one of them shout.

I pushed my way through the knot of the gathered crowd and gasped. In the middle of the exit from the lot a small figure was crumpled on the blacktop. I recognized the electric blue outfit, the blond ponytail, and felt a stomach-lurching pang of fear. But as I got closer, I saw with relief that Susu Jenrette wasn't dead. The skater was lying awkwardly, clutching her left leg and crying; she was streaked with dirt and gravel, and her spandex leggings were torn. I broke through the people surrounding her and knelt down.

"Susu, what happened?"

She looked at me, her blue eyes dazed with shock.

"I don't know," she said. "I was just walking and this car came out of nowhere, Kit. Then I was down on the ground and the car was gone—I don't know what happened." She gave a strangled sob. "It hurts!"

"Jesus," I muttered. Peripherally, I saw that Tony and Joe were getting it all on tape.

"Where's Paul?" Susu sobbed.

"I'm a doctor, please let me through!"

As a stocky dark-haired man knelt beside Susu and began to check her over, I said, "Did you see the car?"

"It was dark," she said. Susu let out a wail as the doctor poked her thigh.

"I know," I said comfortingly, "but did you see anything at all?"

"It was dark," Susu repeated. Then I realized she meant the car that had hit her, not the night itself. "And old . . ."

"The driver?" I pressed eagerly. "Did you get a look at the—"

"Miss," the doctor snapped as he glanced briefly up at me, "unless you're a police officer, would you please get the hell away from this young woman and let me do my job?"

"No!" Susu said, panicked. "I want her to stay!" She grabbed my hand. "The driver was a man," she said. "But I couldn't really see. . . ." Then, as the doctor gently tried to move her leg, Susu's eyes rolled up in her head, and she passed out. Paul Cavanaugh and their trainer, Parks Jentzen, burst through the growing crowd of onlookers.

"My God, what happened?" Paul said. "Susu!" He knelt down on the ground beside her.

"Who're you?" the doctor asked.

"I'm her partner. Is she all right?"

The doctor glanced up. "We have to get her to a hospital," he said. "I don't know if she's sustained any internal injuries."

Paul Cavanaugh went deadly white. Parks Jentzen put a comforting arm around him.

We waited until the ambulance arrived and Susu was loaded gently onto a stretcher and taken away; she hadn't regained consciousness. Paul and Jentzen went with her, and Tony, Joe, and I split off in the KSDG van.

"Hit-and-run in the parking lot of the Bethlehem Arena," Tony mused somberly. "Who'd've thunk it?"

I was worrying this new wrinkle like a terrier. The White Nation wouldn't be likely to target Susu Jenrette, but Joelle Kistler's supremacist friend did drive an old dark car like the one Susu had vaguely described. Was it possible? I wondered. And if so, why? No answers came my way. "I don't get it," I murmured.

"Get what?" Joe asked.

I looked at him in the darkness of the van and shook my head. "Any of it," I said.

12

Susu's condition was listed as satisfactory when I called the hospital later that evening, but no further details were given. I was told the same thing when I called the next morning. Since nurses don't tend to be terribly forthcoming on the telephone, I identified myself and asked for Paul Cavanaugh or Parks Jentzen.

Paul Cavanaugh came to the phone. "Hi, Miss Powell," he said wearily.

"Hi, Paul, how are you doing?"

His voice was a little shaky. "Okay, I guess," he said.

"And what about Susu? What exactly does satisfactory mean?"

"Well," Paul said slowly, "the injury itself isn't really all that serious—I mean, her leg isn't broken, and the ligaments aren't torn through or anything. But she's pretty badly bruised up, and it looks like a tendon may have been pulled."

"So that means she's out for tomorrow night?" I said gently. Susu's last solo shot.

"It . . . looks like it right now," Paul said, clearly struggling to keep his emotions at bay. Tomorrow night and the next night— their pairs finals. This could really be disastrous for the pair, I thought with compassion—their last competition turning into a noncompetition, their hopes for upping the ante on their skating-show contracts vanishing.

"You think Susu might be up for an interview?" I queried. "A little sympathetic publicity might cheer her up." It would make a very nice spot on the news, too, I thought.

"We've got lots of sympathetic publicity," Paul assured me. "Camera crews are practically camped out in front of the hospital. But Susu likes you, so let me check with her," he said, "and I'll call you back."

I hung up the phone and wondered what the police were doing about Susu's accident. It wasn't murder, so I wasn't about to call Nick—this wouldn't be his bailiwick. I'd stick to normal channels of information.

"My goodness, Kit!" Tricia exclaimed brightly, pausing beside my desk. "Isn't it just so *odd* about your stories? I mean, the ones that you actually go out and cover for yourself?"

"Isn't what odd?" I asked mechanically. I should have known better.

Tricia's phony laugh trilled through the newsroom, alerting the staff to her intent to commit nasty shit. "Well, you know, how these silly . . . *jinxes* just seem to follow your stories around."

Silly jinxes? "What exactly are you saying, Tricia?" I asked her pointedly.

"Oh . . . nothing. It's just an observation." She waved a bony hand airily around. "But you know, first it was the Sharks and all that bad luck that followed them around and that cute half-back . . ."

"Quarterback, and he wasn't the killer," I reminded her. I skipped reminding her that most of that bad luck had occurred before the Sharks ever moved to San Diego or I had had anything to do with the story.

Tricia couldn't be bothered with such petty details. "And now," she continued, "it's these poor young skaters and this horrible accident . . ."

"Give it a rest, would you?" I shook my head in disgust.

". . . and those threats . . ."

I felt as if a bucket of ice water had been dumped on me. "What do you know about any threats?" I demanded sharply.

Tricia studied her fingernails. "Oh, you know, just the rumors that are going around about racist intimidation, that kind of thing. . . ."

I was equally angry and surprised. Who had broken the seal of secrecy around the skaters? And why? Even worse, for me, who would break the story? Professional paranoia high-jumped in my system as I pictured another station's sportscaster scooping me on this. "Where did you hear that, Tricia? I need to know!" I stared hard at her, but her eyes—blue today—gave up nothing.

She shrugged ingenuously. "Everyone knows," she said vaguely. "But to get back to my original point, I just find it so . . . *peculiar* that these things always seem to happen when you're on a story."

"You're absolutely right, Trish," I said. I leaned forward confidentially. "The secret of my success is now revealed. I actually instigate all this stuff myself. Threats, blackmail, even murder. Nothing is too extreme for me; I'll do whatever it takes to make a punchy story."

She studied me quizzically, as if she couldn't quite tell if I was kidding or not. Then she narrowed her eyes and smiled a thin smile. "Sometimes it's hard to tell when you're joking, Kit," she said. Imaginary damage done, she drifted off to torture someone else.

I reached for the phone as soon as she was out of earshot, called the hospital again, and asked for Paul Cavanaugh.

"Paul, I'm sorry to be such a pest," I said, "but did you get a chance to ask Susu about an interview?"

"She said she'd be happy to do an interview, Miss Powell," he told me. "In fact, it really perked her up when I told her you wanted to. She just wanted to know when you'd be here, so she could fix up her hair and do her makeup and stuff."

"How about an hour?" I asked, glancing at my watch. It was cutting things close, I knew, but there was no time to waste. If the news was out about the threats, I'd work it into a story on Susu and hopefully get the jump on anyone else who might be privy to the information. I could only hope that the rumor was still confined to the KSDG perimeter.

"That should be fine," Paul told me. "See you then."

"Tony!" I yelled across the newsroom. "Pack up."

Susu was sitting up in bed when we arrived, a little scraped up and wan, but not down for the count. She made that clear as soon as we began talking, while Tony and Joe set up.

"I know this is a rotten thing to say, Miss Powell," she told me, her blue eyes alert, "but I really think that someone is trying to wreck this competition. You know, the competitors have been having all sorts of problems—some of the skaters have even gotten threats."

So the secret was no secret at all. "How did you find out about that?" I asked curiously.

"I, well, I saw the swastika Ari Kotzloff got," she admitted. "I wasn't supposed to, I guess, but I was in the hallway of the hotel when he went into Shannon's room and told her." She looked a little ashamed of herself. "He didn't close the door all the way, and I kind of, um, eavesdropped and peeked. I was curious, because he looked so upset." She looked at me worriedly. "You won't tell anyone, will you?"

I shook my head. "Of course not." I didn't care if she was a snoop. "Did you tell anyone what you saw?" I probed. What I wanted to know was if this was how the rumor had begun to leak.

"Just Paul," she told me. "And he wouldn't say anything."

She sincerely believed that, but I knew that once something like this was leaked, even a little, there was no confining the news; it was too shocking, too titillating to be kept quiet.

"Anyone else?" I pushed it.

"No. Well, I mean I didn't tell anyone else, but Melinda Parsons told me yesterday what happened to her." That was a surprise. "I just put two and two together after what happened to me."

She'd obviously been giving it a great deal of thought. "Personally, I think it's those antitobacco people," she continued. "They just want to spoil the whole thing for everyone."

"Is there anything specific that makes you think it's the tobacco protesters?" I asked curiously. Leads have come from stranger places.

"Just a gut-level feeling," Susu said. "But I trust my instincts." She winced as a wave of fresh pain hit her. "Damn," she said softly.

"Do you want the nurse?" I asked. "A painkiller or something?"

To my surprise, Susu shook her head vehemently. "No way,

I'm not taking anything," she said. "I'm going to be on the ice tomorrow night, and I have to be all clear for it."

I looked dubiously at her bandaged leg and contusions. "You really mean to compete?" I asked.

Susu nodded. "I'm going to skate if it kills me," she said grimly.

Given the circumstances, it was a gutsy thing to say, but her discomfort was clear, and I wondered if she would actually make it onto the ice. I wished her well, then headed for the pay phone down the hall and called Channing Strummer, who sounded pleased to hear from me, but distracted.

"Listen," I said, "have you heard anything about these threats to the skaters?"

"Oh hell!" Channing exclaimed softly. "Just what we need! I just got a call from Bill Bethlehem about it. How did you find out?"

I filled her in briefly, and Channing was silent for a moment. "This is very bad for the city and for Bill Bethlehem's image," she said. "We've got to do some damage control."

"That's why I called you," I told her. I proceeded to fill her in on what I had known and kept secret, and what had transpired over the last few hours. "So since this is going to be public knowledge anyway," I finished, "I'm going to break it on the five o'clock news, and I'd like to get a statement from Bill Bethlehem for the story. Can you arrange it?"

"Sure," she said promptly.

I gave her the number of the pay phone at the hospital, and she called me back four minutes later and told me to go on over to the arena; Bethlehem would see me immediately. We left for the rink right away.

Bill Bethlehem was clearly upset by what he had learned, but he hadn't been at the helm of a huge corporation for twenty years for nothing. He was a controlled and capable man, and he assured me that whoever was responsible for the trouble would be found. He also said he had called in the police, which took the burden of keeping Ari and Shannon's secrets off my back; and whether it turned out to be the tobacco protesters or someone else, Bethlehem guaranteed that the culprit would be found and prosecuted to the full extent of the law. I hoped he was right. Now the skaters had to face yet another emotional upset: talking to the authorities about the very unpleasant secrets they'd been keeping. It was hard to imagine how Melinda or Ari or Shannon, and now possibly Susu, could stay focused on the competition under the circumstances. As for Joelle, she—and possibly to a lesser extent Greta—still had to deal with emotional ramifications of Terese Steiner's death. Maybe Susu was right, maybe Tricia Blaize was right: maybe there was some plot to ruin the competition after all.

I left Tony and Joe watching the skaters while I popped over to the hotel across the broad street fronting the arena, determined to talk to Joelle. But the elusive, mourning Miss Kistler was nowhere to be found. She hadn't been practicing and she wasn't in her room. The concierge had no idea where Miss Kistler or her parents were. Frustrated, I returned to the rink and we headed the van back to the station.

"Well, this is a pretty ugly mess," Doll commented when he stopped into the editing room to look at the piece I was working on.

"Isn't it?" I mused.

Doll glanced sharply at me. "You've got that bloodhound sound in your voice, Powell."

I hated when he did that, when he read me correctly about things I wanted to keep to myself. He was right, of course: I had no intention of simply reporting this one and forgetting it when I walked off the set. I was still determined to tie these loose ends together. I smiled at Doll. "Well, show me a full moon and I'll howl at it for you," I said genially.

Doll snorted. "You don't fool me, you know."

"I wouldn't even try," I said sincerely.

His eyes narrowed down suspiciously. "Ten minutes to air," was all he said.

JOELLE KISTLER should have been practicing, as it turned out. For a seasoned competitor at the top of her class, she skated a mediocre short program, falling twice and boggling badly as she came down from her jumps. Planned triples became weakly executed singles; she was clearly distracted and unfocused. As I kept an eye on her performance, I also scanned the crowd. Joelle's father wasn't around, but Mama Ellen was, looking grim and worried. And not far behind them, I saw the man from the White Nation meeting.

"Tony," I whispered, "as soon as Joelle finishes her program, pan the crowd." I pointed covertly in the direction of the Kistlers. "See the man three rows behind them? The one in the sunglasses and blue jacket? Be sure to get him, okay?" Tony nodded.

Joelle's lackluster performance was in sharp contrast to Greta Braun's; Greta looked sexy and self-confident in formfitting black sequins and skated a tough, flashy short program. She only stumbled once, slightly, as she came out of a triple axel; but just the jump itself was enough to make the crowd go wild.

Melinda Parsons, wearing a dreamy, flowing ice green outfit, skated well, too, a graceful, balletic program that didn't have quite enough of the difficult moves to give her an advantage over Greta. But the crowd liked her—liked her more, I suspected, with a little professional smugness, because of the two reports that had aired in the past two days—the one profiling the pretty skater, and the one that revealed the nasty stress some of the skaters, including Melinda, had been under. Shannon seemed extremely nervous, and her usual power moves were missing completely. She skated a safe, unambitious program, omitting her best jumps, and left the ice looking like she was going to burst into tears. As she rushed by the crew and me, I didn't even try to stop her for a sound bite; she was too upset.

But the real surprise of the evening was Susu Jenrette, who had, true to her word, signed herself out of the hospital and insisted on performing. When Susu appeared on the ice, the crowd went wild; and after a shaky start—her leg was obviously giving her some trouble—Susu skated a very adept program and played right to the audience. For once, the judges, who are notoriously disinclined to go with crowd favorites, seemed to agree. At the end of the short program, Greta ranked first, Susu second, Melinda third. Shannon was fourth and Joelle fifth. Except for the unflappable Greta Braun, the standings had been pretty much turned upside down. Two nights from now, the pairs and men's singles finals would be held; two nights after that, the women's singles. I wondered what else would change over the next four days.

Sandy Harrow joined me as the event ended and gave me a friendly hello hug. "Hey," I smiled at him. "Listen, I want to try to catch Joelle Kistler in the dressing room—I'll meet you outside in ten minutes, okay?"

"Okay," Sandy said obligingly. "But don't be longer—I worked up a powerful thirst watching those kids expend all that energy."

I told Joe and Tony to go ahead without me. My professional evening was technically over; I just wanted to see if I could get Joelle Kistler to say something, anything, that might shed some light on the bizarre events surrounding the competition.

As I pushed open the swinging doors to the women's locker room, Shannon Ngao rushed out past me, clearly upset. Inside, I found a frozen tableau—well, at least Melinda and Susu were frozen, watching in shock as Greta Braun and Joelle Kistler stood toe-to-toe, verbally jabbing at each other.

"It's you, isn't it, Greta?" Joelle was saying. "I know it is—all you care about is making sure you win!" Behind her, in her open locker, I saw something that struck me as out of place, but then my attention was promptly pulled back to the two young women.

Greta stared at Joelle with pure disdain. "I am very sorry for you that you are so upset, perhaps that is why you skate so badly tonight. But don't you forget, Terese was my coach long before she was yours, and I'm sadder than you could ever be at what has happened."

"I'm not talking about Terese, and you know it!" Joelle's voice was high-pitched, edging on hysteria. "You . . . you're the one who's behind all these awful things that have been happening to everyone. . . ."

"Joelle, don't . . . ," Susu began.

Joelle waved Susu's attempt at intervention off angrily. "Don't try to protect her," she said.

Greta took a threatening step forward. "You are crazy, Joelle," she hissed. "You are unbalanced."

"And you're a Nazi psycho!"

Greta's eyes dilated with fury. She hauled off and slapped Joelle so hard that the younger skater stumbled back into the lockers. "Fuck you, you miserable loser!" Greta spat.

I jumped in to separate them just as Joelle came flying back up at Greta, damage on her mind. I caught an elbow to my ribs as I struggled between them, then was yanked away by Ellen Kistler, who'd entered the locker room right behind me.

"Stop it!" she yelled at her daughter. Then she whirled on Greta. "And you stop it, too!"

Her words had the desired effect; the two skaters were shakily separated, although neither looked as though she really wanted to stop. Ellen Kistler turned to me. "Please get out of here, Miss Powell," she said. "And stay away from my daughter."

I was in no position to argue. But before I left I glanced quickly into Joelle's locker and verified what I thought I'd seen—a stack of what appeared to be letters, rubber-banded. They could have been fan letters, they could have been threats. There was no way of telling. Outside, I found Sandy Harrow leaning up against a wall, looking calm and friendly, and I told him what I'd just seen.

"Jesus," said Sandy, shaking his head, "the vitriol is flowing, isn't it?" I nodded. "Hey, Kit, let's forget it for just a little while, okay?" I nodded again. "So where's this best martini place?"

I had to laugh. "I don't know, I just said that to be cute."

"Cute you are," Sandy smiled.

We drove to a dark, pleasant club in Gaslamp Square and snagged a booth. I decided to do what Sandy said, just forget the craziness at the arena for the moment. We ordered drinks and listened to a better-than-average jazz trio and unwound quietly. Then we began to talk—ordinary talk after my account of the White Nation rally with Donny was out of the way. Sandy was a good listener and easy to talk to; he had a very direct approach, the kind that can make even a cautious type like me open up.

"So," he said, "do you want to spend your life at KSDG?"

"Actually," I said slowly, "I've been thinking about that lately. You know, I told Donny that I wanted to move up and out, and . . ." I shrugged. "I'm beginning to think it might be true."

Sandy laughed. "Life imitating art?"

I laughed, too. "Life imitating spur-of-the-moment lies is more like it."

Sandy's deep blue eyes were sharp. "Have you sent out any audition tapes?"

"Not yet," I said, tracing a line in the condensation on my glass. I looked curiously at him. "How about you—destined for nonprofit forever? D.C. office of CEO in the future?"

He pushed a lock of dark hair off his forehead and shook his head. "I don't think so," he said, "although D.C. is a possibility."

"Oh?" I felt an unexpected letdown.

"I was a speechwriter for ten years," Sandy said. "I'm thinking about jumping onto that ship again."

"Political speechwriting?" I asked, surprised.

Sandy nodded. "Uh-huh, and I'm damned good at it. But it got, well, let's just say times changed and what I was trying to help people say didn't seem to be what most people wanted to hear."

"And now you think they do?"

He shrugged. "I don't know about that. Maybe I'm just restless. Just when I think I've successfully beaten the life out of any ideals I still have, they begin to raise their troublesome little heads again."

"Ideals?" I echoed with a smile. "What an unusual word to hear used in a sentence."

He grinned cynically. "Don't worry, I use the word advisedly, and with the wisdom of a decade or two of beating my head against various unyielding walls behind me."

I raised my glass. "To breaking down walls."

He clinked his against mine. "Of various sorts," he said.

I was definitely attracted. In well-worn jeans and a sports jacket, his lankiness was both graceful and sexy, and his dark blue eyes were lit with the same intelligence and humor as his conversation. I could feel a softening inside that hadn't happened in a while. I wasn't sure how I felt about that.

When Sandy dropped me off at my car in the station parking lot an hour later, we both agreed it would be nice to see each other again. Then Sandy leaned over and kissed me lightly. The friendly kiss turned into something more complex and interesting. I finally pulled back. "I have to go," I told him abruptly.

"Did I do something wrong?" he asked, one eyebrow lifted a little quizzically.

"No," I said after a moment. "Not at all."

He leaned back and surveyed me. Then he smiled. "Okay," he said. "Then I'll call."

I smiled back. "Okay," I said. "Good."

13

MASON DROPPED BY the station the following day around noon-
time and hauled me off for a cheap burger. It's always been my
favorite brother's favorite lunch; even marriage to a health-con-
scious woman like Felice hadn't changed that. "Come on," he insisted, brushing his thick brown hair off his forehead. "We haven't
talked in ages."

"Dad told me about the baby," I said to him as we settled ourselves into a tacky orange vinyl booth at a nearby coffee shop. "I
think it's terrific, Mase, I'm really happy for you guys."

"Me, too," Mase said easily.

I asked bluntly, "Are you both okay about this not being your
biological child?"

Mason wore his usual unruffled expression. He's as cute as they
come, a young thirty-two who looks twenty-five. And to me he's
still—despite his marriage and his financial success with the
aquatic sports shop he and his lifelong friend and partner run—
the shiny-haired surfer, the perpetual little brother of my child-
hood. Actually, we have an even younger brother, Drew, but by
the time Drew was born, Mason and I were already nearing ado-
lescence and our ranks had closed tight.

Mason's hazel eyes, which are much like mine and much like
our father's, were bright. Unlike mine, his are serene. He nodded.
"You know, Kit," he said thoughtfully, "ever since Felice and I
started to go through this, all the medical trips, learning about the
adoption channels, I've come to realize that I never really cared

that much about the whole replicant syndrome. I mean, I don't have a thing about seeing a little Mason or Masonette running around. I just want a kid, and I'll be thrilled to get a baby that someone else can't take care of and give it a home."

It made me happy to hear him say that. "And Felice?"

Mason shrugged through a bite of onion-laden burger. "I think she was a little more disappointed at first," he said. "But now, she's really into it, she feels the same way I do."

"So . . . what exactly do you know about the parents of the baby?" I asked cautiously, trying to keep any note of worry from showing in my voice.

"We've met the mother a couple of times, and she seems like a really sweet kid. She's nineteen, and she's a junior-college student in Palm Desert," Mason said, "and she's perfectly healthy. She got an AIDS test, all that stuff—hepatitis, TB. She's just too young and unsettled to take on the responsibility of a child at this point in her life."

"What about the father?" I enquired.

"He's out of the picture."

"How so?"

Mason shrugged again. "Just . . . gone, I suppose. I'm not sure if it was a one-night stand or what. We didn't really want to probe."

"Uh-huh." And the mother clearly didn't want to volunteer the information, which didn't make me too happy. "This is all kind of . . . expensive for you, isn't it, Mase?" I asked gently.

Mason grimaced. "Twenty grand with the lawyer's fee." Then he smiled. "But, hell, Kit, I guess we can afford it for something we want so much."

But can you afford to lose it? I wondered. Not only could the entire thing turn out to be a scam on the young mother's part, but even supposing it was legitimate, the girl could still, under California law, change her mind for up to six months after handing the baby over to Mason and Felice. And the "just gone" dad sounded like potential trouble to me as well. At any given time, the biological father could show up and—especially if he hadn't been told about the pregnancy, hadn't ever had the chance to voice his opinion—lay claim to his biological child.

I didn't want to raise these issues with Mason, not really. I was certain that Felice, being as sharp a person as she is, would have thoroughly investigated the entire matter. And at this stage, what was the point of questioning the process anyway? Mason and Felice were already wallet deep into whatever was going to happen, aside from the emotional consequences. But Mason must have read my mind—it's something he's always been able to do—because he finally lost the smile.

"I know exactly what you're thinking, Kit," he said seriously. "And I know the potential for problems. Believe me, Felice and I have discussed it to death. But what else were we going to do?" His eyes had darkened perceptibly, and it made me a little sad for him. Mason is an upbeat person by nature, not given much to self-reflection or dwelling on the negative. But Mason was growing up, finally, and some of the realities he was dealing with were almost guaranteed to dim even the sunniest soul.

I reached across the table and gave his tanned wrist a squeeze. "I know, honey," I said. "I know all about it, too. But statistics are on your side. Chances are things will turn out all right; it's the ones that don't that get all the publicity that are the norm, not the headline grabbers. Try not to worry." I wasn't even sure if I believed my own words, but they seemed to reassure Mason. "Have you picked out any names yet?" I asked to change the subject.

We spent a few minutes wrangling over the choices, and I was happily surprised and more than a little touched to learn that if the baby was a girl, her middle name would be Kathleen.

"I'm very flattered," I said. I told myself that if this baby turned out to be a girl, I'd have to make sure I never forgot a birthday. "You're a sweetie," I told my little brother.

"It was Felice's idea, not mine." Mason grinned wickedly at me. "She thinks you're doing really well, professionally, and believe it or not, she has a superstitious streak."

"What do you mean?" I asked.

"She thinks naming babies after people whose lives are successful is empowering to the kid."

I burst out laughing. I'd never thought of my life as all that successful, nor would I have suspected my pragmatic sister-in-law of such mystical leanings. "Well, I hope it works."

We drifted into a different discussion, and it was Mason's turn to ask the questions. I've never bothered to try to hide anything about my personal life from my brother. He knew more than anyone else in the family about the string of disasters that had led to the end of my marriage to a ballplayer named Terry Brody; he knew all about Nick. He knew everything in between and before. So I brought him up to date on the internecine KSDG battles and on my romantic situation—or lack thereof. Mason nodded judiciously when he heard about my encounters with Nick, my date with Sandy Harrow.

"From a brain-dead professional athlete to a deadpan homicide dick to a crusading liberal—that's my sister." Mason shook his head ruefully. "What I love about you is that you're so consistent."

"Oh, shut up," I said crossly. "Terry wasn't exactly brain-dead, he just . . ."

"Had other attributes?" Mason winked at me.

I had to laugh. "And don't you dare mention it to Betty," I cautioned him. It was Betty from whom, I suspect, I inherited my bloodhound sensibility, although Betty, a true mom of the 1950s–1960s variety, had never used that particular skill professionally—she preferred to make keeping track of her five children her full-time job, and she did and still does an unnervingly good job at it. Mason and I had allied early against the constant privacy invasions, and we still got permission before telling our parents anything about each other.

Mason hooted. "As if I would," he said.

When I returned to the station, I was surprised to find two messages from Nick on my desk. They were marked urgent. What could be so urgent? I wondered as I punched out the number of the San Diego Police Department; this definitely had the earmarks of professional rather than personal contact.

"Strummer." When I finally got through, his voice was tighter than a drum.

"It's me," I said. "I just got in and got your messages. What's up?"

"I need you to come down here to make a statement," Nick said tersely.

"To the station? A statement about what?" I asked.

"Just come, okay?" Nick said. "This is official. I'll explain when you get here." He hung up the phone, leaving me no choice.

I picked up my purse and left, wondering what could be going on that required a statement from me. Even for Nick, who's a cipher by nature, this was an unusually cryptic communication. I drove over to Broadway and parked behind the station, feeding coins into the meter.

I entered the building, signed in, and made my way upstairs to Nick's office, rapping lightly on the door. Inside I found Nick, Stan Mardigian, and two other officers I recognized but didn't know by name, along with a man in punky street clothes and a buzz cut, who had to be undercover. Their conversation came to an abrupt halt as I entered, and when Nick nodded, everyone except Mardigian silently left the room.

"What's wrong?" I asked without preliminary, looking from one to the other of them. Their expressions were somber. "Why am I here?"

Nick looked back at me, his eyes unaccountably reddened. "Will Merriwether is dead," he said quietly. "Murdered."

I stared blankly at him. "Who's that? Another transient?"

"Your guide to the inner workings of the White Nation," Nick snapped.

"Will . . . no. That's not his name," I said. "His name is Donny, and . . ." Their expressions hadn't changed. "I'm sorry, I don't understand."

"Donny Duvall was Will Merriwether's undercover name, and his body was found early this morning," Mardigian told me. "In his car. He was shot in the head at close range." Mardigian looked positively grim; even his plaid sports jacket, usually good for a laugh, didn't dispel the pall in the office.

"Undercover name?" I echoed blankly. "But how did you know . . . I mean, how did you know that I knew . . . ?" My question trailed off.

"Donny was a cop, Kit," Nick told me, his voice leaden with fatigue. "His real name was Will Merriwether."

I shook my head to clear it. "No, not the one I know," I said. "He isn't a cop. This must be a different man. The Donny I'm talking about is a junkie."

There was a moment of heavy silence. "That, too," Mardigian said softly. He glanced at Nick, who nodded. Then Stan looked at me. "Merriwether worked undercover for the past six and a half years. It's way too long for most people, and it turned out to be too long for him. He . . . got strung out somewhere along the way. It happens."

I said nothing. Stan got up and patted Nick awkwardly on the shoulder. "I'll be in my office," he told him. "Good-bye, Kit."

I nodded, trying to digest this information. I looked closely at Nick and knew I'd never seen him this upset. "Nick? Did you know him well?" I ventured.

"Very well. We were at the academy together," he said. "He was the best man at my first wedding." He smiled joylessly, the irony of that particular admission to me not lost on him.

"What happened to him?" I asked gently. I'd heard all the stories about undercover cops going bad themselves but had somehow never connected it to real life, had never thought that someone I knew or Nick knew could be among those ranks.

Nick squeezed his eyes shut and rubbed hard as if to rid himself of an image. "We were close friends back then, but we never wanted the same things. After the academy, I went the corporate route and Will went to the streets. We drifted. He loved it, loved the edginess and the subterfuge and the mind games and . . . the payoffs." He stared somberly at a spot on the wall. "Somewhere along the way, it all got very real—real enough to need a needle in his arm."

I sat in stunned silence for a moment. "Was he still on the force?" I asked. "I mean, with an addiction . . ."

"He was supposed to have gone through rehab, he was supposed to be getting counseling," Nick said angrily. "But yes . . . he's still . . . was still a cop. He begged the brass to let him stay undercover—he's been tracking Eugene Ebberly and his bunch for a long time and he was certain he could link them to the transient deaths if he just had a little more time." He glared at me. "Remember the San Jose killings I told you about? Will had been on the case since then."

"Do you think they killed him?" I asked. My stomach turned as I asked the question.

"I think they found out he was a cop," Nick said. "And I think they killed him. Yes." His eyes stared off at something I couldn't see. "He lost his gift, Kit. He turned his brain to mush. Christ, he used to be so damned good at getting into his parts and staying in them—we used to joke that he could have been a great actor."

"He did a pretty damned good acting job with me," I said softly. All that racist rhetoric had convinced me he was a true believer.

"Well, he fucked up," Nick said harshly. "He fucked up the night he took you to that meeting—Christ, somewhere on the outskirts of that brain of his, he was still keeping track, he knew you and I were—" He stopped abruptly. "And he just *forgot* until he was driving you back from that celebration of the Third fucking Reich!" He glared at me. "He got careless, he got stupid, God knows what else he forgot, but he slipped and he got himself killed."

There was a thick silence in the room. Nick isn't given to emotional outbursts. Finally, he looked up at me, more composed. "I don't think I can talk about this anymore right now," he said calmly. "Can I just get a statement from you?"

"Nick," I said, still unable or unwilling to believe what I'd been told, "are you absolutely certain we're talking about the same person? I mean, maybe my Donny Duvall wasn't your . . ." It sounded lame, even as the words emerged.

Nick's look was one of exhaustion. "I know who he is, but I suppose we should at least verify that the deceased is the same man. Are you up to looking at the pictures?" he asked doubtfully. He'd seen my reaction to dead bodies before. I nodded.

"Okay," Nick shrugged, resigned. "Just to be on the safe side." He opened the official-looking folder on his desk and passed me four photographs of better quality than I might have wished. I stared down at pictures of the dead man. Half his face was gone, reduced to a pulpy mass of body parts I didn't want to know the names of. But the one pale eye and the straw hair, the pockmarked skin and the gaunt half face that was left were those of Donny Duvall aka Detective Will Merriwether. I felt whatever color remained in my own face drain abruptly away, and I handed the pictures back to Nick. "It's the same man."

Nick slammed the folder shut. "Of course it is," he said, anger hovering in his tone. "Can you give me a statement now?" he asked.

"Of course." The quicker I was out of here, the better, I thought, longing for fresh air.

Nick got a stenographer in the room, and I shut the mental picture of Duvall resolutely out of my mind in order to give the clearest account of my activities that I could. I was nearly through with my recitation when there was a rap at the door; it opened and Sandy Harrow walked in. He looked surprised to see me and gave my shoulder a reassuring squeeze before he held out his hand and introduced himself to Nick. I saw Nick's eyes flicker from me to Sandy, but a veil of professionalism hooded his expression before I could read it.

After Nick went through the preliminary explanation again, he asked Sandy if he'd had any idea that Donny was a cop.

"No," Sandy said, "not a clue. I thought he was just another ex-con with connections to one of the groups CEO tries to keep an eye on. And . . . I thought he sold me the information to buy narcotics." He looked quizzically at Nick.

"He did," Nick concurred tersely. He turned to me. "Kit, why don't we finish up your statement, and then I can get to Mr. Harrow." He made sure that he used my first name, Sandy's last. And Sandy caught it, too. I thought irrelevantly that maybe we should just get Channing Strummer in here and complete the incestuous circle.

I finished my statement and made for the door without ceremony, eager to get away from all of it. At the same moment, I heard Nick and Sandy both start to say, "I'll call you later. . . ."

I turned and saw them staring at each other. Nick's eyes were narrowed, Sandy's a little surprised. Under any other circumstances, it probably would have made me very happy. I got out of there as quickly as I could.

ONE OF MY AUTOMATIC REACTIONS to trauma of any kind is to return to something familiar, something soothing. I knew I should go back to the station, but I just couldn't face the frenzied chatter of the newsroom or the questions I was sure to be asked quite yet.

Instead, I used a pay phone to call Max Flores and tell him what had happened; the story was logically his.

Then I got into my car and drove aimlessly for a while. Eventually, without planning it, I wound up on Point Loma, not far from Mason's shop, but didn't stop there. I had no desire to talk to anyone, not now. I finally stopped and parked at Sunset Beach. The sky was overcast and the sand was still damp from the recent rains, and although the beach was pretty much deserted except for a few people walking their dogs, the surfers were out in the water, cruising.

I walked restlessly up and down on the shore, trying to allow the rhythms of the breaking waves and the patient up-and-down motion of the surfers, waiting for the next good wave, to take me down a notch. And eventually, as it usually does, the beach had a calming effect on me, returning me to a past in which I had been as ignorant of life's potential disasters as these kids were.

But, of course, there was no escaping from the present, from what had just happened. The image of the man I'd known as Donny Duvall—with his destroyed face and blood-drenched blond hair—flickered in and out of my thoughts. I couldn't allow myself to dwell on the picture, so instead I concentrated on the back story, wondering what it was that had gone so wrong for him. The cliché about cops and criminals being two sides of the same coin predictably came to mind, but this seemed far more complex than that. According to Nick, he'd been a very good cop, but somewhere along the way, it all went wrong. Apparently he'd wound up doing a lot more than his job: he still worked undercover, still fed information to the police, but he also sold that same information to people like Sandy Harrow and me. It was a game that seemed predestined to end badly.

If Nick was right, and I had no reason to think he wasn't, Will Merriwether's murder was tied to the White Nation. But did any of this tie in directly with the messages sent to the competitors at the Bethlehem Invitational, or was I trying to create a case where none existed? My thoughts returned to the ugly locker-room confrontation between Joelle Kistler and Greta Braun and the accusations that Joelle had made; I wrangled with the possibility that Joelle could have been right, that Greta was somehow responsible for the threats against the other skaters. But I couldn't make it add up: Greta was just too damned good at what she did. She was an international star, quite possibly the best female skater in the world—she simply had no need to cut her competitors off at the knees with psychological warfare. And the possible involvement of the tobacco protesters had yet to be proved or disproved. Vague, vague, vague, I told myself, kicking up a small sandstorm in frustration.

After more than an hour at the beach, the inner peace I had sought still eluded me, and I was stuck very much in the present tense. I couldn't get the thought of the skaters out of my mind, and over and over, it was Joelle Kistler to whom my thoughts kept returning. Her rocky skating even before Terese Steiner's death, her bizarre connection to the man from the White Nation rally, the very public blowups with her parents and with Greta. This was a girl on the edge of . . . what, I didn't know. But she was there, all right, I thought, not just on the edge but somehow at the darkening center of this puzzle. I wanted to know what was really going on with Joelle. Instead of returning to KSDG, I drove to the Bethlehem Arena.

The parking lot was nearly deserted, but the extra security posted by Bill Bethlehem was in evidence. I waved my press credentials at the two guards at the entrance and strolled into the arena, uncertain exactly what my plan was. Then I saw Joelle on the ice, sans coach, of course, trying to make up for her foul-ups the previous night. Naturally, Ellen Kistler was right down in the front of the stands, giving her pointers and advice. I stayed at a distance, not wanting to be seen and unable to read the mood between mother and daughter. There was no question of approaching Joelle directly, certainly not with her mother there. I was certain that Ellen Kistler's admonition to stay away from Joelle during the fight with Greta applied to the entire competition; I suspected she was trying to shield her daughter less from any public grieving over Terese Steiner than any public displays of an increasingly off-kilter temperament.

A thought had been at the back of my mind ever since that locker-room brawl, and it was what had sent me here. Those letters in Joelle's locker had strongly piqued my interest: why would she have put them there unless she wanted to keep them out of her nightstand or jewelry box or whatever—in other words, to keep them hidden safely away from prying parental eyes? They could, of course, be love letters or some other kind of very personal correspondence, but given her hysterical accusations at Greta, wasn't it also possible that Joelle herself had been the target of hate mail or threats? At least it was something to look into.

I left the rink area and headed upstairs to the security office, where I identified myself to the man in charge. I was in luck: the head of security, a man named Burton Oliver, turned out to be a fan. He chatted pleasantly with me about a piece I had done a few months back about his son's high school volleyball team.

Oliver didn't question my report about suspicious-looking vehicles cruising the lot, cars I claimed might contain more protesters with surprises up their sleeves. He heaved himself out of his chair. "I'll go take a look," he said, "and talk to the staff downstairs while I'm at it. These people are sneaky and determined. You can't be too careful."

"That's what I thought," I told him, nodding in agreement. "I'm going to see if I can find Shannon Ngao," I added by way of explanation as I headed off down the corridor in the opposite direction. I looked at my watch. When Oliver had been gone for two minutes, I padded quickly back into the office and snagged the ring with the master locker key off the Peg-Board it was hanging on; the built-in combinations could be opened only by the locker's current user, but all it took was one key to solve that problem. It was so easy I felt like I was in a Nancy Drew book. Then I jetted down to the deserted women's locker room and entered. Without giving myself time to reconsider the complete impropriety of what I was doing, I opened Joelle Kistler's locker, then raced back to security, replaced the key ring, and returned to the locker room barely out of breath. If anyone was in the locker room when I returned, I thought, I'd just lie my way through it. It wasn't like I didn't have a legitimate reason to be there. Well, I could no doubt dredge up *some* legitimate reason if it came to that.

But the locker room was still empty of occupants. I pulled the small stack from Joelle's hiding place behind her sweats and, using one foot to prop the swinging door partially open so I could see anyone heading my way, I rapidly scanned through the four letters I held. Written on plain white paper in a blocky hand, they didn't read like romantic, private messages or the kinds of intrusive veiled threats that might come from an obsessive fan, a potential stalker.

The first one was addressed to "My Dear Joelle," and it was a plea from the sender to meet with him, saying it was a matter of utmost importance and that it had to do with her family. It was signed with the name Gary Held, which meant nothing to me. The second one was very similar, a little more urgent—apparently, Joelle hadn't responded to the initial contact. But the third letter was markedly different. It indicated that the writer and Joelle had met and that Gary Held was "happier than I've been in many years" about what had taken place. The fourth letter revealed a growing intimacy of a sort I couldn't quite fathom; with its vague allusions to "the things we discussed" and "the wishes of your beautiful mother," it just left me more puzzled than ever.

I could have pored over that correspondence at much greater length in an attempt to decipher the subtextual meaning, but I figured I was already pushing it. Joelle might well be intimidated by me, or just plain scared to have the existence of these letters made known to her parents; but I knew if Ellen Kistler walked in and saw what I was doing, I'd be in so deep I wouldn't ever be able to climb out. I put the letters back where I found them, spun the combination lock, and got myself rapidly out of the locker room. Just to cover my rear end completely, I waltzed back up to security and asked Oliver what had happened in the parking lot.

The head of security shrugged. "We didn't see anyone," he told me, "but thanks anyway, Miss Powell. I want everyone on their toes at all times. We just don't know what's going to happen next around here."

"I know exactly what you mean," I agreed.

14

BACK AT THE STATION, I did my best to ignore Tricia, who was nattering on about how she thought I was stepping on anchorperson territory with my forays into hard news—this, despite the fact that I'd happily handed the story of Will Merriwether's murder over to Max—as well as John Weidendecker's pitiful attempt to correct my description of a triple-triple (I was right, he was wrong; nothing new here). Instead of getting bogged down in petty office politics, I went right into Doll's office and began to outline everything I'd done and learned, hoping to see some cohesive pattern emerging as I talked.

"I'm really very sorry to hear about the cop," Doll said, shaking his head somberly. "It's like a bad movie, isn't it?"

"Nick said Merriwether was the best at what he did," I mused, "at least at the beginning."

Doll peered sharply at me. "Are you okay, Powell?" he asked.

"I guess I am," I said. I stared down at the linoleum, trying to collect my thoughts. "No," I admitted finally, "I'm not doing so well. I've got this gut-level feeling that all of this connects, but every time I try to make sense of it, the pieces slip out of pattern." I needed a sounding board, and Doll is as sharp and logical as they come.

"Is it possible that you're trying to make a case where there isn't one?" Doll asked, echoing my own earlier thoughts. "Maybe there just isn't a pattern to find, Kit; maybe none of this really does connect."

"You think I'm dancing without a partner here?" I frowned.

Doll shrugged. "It happens, Powell. Not every hunch is a good one, even for a bloodhound like you."

"I know," I sighed. "But I swear, Doll, I really believe there's something here that I'm missing, and I think whatever that is, it's the key to the entire thing. And I think it has to do with Joelle Kistler, somehow." Then I told him about the correspondence I'd found, for lack of a more accurate word, in Joelle's locker.

Doll's forehead creased in a series of worried horizontal lines. "You can't pull stuff like that, Powell," he admonished me. I figured it was just said to have it on the record; Doll wants us to do whatever we have to in order to dig up the facts on a story.

"Okay, okay." I waved the admonition aside. "Duly noted."

"And another thing," Doll continued. "I don't want to hear about it if and when you do—I know I'm going to be stuck for bail one of these days anyway." He fixed me with a stern eye. "You know you're incredibly lucky you didn't get caught."

"I was very careful." And pretty lucky, too; he was right about that. "But about those letters, what do you think?"

The horizontal lines stayed in place as he worried the idea silently. "Could be just a fan, I suppose," he said, "although it really doesn't sound like the typical stalker approach."

"I know." I nodded in agreement.

"Doesn't sound like a lover, either. . . ."

"Not with all that family stuff mentioned. And Ellen Kistler is an attractive woman, but she's no beauty," I mused, remembering Held's phrasing.

"Maybe it's Ellen Kistler's lover," Doll shrugged. "Maybe it's some kind of blackmail."

It was an interesting thought. "I think I'm going to poke around and see if I can turn up anything about this Gary Held guy."

Doll rolled his eyes. "For Christ's sake, Kit, this is really reaching for straws—it has nothing to do with the stories you're working on. Besides, you don't even know where those letters were mailed from. Where are you going to start?"

"Don't worry," I assured him, "I won't neglect my gig." Although I knew Doll wasn't worried that I would.

"I hate that word," Doll muttered, "and I think you're wasting your time."

Which meant, don't tell me if you're about to do something that might be considered legally hinky. "See you later," I said.

I got Tony to blow up a frame of his footage that showed Joelle's admirer for me; I pocketed the grainy image, then returned to the police station downtown. Nick and Mardigian were poring over some computer printouts when I walked in.

"Hey, I'm sorry to interrupt," I said. "I know how busy you are, but could you do me a favor and just look at this photograph?"

"Hand it over," said Nick. He and I seemed to have come to some sort of unspoken truce over the past few hours, a silent agreement to put personal problems aside while we wrangled with overlapping professional ones.

I showed him the picture, and he studied it for a moment, then shook his head. "I can't tell a thing from this," he said. "Stan?"

Mardigian looked at it and shrugged. "Sorry, Kit, but this could be anyone. What's the deal?"

I told them briefly where and how I'd seen this man, both the Joelle Kistler connection and the fact that he'd been at the White Nation rally. Neither man registered much of a reaction to the news about Joelle Kistler's strange friendship, but their interest was sharply aroused when I mentioned the man's presence at the meeting and recounted Merriwether's offhand remark about his affiliation with the "inner circle" of the supremacists.

"If we can get an ID on him from this picture, that would be excellent," Nick said grimly. "I'll be happy to shake the asshole up a little, make life miserable for anyone connected with White Nation—even if they didn't have anything to do with Will's murder. Which I'm certain they did." He sighed. "Shit, I can't even think straight. Listen, go on down to records and tell the officer at the desk I said to give you a hand."

"Okay, thanks."

Downstairs, in records, a uniformed officer offered to let me look through the county mug books while she ran Gary Held's name through the computer. It was a long shot, but the Kistlers were from Orange County; it's not that far north of here, and I thought perhaps Held—if he was a convicted criminal at all—had some kind of local record. I flipped idly through a couple of books but wasn't able to find anyone who I could swear was Joelle's friend, although a lot of the men looked vaguely like him. Bony, pumped-up white cons with slicked-back hair seemed to be a type. A very common type.

For perhaps the first time since I'd started on the Bethlehem story, luck was on my side. Gary Held did have a local record, a long if fairly minor one. Seven times in the past twenty years, he'd been picked up. It was no earthshakingly dark criminal portfolio; a couple of times the charges were vagrancy, several times he'd been busted for drunk driving, once for B & E—which had been pled down—and once for an inebriated assault on an ice-cream vendor. The last arrest had occurred more than five years ago, and the last address on the parole document was a local halfway house.

"Drug addict?" I asked, my interest aroused. Donny had denied knowing him, but if they were both connected to the drug world, perhaps there was someplace to start.

The desk officer frowned as she read through his record. "It says . . . no, it's substance abuse, but it's alcohol. No other drugs mentioned." She looked up at me. "This guy's a loser, but he's not exactly your big-time criminal," she added.

"What do you think?" I showed her the picture, and we compared it to the old mug shot. The hair was the same—thinner, now, but dark brown and slicked back; but otherwise, the shot from the rink was probably useless to anyone who didn't know the man. I'd never seen him without his sunglasses myself, and I certainly couldn't have given an accurate description to anyone who wanted one.

She shrugged. "Could be," she said. "Maybe not. Not much help, huh?"

"Well, thanks anyway," I said, copying down the address of the halfway house and that of a sister who lived in Chula Vista.

"Good luck," she said, and went back to work.

Even with Gary Held's last known address in hand, I still couldn't shake the desire to confront Joelle Kistler with what I knew—what little I knew—first. I figured I was a lot more likely to wheedle or trick information out of a young skater than a professional criminal. And besides, I knew where to find Joelle. I figured that if I hung around the hotel and the arena long enough, I'd find an opening, a way to get to her when she was rid of her parents. And I definitely wanted to approach her when she was alone. With picture and rap sheet in tow, I returned to the arena and smiled blithely at the guards. Darkness was beginning to fall, but with no competition or exhibition scheduled for the evening, the lot was empty.

"Back so soon?" one of them asked genially.

I shrugged. "I've been trying to track down Shannon Ngao all day," I said. "Have you seen her?"

"Nope, not this afternoon."

I tried to look disappointed. "How about the others? Is Susu Jenrette here? Or Joelle Kistler?"

"I saw Joelle Kistler and her mother going across the street to the hotel," one of the guards offered. "About an hour ago."

"Maybe I'll see if I can catch up to them there," I said, all business.

I settled into a corner of the hotel coffee shop facing the lobby and ordered some hot tea and an English muffin. I realized I hadn't eaten since lunch with Mason. That had been seven hours ago, and although I wasn't hungry—the morgue pictures of the man I'd known as Donny Duvall had knocked that out of me—I knew I needed something in my system to keep me going. I didn't have long to wait. Joelle's parents appeared in the lobby, dressed up and clearly on their way to a chichi dinner somewhere, no doubt in the continuing effort to promote their already highly visible daughter. Ellen Kistler looked overly made up and distracted; John Kistler looked bored and unhappy. I watched them get into their gold Mercedes and drive away, and forced myself to wait a full five minutes, hoping their daughter wasn't sneaking down the back stairs even as I bode my time. Then I took the elevator up to the fourth floor and knocked on the door of Joelle's suite. After a moment, I heard Joelle ask who it was and I identified myself.

"Oh, Miss Powell," she said, opening the door a crack, "I'm sorry, but I really can't talk to anyone right now. I'm trying to rest."

"Just for a minute," I said, trying the polite, neutral approach first.

Joelle's eyes hardened a little; I had the sense that people seldom challenged her in that rarified atmosphere in which she lived. "I'm afraid this isn't a good time," she said, shaking her head. "My mother is just across the hall, and she really doesn't want me talking to the press right now."

"Your mother and father just left the hotel; I saw them go," I said, abandoning the polite approach. "And I have the feeling they'd have a lot more to be upset about than just press relations and publicity if they knew who you were hanging around with."

"What do you mean?" Joelle asked, widening her eyes guilelessly.

I pulled the grainy photograph out of my purse. "This is what I mean," I said.

Joelle glanced down at the picture, then looked up at me. In contrast to the phony innocence of a moment before, Joelle's expression of shock was very real. "Come in," she whispered.

The suite was done in pastel colors, very nicely appointed and completely lacking in character. Joelle walked restlessly across the large room to the phony marble fireplace. "What do you want?" she asked, turning to face me. Her hand was on the mantel behind her, and I noticed that her knuckles were white.

I pointed to the photograph. "First, I want you to tell me how you know this man."

"I don't understand," she said. She had recovered her equilibrium, at least partially. She might be young, but years of public appearances, the toughest kind of competition, and stringent self-discipline had taught her about poise. And stonewalling.

"It's a simple question," I countered. "I've seen you with this man and I need to know what your relationship is to him."

She shrugged. Standing there in front of the phony fireplace, dressed in black leggings, flat ballet slippers, and a long striped sweater, she looked the picture of healthy naïveté. "I don't really know him," she said with a smile. "He's just a fan. . . ."

"Skip it," I told her. "You don't go sneaking off with 'just a fan' the way you have, you don't hang around with people like this at all."

"People like what?" she asked a little defensively.

"Joelle, this man is a lowlife," I said, "and I don't for a minute believe that whatever is going on between you is normal."

"Normal?" she echoed.

"Yes, normal—like a friendship. I think he has some sort of hold over you," I said. "Why don't you tell me what it is? Is it blackmail?"

"Blackmail?" Her jaw dropped. "No, of course not—what could anyone blackmail me about?"

The reaction seemed genuine, but maybe she was a good actress. "Why don't you tell me?"

"I don't understand what this has to do with you," she said stubbornly.

I didn't want this to turn into a bargaining session; I had no intention of giving her any details before she gave me some basic facts. "Look, Joelle," I said as kindly as I could, "I'm not just a sports reporter, I also do other kinds of work. Investigative work for the news. And this guy, well, I think he might be involved in some shady things."

"He isn't mixed up in anything bad," she flared. Then she flushed as she realized her slip; she had just admitted this was no casual acquaintance.

"What's going on, Joelle? Are you having an affair with him?" I hazarded.

She looked shocked. "No! Oh my God, no, it's nothing like that!" Suddenly, inexplicably, she seemed to be on the verge of tears.

"Then what is it?" I asked insistently.

She shook her head silently.

"If it's not blackmail and it's not sex, what is this man to you?" I persisted.

One tear finally spilled over and coursed down her cheek. She walked over to a chair and sank down into it. "He's my father," she said, very softly. "My real father."

Whatever I might have expected to hear, this had never entered my mind. "Your father?" I repeated blankly.

"My biological father." Joelle looked defiantly at me. "I'm adopted."

It certainly explained the letters—those cryptic allusions to her beautiful mother, to family, finally began to make some sense. "And you just found out?" I asked more gently.

Joelle nodded. "I mean, I knew that I was adopted," she said, "but my parents—I mean, my adoptive parents—told me that both of my real parents were dead, that they'd died in a car accident." Once the words began to come, she seemed eager to reveal the truth to someone, to tell her story. I was handy, and I was obviously willing to listen. "And I just never questioned them about it; I mean, why would I?" The last question was both rhetorical and defensive; Joelle was clearly upset that she had never bothered to inquire into the truth of the situation.

But she was right: why should she? She had everything a girl could ask for—talent, looks, parents who encouraged her every step of the way. A different kind of kid, one who wasn't so seemingly blessed or so singularly driven might have asked questions, but it was understandable to me that this one hadn't.

I nodded sympathetically, hoping to keep her talking. "And how did you find out about . . . your father?" I asked, even though I knew exactly how.

"He wrote me," she said quietly. "I didn't want to believe him at first. I wanted to think he was just some crackpot who, I don't know, followed my career or something." She looked at me. "You know, some people get kind of . . . obsessed." She shrugged. "I mean, it wouldn't be all that hard to learn some of the things he knew, like my birthday. But I got more curious after he wrote a second time, and we were coming down here for the competition anyway, so I decided to make a preliminary trip. I told my parents I just wanted to check out the area, but I . . . I arranged to meet him." She looked down guiltily.

"And?"

She looked up again, focusing on some distant point, as if looking at me directly while she spoke would be too painful. "And after I met him, just once, I knew he was telling the truth. He has this place on Marine, just a little run-down place he rents. But"—her eyes went liquid again—"he's got all this memorabilia—pictures of him and my mom, and some baby stuff of mine and a copy of my birth certificate. And this old picture of him and my mom and me when I was just a few weeks old." Something between a hiccup and a sob escaped.

"But . . . what really happened?" I asked quietly. "To your biological mother, I mean?"

"She *did* die in a car crash that they were in. At least they didn't lie about that," she added bitterly, now relegating the Kistlers to the distancing "they" category. "But my father—his name is Gary Held—didn't die. He was in the hospital for a long time, but he didn't die. I was put in foster care and then my parents—the Kistlers, that is—got me. But Gary says he never signed any papers that made an adoption legal."

A sick feeling churned up suddenly in the pit of my stomach. Coming on the heels of my luncheon discussion with Mason, there was an eerie, uncomfortable echo to what Joelle was telling me. I wondered to what lengths the Kistlers had been willing to go to obtain the baby they must have wanted so much; I wondered if what Gary Held had told Joelle was true. And if it was, if the adoption hadn't really been an adoption at all, what were the legal ramifications of any of this?

"Joelle," I said quietly, "I can only imagine how confusing and upsetting this is to you, to find out that you have a living biological parent. But your parents—your adoptive parents, that is—probably did what they thought was best for you."

"Best how?" Joelle asked bitterly. "Keeping the truth from me?"

"I'm sure they believed they were doing the right thing," I said gently. "The thing is, your real father, well, that's why I insisted on talking to you about him. I looked into his background, and he's had"—I tried to phrase it as delicately as possible—"some problems."

"I know he has," Joelle said defiantly. "He told me *everything*. I know about the trouble he's had with drinking and I know he's been in jail. But it's not his fault, Miss Powell. Don't you understand?" Her eyes were intense and angry. "He got out of that hospital twenty years ago and everything was gone. He had nothing left to live for. No wife, no baby, nothing! It's so unfair! Just think, if I hadn't been taken away from him, his whole life might have been so different."

What about your life? I thought. But I refrained from asking the question. "I understand what you're saying, Joelle, but . . . what does he want? What does he want from you?"

"Nothing," she said angrily. "You can't understand that, can you? I know my . . . the Kistlers wouldn't understand it! All they want is a trophy case!" She glared at me. "My father hasn't been in any trouble for years and he doesn't drink anymore. He just wanted to meet me and tell me the truth and maybe . . . see if it's possible for us to have a relationship."

I winced inwardly at the revelations that lay ahead for this sheltered, sensitive girl about the man I'd seen at the White Nation rally. Gary Held might have told Joelle that there was nothing he wanted and gotten her to believe it. I didn't.

"Gary believes in telling the truth," Joelle said proudly. "Not like—but why did you want to ask me about him anyway?" Joelle asked suddenly.

"Oh, I just, well, you know about these things that have been happening to some of the skaters," I improvised quickly. "I found out about them several days before any of it became public knowledge, and I saw you with this strange man. I suppose it's just journalistic suspicion, but I was worried that he was—someone like you thought he might be before you met him—a crackpot who was hung up on you. A stalker. With his arrest record and all, I was just worried he might have had something to do with what was happening to the other skaters, as a way to insure you'd win or something."

It sounded weak to me as I said it, but Joelle was so wrapped up in her own inner turmoil that she appeared to accept the explanation at face value. She nodded. "I understand," she said. "But believe me, he had nothing to do with those awful things that happened. He's just not like that—he's really a very kind man. And he's had such a rough life." She sighed. "I don't know why I told you all this," she said. Then the professional Joelle made a brief appearance. "You won't make any of this public, will you?" she asked worriedly.

"Of course not," I assured her. "You have enough to deal with. And I can imagine how difficult it's been for you."

Joelle stared sadly into space. "I haven't skated this badly since I was six years old," she said. "It's been so hard to concentrate. And I miss Terese. I could always talk to her about things that upset me."

"Did you ever talk to her about what you had learned about your . . . about the adoption?"

Joelle shook her head. "No. I wasn't ready to talk to anyone about that." She seemed exhausted, overwhelmed. "I can't believe she's really dead. Somehow it makes me wonder if there's any point to even skating at all."

"You're a world-class athlete," I told her gently. "Don't forget that."

"That was Joelle Kistler," she said softly. "And she was what she was because she was pushed and pushed and told that's what she should be." She sighed. "But there is no more Joelle Kistler. There really never was. She was all made up."

I wondered if she planned to confront the Kistlers with her new knowledge, but I had no excuse to pry further. And I wasn't about to tell her where I'd bumped into her biological father. She already had plenty to think about. I got up to leave, and Joelle walked to the door of the suite with me.

"Listen to me," I said to her as I stood in the doorway. "There *is* a Joelle Kistler. And she's a great skater."

She shook her head. "No. My name is really Angela Held, and I don't have any idea what or who Angela Held is." She smiled sadly at me. "Thanks for listening, Miss Powell," she said. Then she shut the door behind me.

15

As I PULLED OUT OF the Bethlehem Vista parking lot, I was feeling both surprised and a little depressed by what I had just learned. Joelle's anger and confusion made me think about Mason and Felice and what they might face somewhere down the line themselves.

At least there was a logical reason for Joelle's strange behavior, I mused, and for the appearance of Gary Held in the picture as well. But there were also things that still begged explanation. There was Held's troublesome connection to White Nation and the still-unsubstantiated link between the supremacist group and the transient killings, one of which had occurred right where Joelle's own coach had been found. I still couldn't quite make myself believe that that was purely coincidence. There was the fact that the car that had hit Susu Jenrette, while vague in Susu's mind, did seem to fit the description of Gary Held's car. Well, if I stretched it, anyway: it was old and dark and driven by a man. It wasn't really much to go on, I thought. But at least I could pat myself on the back for one thing: I'd been right about Joelle being near the center of all that was going on. But that still didn't tell me much of anything.

As I drove along, lost in thought, I became aware of bright lights shining annoyingly into my rearview mirror; a car was following far too closely behind me. With a few miles left to travel before the freeway entrance, I shrugged it off dismissively and sped up around the wide, approaching curve—as much as it is possible to speed in an old VW wagon—in order to clear the dark road for the insistent vehicle right behind me.

When speeding up didn't seem to help, I moved obligingly to the right-hand lane. The headlights stayed right on my tail, refusing to pass or slow down on the semi-isolated, winding road, and I began to feel very alone in my car. Don't worry, I told myself, it's nothing. But as the lights stayed glaringly apparent in my rearview mirror, blocking out any clear view of the car following me, I could feel my pulse jitter with anxiety, and suddenly I wished that I hadn't spent quite so much time making fun of people who have cellular phones conveniently located near their steering wheels.

I was thrown forward in my seat when the car behind me tapped my bumper. As I pulled my own car straight ahead, I tried to tell myself that whoever was driving it had seen too many car-chase movies and thought he was having some fun at my expense. I looked around for a place to pull off the road, for a lighted phone booth, for a cop. But this stretch of road was still mostly undeveloped fields, and I sped up again, just trying to get somewhere, anywhere out of range of the car behind me.

Finally, I spotted one of the new malls and, immensely relieved, I veered sharply to the right and into the parking lot, looking for a spot where I could see and be seen by other people. The bigger car turned in right behind me. I saw my mistake with an abrupt sinking feeling: the shopping mall wasn't completed yet. It was barely rented out, and the few lights that came from the closed businesses at one end were there purely for security against nocturnal break-ins.

I frantically tried to turn the wagon around and get back out the way I'd gotten in; but my car was hit again, a hard smash on the right rear bumper. The wagon spun around away from the road, its nose plowing into the high oleander bushes down at the end of the lot farthest from the street. The car that had hit me, a big American model, stopped right on my bumper and blocked my way out. My heart thumping in my throat, I left my engine running as I scrambled under my seat for the wrapped baton I carry; but before I could get a grip on it, my door was jerked open and my seat belt severed by something with a glinting blade, and I was pulled out of the car with a force that nearly yanked my arm from its socket.

The two men who had pursued and trapped me wore dark ski masks. As I began to scream, the one who had grabbed me slapped his hand across my mouth, tugging sharply on my hair. I felt tears of pain come to my eyes as my head was jerked back by the motion and I instinctively attempted to bite the hand across my mouth. Then I remembered AIDS and blood and stopped trying to bite. Instead, I kicked out backward, connecting with a shin, but the man holding me barely reacted to the impact. From behind his hand, I tried to scream again.

"Shut up, you fucking cunt," the man whispered. "There's no one around here to hear you no matter how much noise you make, so just shut up and watch carefully and listen." He leaned close to my ear, holding me tightly while he spoke, and I could smell the sharp odor of sweat on him.

As I kicked back again, trying to dig my heel into his instep and squirming frantically, he held tighter and pointed me in the direction of his partner, who was methodically slashing the tires on my car. "See how easily those tires cut?" he whispered. "Do you?" He jerked back on my hair and forced my head up and down in a nodding motion, his thick fingers digging into my jawbone. "Sure you do," he said. I felt as though the breath were being squeezed out of me as he pressed hard on my solar plexus.

The man who had slashed the tires went to the trunk of the Chevy and opened it. Oh Christ, I thought, a whimper choking in my throat. I struggled harder and earned another jab beneath my breastbone. But instead of throwing me into the trunk, the tire slasher removed what I recognized with horror as a can of gasoline, then efficiently began to douse my car. "Are you watching carefully?" the man holding me said, jerking my head up and down again in a puppetlike motion. "Are you?"

I made a sound from behind the hand that held my face.

"That's very good, *Ilene,*" he whispered. "That's what we want to hear."

The use of the name sent an even sharper pang of terror through me: White Nation knew who I was, had probably known all along. I began to shake. Some objective, removed part of me observed this phenomenon and thought, How strange—I'm shaking so hard that if this man weren't holding onto me, I'd probably just fall down. Isn't that odd? Something to be grateful for. His words jerked me back to reality.

"I really do hope you're paying close attention, Ilene, because we want you to remember this and think about everything you see here the next time you're tempted to pull any more stunts like that last one. We're a force to be reckoned with, and we want you to keep that in mind. Think about how much easier it is to slice through skin than it is through rubber." He chuckled. "And how easy it would be to turn someone into a Crispy Critter."

He nodded at the other man, who had apparently finished his dousing task and who now walked calmly toward me. As he got closer, I could see that from behind the slits in his black ski mask, his eyes glittered happily. "He's right, you know? You should stick to sports, sweetie," he said, a cheerful lilt in his voice. "It's much safer. But hey, Kit . . . ?"

I felt faint, nauseated, as he leaned over and stuck his face right up to mine. "Why don't you think about changing focus? Why don't you start telling the truth about the really great athletes? The white athletes. That way you'll be in practice for when we take over."

Without warning, he pulled back and punched me hard in the stomach. "By the way," he said conversationally, "that disguise wasn't very good, but I guess you can tell now if blondes really have more fun." This got a chuckle out of the man holding me. Then the clever one hit me again.

The first punch had left me gasping helplessly behind the hand that was still pinned over my mouth. With the second punch, a wave of thick fog descended. I felt myself dragged some indefinable distance, my knees collapsing weakly beneath me. Then I was thrown against a chain-link fence that separated the unfinished and the completed parts of the parking lot. I automatically grabbed the links in the fence to keep from falling all the way down, choking for breath. Behind me, I heard a squeal of tires and turned feebly. Something was tossed from the departing car, and the VW wagon went up in flames, bright orange and yellow licking at the night. When the huge explosion shook the blacktop, I could feel the heat even from my limp position some fifteen yards away. Nausea washed over me again, and I fell all the way to my knees as I watched my car burn up. Time went all sorts of ways. Eventually, I heard the approach of sirens.

APPARENTLY IT WAS MY LUCKY NIGHT. Not only was I alive, but since it was still early in the evening and there hadn't been any gang shootings or stabbings brought into the small Pleasant Valley emergency room, I was also checked over right away. Not that there was really any need for it—I felt like hell, but even I knew that a couple of hits to the stomach probably wouldn't produce any lasting damage. My shoulder was a little worse off; it was dislocated when I was jerked from my car. But that, too, was an injury in the not-very-serious-considering-the-potential category. Doll and Alan McGill rushed into the small hospital just as I was getting ready to call a taxi to take me home, and they clucked over me like double mother hens.

"I'm all right," I insisted. "More frightened than hurt."

"Which is just what those bastards wanted," Doll seethed.

"That's right," I agreed, fatigued.

"You're coming home with me," Alan insisted. "And bunking in the spare bedroom."

"No, I'm not," I said. "But thanks anyway."

"Powell, go home with Alan and don't be a jerk," Doll snapped. It's his way of showing his concern. "These people know who you are, they damned well might know where you live!"

"They've done exactly what they set out to do, which is make me too scared to try to investigate them," I said with a shrug that proved to be too painful to complete. "Nothing else is going to happen."

"I called Jay already and told him to make up the spare bed," Alan said.

"And I called Nick Strummer," Doll informed me.

"Oh, for Christ's sake," I groaned. I knew Nick was going to hear about this soon enough as it was; the uniforms who'd come to the scene and taken my statement were from downtown, and I'd seen them exchange those looks that meant they knew that I was somehow connected to Strummer. But for Doll to have called him, too—Jesus, I felt like I was about four years old. "Anyone remember to call my parents and tell them, too?"

Doll and Alan looked at each other in surprise. "I forgot," Doll confessed.

"Me, too," Alan said.

"I was kidding," I said tightly. "Believe me, it will be much better for everyone concerned if I break it to them in my own way." The idea of their horrified reactions to the danger I had put myself in, the thought of Betty shrieking in my ear about how I should get a normal, safe job—if it was too much to ask that I actually settle down like a normal person—was more than I could deal with at the moment, and I put the thought of that phone call right out of my head.

"Are you sure you won't come home with me?" Alan asked again anxiously. "I'll fix you a great hot toddy."

My tender stomach heaved at the thought. "No, really." I shook my head. "But how about a ride?"

Doll glared. "I think you're being stubborn, Powell," he said. "I think you're trying to prove how tough you are, and this isn't the time for it."

"I'm not tough," I assured him. "Believe me, I think I just discovered exactly how tough I'm not. I just want to be in my own bed tonight and think about what kind of car I'm going to get."

During the ride home, I recounted what had happened again to Alan, who wore a much grimmer expression than usual. "Those sons of bitches," he muttered.

"It could have been worse," I said.

Alan's lips compressed. "I know."

"Let's change the subject," I suggested.

Alan smiled gamely. "Okay, but I'm afraid I have some news you won't be happy to hear."

I groaned. "What now?"

"I had a heart-to-heart talk with Charity and Albert Killough, the leaders of the antitobacco protesters here, and they swear on a stack of Bibles—which, by the way, they believe in—that no one in their organization has anything to do with the stuff that's been happening to the skaters."

"And you believe them?" I asked.

"I'm afraid I do," Alan sighed. "They may be fanatic, but they want sympathy for their cause, not bad press. At least, that's how I read it."

"I trust your reading," I said glumly.

"So when do Jay and I get to hear all the juicy backstage details about the competition? That drinks date has been on hold for a week."

"I know," I said. "I'm sorry. This whole thing has mutated into something so foggy and weird, I've just been too busy to sit down. As soon as the women's finals are over, it's a date, I promise. But, hey, listen to this. . . ." As we drove through the night I proceeded to tell him what I'd heard from Joelle earlier that evening—it seemed like days ago.

By the time we reached my neighborhood on Coronado, we'd made up a whole bunch of comic scenarios about the newly found father and daughter, winding up singing a couple of verses of "Getting to Know You" as we headed up my block. It was defensive humor, to ward off the ghouls of the reality I'd just dealt with. Alan had stopped pushing for me to stay at his place, but he did insist on coming inside with me and checking the place out. That was fine with me. It was empty except for Dancer, who looked curiously at me, then trotted to his food bowl. I shooed Alan out, repeating that I was fine. Then I fed Dancer and put the kettle on, familiar actions that gave me a sense of security.

I'd seen the blinking light on the phone machine, but had no intention of talking to anyone, at least not right away. I'd done enough talking to the police and the emergency-room doctors and Doll and Alan. What I needed now was to pamper myself a little, to relax in a place where I felt safe. I put a jazz station on the radio, low.

I ran a hot bath and added chamomile salts to the water, and as the tub filled, I reassured myself by studying my surroundings, looking at the original deco tiles, pale yellow and purple, the pedestal sink and glassed-in shower, the lace-curtained windows. I felt incredibly grateful to be there. Then I looked into the mirror over the sink. My face was paler than usual, accenting the three purple marks where my captor's fingers had dug brutally into my face.

165

My hair looked greasy; my eyes looked tired, frightened, and stunned. I might have been keeping up the jaunty attitude in my verbal exchanges, but my physiology told the truth. I was a mess. Still, I reminded my pitiful reflection, you lived to tell it.

I ignored the ringing phone while I poured a mug of steaming water and added lemon and honey to it. Then, reversing my previous course, I put in two shots of brandy and popped one of the painkiller pills the emergency-room doctors had thoughtfully provided for me. What the hell, I thought as I returned to the bathroom with the mug in my hand. If I hadn't thrown up by now, I probably wouldn't, and maybe the brandy would help lull me to sleep. I stripped and sank gingerly into the tub, using my one good arm to brace myself. Then I called Dancer. It was a true mark of my state of unnerved desperation, wanting that schizy creature with me for company. It was a true mark of his schiziness that he obligingly came into the bathroom and sat on the sink grooming his whiskers while I soaked; normally, he does the opposite of whatever I want him to do. My precarious sense of well-being increased incrementally as the soothing effects of the brandy, the pill, the hot bath, and the big orange cat combined to reassure me that I really was safe at home.

I soaked until the water went lukewarm, then pulled myself out of the tub. I was almost dry when the doorbell rang. Dancer and I both jumped a foot into the air at the shrill noise; then I threw on my old terry-cloth bathrobe and padded through the living room to peer through the peephole. The bell had startled me, but I wasn't really surprised to see Nick at the door, and moreover, I was glad he was there. I threw open the door and let him in, then just stood in his arms while the shakes returned for a minute or so.

After a while, Nick tilted my chin gently up to examine my face and winced when he saw the purple bruises. "Come on," he said, "sit down and tell me about it."

Alternating waves of exhaustion, nervous energy, and fear washed over me as I recounted the events of the evening to Nick. From the start of the night and my strange conversation with Joelle Kistler all the way to the prescription in the emergency room, I tried to cover everything in clear detail; when I got fuzzy and went off track, Nick brought me back to the point with specific questions and gentle reminders about where in the story I'd been. "There's no way you'd be able to recognize these men, is there?" he said, resigned.

I shook my head. "Maybe their voices but not their faces. I wouldn't even be able to recognize their goddamned car."

"I'm not at all happy that they know who you are, Kit." Nick's eyes were darker than usual, dark with fatigue, grief, worry.

"I'm not either," I assured him. "Believe me."

He reached over and stroked my cheek, his fingers pausing where my face had been gripped and bruised. "I don't know how," he said quietly, "but I'm going to pin Will's murder on these people and get a conviction. And I'm going to get them for what they did to you."

I put my hand over his. "Thanks."

Nick surveyed me with tired eyes. "Maybe being sensibly frightened off this whole thing is the smarter course of action for you right now," he suggested quietly.

"Maybe it is," I agreed.

The phone rang, then rang again. The third time, I shrugged with my one good shoulder and got up to answer it. Whoever was calling was clearly going to keep on trying until they got me on the line. I was right about that: the call was from my parents, one on each extension, freaking out in stereo about what they'd just seen and heard on the late KSDG newscast.

I waded my way through the hysteria and figured out that Tricia Blaize had broken the story about the vicious assault on part-time sportscaster Kit Powell in a deserted parking lot in Pleasant Valley.

"She called me part-time?" I asked in outrage when my parents had finished their account.

Specific details about the incident were vague, still to follow, but Miss Powell was reported to be doing well and Tricia Blaize would, of course, keep the audience up to date on the developments surrounding the inexplicable and brutal attack on her colleague.

"Shit," I muttered.

"What did you say, Kathleen?"

"Nothing, Mom. Listen, Tricia exaggerated. I'm fine, really I am. . . ."

"Kathleen Powell, I don't care how old you are, I want you to tell me right this minute what on God's green earth were you doing out there in the middle of the night!" My usually unflappable father was on the edge of panic. "I saw the news at the Ringside, Kit. The entire bar was in an uproar—I rushed right home, and don't you ever check your messages? What do you have that machine for anyway if you aren't going to use it? Why didn't you call us? What *happened,* for God's sake?"

"Listen," I said soothingly, "calm down. It isn't the way the news made it sound. I was working on a story and it wasn't the middle of the night"—I looked at the clock—"well, it wasn't then, anyway. And this was no random attack—it was very deliberate and it was meant to warn me off something I've been investigating. . . ."

"Well, then stop investigating it!" Betty interjected hysterically.

"Of course I will, Mom," I reassured her. "Do you think I'm crazy?" Betty didn't reply. "Listen, I just got home a little while ago and I'm sorry I didn't call first thing. I was going to call you, honest. And, Mom," I added before she could dither in and talk around her real concern, "I just got a little beat up, not raped, so don't flip out, okay?"

"What do you mean, a little beat up?" she wailed. "Your face?"

As if it were my fortune. "No—well, yeah, I've got a couple of tiny marks on my face . . ."

"My God!"

". . . but nothing makeup won't hide. My shoulder's kind of . . . dislocated and my stomach's a little tender."

My father let out a strangled roar.

"I'm fine," I insisted.

"Are you there alone, Kathleen? Because if you are, I'm sending Drew right over to spend the night," my mother said.

The thought of my sloppy, immature youngest brother barreling around my house to the accompaniment of the loud metalhead music he favors sent a fresh wave of nausea over me. "No! You don't need to send Drew—Nick's here," I said hastily.

There was a beat of silence. "Oh, really?" Betty said, putting a world of meaning into the simple phrase. Well, I have to give her marks for consistency—once reassured I wasn't badly damaged, she reverted promptly to form. "Is he staying?"

I didn't know. "Yes, Mom," I assured her. "I'll call you in the morning. And I'm fine, really, so stop worrying and go to bed, okay?" After hearing about how many calls they now had to make to reassure concerned friends and relatives about my well-being, I finally got them off the phone and made my way back to the couch, even more worn out than before.

Nick was looking at me with a faintly amused glint in his eyes; it was like seeing the lifting of storm clouds. "I didn't think anything could make me smile after this day," he told me, "but that was quite a conversation, even the half of it I heard."

"Well, you know Mike and Betty—ouch." I had forgotten my shoulder again and tried to shrug.

"Did she ask if I was staying?" Nick said.

I laughed. "Of course."

He leaned over and kissed me very gently on the lips. "Am I?" he asked.

The phone rang.

This time it was Mason and Felice, and as soon as I'd hung up with them, I got a call from Sandy Harrow and had to go through the entire explanation again.

Sandy sounded stricken. "First Donny Duvall, now you," he said. "I can't help thinking this is all my fault, somehow."

"It's not your fault," I reassured him. "We're all doing what we're paid to do. And we're all taking the risks that come along with that. You do it all the time," I reminded him, thinking about the bomb scares at CEO.

"Are you sure you're all right, Kit?" he asked worriedly. "Do you want me to come over? It's no problem."

That's what you think, I thought. "No, Sandy, but thanks," I said hastily. If everyone who had offered had actually arrived on my doorstep to baby-sit me, I mused giddily, I'd have a house so full of testosterone at this point that the roof might well blow off. "I'm fine, honest. I'll call you tomorrow."

When I returned to the couch this time, Nick's expression had cooled a little. "Was that . . . what's his name? Sandy Harrow?" he asked neutrally.

I knew that he knew Sandy's name perfectly well—after all, he'd taken a statement from him less than twenty-four hours ago. But I just nodded, keeping my expression as studiedly blank as his. "Yes, it was," I said.

Nick was quiet for a moment. "Is there . . . something I should know about, Kit?" he asked.

"I don't know," I said honestly. "We just met, we've only been out once."

Nick nodded judiciously; he's maddeningly unreadable when he chooses to be, and this was one of those times. "He seems like a very smart guy," he said.

I smiled coolly in agreement. "And good-looking, too," I said. I couldn't help it.

Nick glared at me. Suddenly, I didn't care what he thought or what was going to happen. I could barely keep my eyes open, and I knew that if I didn't get to bed in the next three minutes, I'd just pass out on the couch and wake up even more sore—and in different places—than I was right now. I also knew I didn't want to be alone.

"Come on," I said quietly, taking his hand. "Let's go to sleep."

He looked quizzically at me but came obediently with me into the bedroom. And sleep is exactly what we did. Nick held me comfortingly as I fell into a deep slumber that was nonetheless troubled by anxious dreams of death by fire and blood on the ice.

16

TRICIA SURVEYED MY FACE the next morning with her currently aquamarine eyes and made cooing sounds of sympathy. "Oh, Kit, look at that! And that! Ugh—how terrible for you—I do hope those bruises won't last for long. They're so . . . purple!"

"Thanks for the memorial piece last night," I said with a sweet smile. "But I'm not dead yet."

Tricia looked appalled. "Kit, you must have been hit on the head," she said sadly. "You're positively paranoid."

"Powell!"

"I have to go talk to Doll," I said, walking away from Tricia and the rest of the newsroom staff who'd gathered to check out my wounds and offer their sympathy.

Max was sitting in Doll's office when I went in, and he hugged me briefly. "You know," he said, studying me as closely as Tricia had done, but with genuine concern, "there's no such thing as a story that's worth exposing yourself to this."

"Believe me," I said, sinking into a chair, "it wasn't my intention. I had no idea that I could have been recognized."

"The point is, no more undercover work for you, Powell," Doll informed me crisply, all traces of the previous night's concern erased. "At least, not until you get better at it."

"No problem," I said, my hands in the air. "I have no desire to come home and find a cross burning on my little lawn one night."

"You'll stick to sports for the time being," Doll went on.

"Okay," I told him. "I already said I would." I pointed to my face. "Do you still want me to go on camera?"

Doll grinned. "Mr. Hoenig called." Hoenig owns the station. "And he said if you didn't look like a bad Irish fighter after ten rounds with any good heavyweight champ, to put you on."

"In other words, if your contusions aren't disgusting enough to cause the audience to turn to another station, smile for the camera," Max added.

"He thinks it will increase ratings, doesn't he?" I asked. "That people will tune in just to see the local sportscaster woman— freaky enough by herself—who survived such a brutal attack, right?"

"Your cynicism can't hold a candle to that of our station owner's," Doll agreed.

I smirked. "Want me to ask makeup to darken the bruises?"

"Not a bad idea," Doll said, deadpan.

I got up again, wincing as my shoulder reminded me it wasn't currently located where it was supposed to be. "I'm covering the pairs and men's singles finals tonight, then," I told him.

"Any more hate mail?" Max asked.

I shook my head. "Not that I know of."

"Stay away from that angle, too," Doll said sternly. "Just in case it's linked to the supremacists."

I rolled my eyes heavenward. "There must be a God," I said. "Doll has taken my theory seriously."

"Get out of here," Doll said, annoyed. "And stay out of strange neighborhoods after dark—I hate losing sleep over staff problems."

"You like me!" I gushed. "You really like me!"

Max began to laugh.

So many people brought me tea while I worked that morning that I thought my kidneys were going to take the next hard body hit. I prepped my coverage for the evening but couldn't keep my mind on just sports, as I had promised Doll I would. Around lunchtime, flowers arrived from Sandy Harrow. Then flowers arrived from Mr. Hoenig. Then flowers arrived from a bunch of the Ringside regulars.

"Looks just like a hospital," Tricia remarked, reaching for the cards. I slapped her hand away. "Uh-oh," she said, "nothing from the boyfriend?"

Before I went looking for Tony to ask him for another blowup of the picture of Held—the first one had burned up in the wagon, along with my purse—I took the cards off the flowers and slipped them into my pocket.

"Hey," Tony said as he made another print for me, "are you supposed to be needing this anymore?"

"Not exactly," I admitted.

He fixed me with a knowing eye. "Uh-huh," he said, handing the print to me. "That's what I thought."

Of course, I'd lied through my teeth to Doll when I had placidly agreed to stay away from any more poking around where I so clearly wasn't wanted. It's not that I think I'm a particularly brave person, but tenacity is a quality I have in spades, and despite what had happened, I couldn't shake the need to find out more about Held.

I drove my rented car to the address I'd been given for Gary Held's sister in Chula Vista. The run-down house looked to be about eight hundred square feet, in need of roof repair and paint; it was planted in the middle of a tiny squalid lot on a block of similar houses on identical lots. Although a dog barked and barked, no one answered the door. I moved on to the National City address of the halfway house Held had lived in after his last release from prison. The place was located in an area that made Held's sister's neighborhood look like Bel Air in comparison.

Groups of people loitered on corners, graffiti was rampant, and iron bars of the distinctly nondecorative type covered doors and windows of every shoddy building. Men with rags tied around their heads leaned into the windows of cars that were far too expensive for the area. Drug deals right out in the open in the middle of the day—what a great place to stick a bunch of ex-cons who were supposed to be continuing the fabulous rehabilitation that they'd begun in prison. Not that other, more upscale neighborhoods tended to hang out the welcome banner for such establishments. But the places have to wind up in someone's backyard.

I suppose the only reason I wasn't really nervous about getting out of the car was that the boxy little rental looked nothing like a vehicle cruising for a drug buy; or maybe it was just the painkillers smoothing out the edges. But I did think, as I mounted the wide cracked-stone steps leading to the house, that Will Merriwether might have spent a lot of time around here in both of his capacities—as cop and as buyer. And it made me sad.

The man who answered the door was fat and unshaven. He looked me up and down, noted the bruises on my face, and said, "Yeah?" in an uninterested voice. "Who do you wanna see?"

"Whoever runs the house," I said crisply, affronted at his clearly having mistaken me for the wife or girlfriend of one of the residents.

"May I help you?" A lively-looking middle-aged woman in a faded but clean blouse and slacks appeared in the doorway as the man, a resident, I assumed, faded back into the dim hallway. "I'm Helen Blasucci. My husband and I run Merit House."

I identified myself to her and we shook hands. "I'm sorry," said Helen Blasucci, "but I don't watch too much TV except the national news."

I smiled. "I understand." Then I told her whom I was looking for.

Helen Blasucci's graying dark brows knit while she thought. "Yes," she said, "of course I remember Gary, he was no trouble at all. He attended his AA meetings and got a job, let me see, working down at the docks, I believe." She looked at me, puzzled. "But that was several years ago now."

I shrugged. "This is the last address I have for him," I told her. "This might sound odd, but did he ever talk about a daughter to you?"

"Oh dear." Mrs. Blasucci bit her lip. "Let me try to remember. . . ."

"Remember what?" A man appeared beside Helen Blasucci, and she introduced her husband, Raymond, and told him what I wanted to know. Raymond Blasucci was a big, spare man with calm, intelligent eyes.

"Do you remember Gary Held ever talking about a child, a daughter?" Helen Blasucci asked her husband.

"Yes," Raymond Blasucci said promptly. "I remember because he brought it up several times in the group, and he was very emotional about the child. He'd lost her or given her up for adoption or something. I'm afraid I don't remember the details, though."

"And did he seem inclined to, um, racial prejudice? Extremist views?"

Helen Blasucci shook her head. "Not that I recall," she said. "He was a rather gentle man, kind of sad and beaten down."

"Is he in some kind of trouble?" Raymond asked.

"I don't know," I said slowly. I showed them the picture. "Is this Gary Held?" I asked her.

Helen Blasucci put on the glasses that hung from a beaded chain around her neck. "It could be," she said, frowning. "But I can't really tell from this."

Raymond Blasucci just shook his head.

It felt like a dead end again. "Do you remember if Gary had any friends, anyone he hung around with?" I persisted.

Raymond sighed. "Gary hung around with two of the other residents, at least while he was here," he told me. "Marlis Hasper and Frank Pyne."

"Oh yes," Helen said, frowning, "now I remember."

"You have to understand the men who stop here are just as likely to go one way as the other, Miss Powell. We try our best to help them go straight in the outside world, but we're not always successful. Those two, well, Gary would have been better off making friends with some of the others." He looked at me calmly. "But that's my personal opinion, understand."

I understood that the Blasuccis were thoughtful people who didn't incline toward gossip. I thanked them for their time and left. Helen Blasucci's description of Gary Held had dovetailed with what Joelle had said about her father, but something had changed. Something had turned a sad harmless man into a charter member of White Nation. That insistent finger that pointed to something not adding up here was tapping at me again.

I returned to Chula Vista. This time, the door was answered. Gary Held's sister was a beat-up-looking woman of about forty, with eyes that were alternately suspicious and calculating.

When I told her who I was and what I wanted, she shrugged dismissively. "I haven't seen my brother in over a year," she said. "And that's fine with me. All he ever wanted from me was money for his rotgut liquor and a place to crash when he couldn't find a mission or something open. I figured he must've moved on by now, up to Reno or somethin', that's what he was always talking about anyway." She snorted derisively. "I don't know what all he thinks he'll find there—he's always got himself to deal with no matter where he is."

The milk of human kindness, I thought. "But you haven't heard from him?"

"Uh-uh." She shook her head. "He don't keep in touch unless he needs something."

"Do you know if he's in touch with his daughter?" I asked.

"The baby—nah, he gave her away," she told me with a shrug. "Gary wasn't no fit father. I think she's some kind of famous dancer or something; at least that's what he claims."

I showed her the photograph, and she shook her head. "No," she said. "I don't know who that is, but it ain't Gary."

"Are you sure?" I pressed her.

She looked offended. "We ain't close, honey, but I know my own brother. And that ain't him."

"Do you know a Marlis Hasper or Frank Pyne?" I asked.

She shook her head. "And if they're friends of Gary's, I don't want to." Her phone rang and she shrugged. "I got nothin' else to tell you," she said as she shut the door.

As soon as I arrived back at KSDG, I phoned Nick but got Mardigian instead. "You okay?" he asked.

I assured him I was fine. "Listen, Stan, I turned up something on the man I saw at the White Nation rally, the one claiming to be Joelle Kistler's father. Did Nick tell you about that?"

"Uh-huh," he said.

"He's not," I told him.

"Not what?"

"Not the real Gary Held."

Mardigian was silent for a moment. "Then who is he?" he asked.

"That's the sixty-four-thousand-dollar question," I said. "I think I know where to start looking, though." I gave him the names Marlis Hasper and Frank Pyne.

"Just out of curiosity," Mardigian said, "weren't you supposed to back off?"

"Well," I began.

"That's what I figured," he said.

"Hey, I'm sitting safely at my own little desk right now," I protested. "And soon I'll be surrounded by crew and spectators while the Bethlehem Invitational finals come to their glittering finale."

"Save the evasions and the promos for someone else," Mardigian said, not unaffectionately. "And just please be careful."

"I will," I assured him.

"I'll tell Nick you called," he said.

Nick checked in a few minutes before I left the station for the Bethlehem Arena. "Interesting stuff, Kit, but I don't know where it's going to go. These two guys—well, there's only one left. Marlis Hasper died in Tehachapi last year—but they both had extensive records. And listen, you were sort of on the right track. Frank Pyne is a dyed-in-the-wool charter member of White Nation; he's suspected of having killed two Muslims while he was still behind bars, but nothing was proved."

I felt a shiver run up my spine. "Do you have a picture of him?" I asked.

"Of course."

"I want to take a look at it. And, Nick, listen, there's one more thing. . . ."

"Spit it out," he said, resigned.

"Why don't you see if you can match the dental records of that unidentified transient to Gary Held?"

There was a moment of silence. "Jesus Christ," he said. "Okay."

After we hung up, I sat at my desk staring at my blank computer screen, trying to make the pieces add up; they were beginning to, and I didn't like what I saw, not one little bit. If the man who claimed to be Gary Held was really Frank Pyne, then what did he want from Joelle Kistler?

"Come on, Kit." Joe and Tony appeared by my desk. "We're running late for Pleasant Valley."

Tony nodded toward the exit, where an overdressed Tricia

177

Blaize and her crew were on the move. "Tobacco protesters have put the word out that they're going to be out in full force for the last two nights of the competition," he told me, "and Tricia is going to be very, very visible—let's see if we make ourselves even more visible."

"Not likely," I muttered.

We traveled down the same road I'd been attacked on the night before, and I showed Joe and Tony the parking lot where it had happened. The scorched blacktop still smelled, but the remains of my charred car had been removed. I felt myself begin to shake as I gave the guys a guided tour of the scene of the crime.

"Let's get out of here," I said abruptly.

Tony nodded and pulled the van quickly out of the lot.

"Hey, what kind of car are you going to get?" asked Joe by way of turning the subject to something more upbeat.

"I don't know, but whatever it is, it's going to have a phone," I confessed, a little embarrassed.

"Good idea," the guys agreed somberly. That made me feel a little better and a little worse simultaneously.

The arena lot was jammed with cars, news vans, and, as Tony had predicted, protesters. A huge picket line of vocal antitobacco marchers circled repetitiously in front of the entrance, hassling spectators as they arrived for their support of the poison Bill Bethlehem was promoting. To my surprise, there was an equally large counterdemonstration of local residents who wanted to show their support of Bethlehem Enterprises for moving into the area. I saw a clash break out among three or four opposing protesters, and a few people fell to the ground in a scuffle. The arena guards had called in extra protection, and several police jumped into the melee, separating the protesters and antiprotesters and hauling two of them off to be booked. Tricia was there, covering it all in her perky, breathy, every-hair-in-place style.

"Jesus," I muttered, "if there's even a half minute left for a sports segment tonight, she'll have failed miserably in her mission."

We slid by the heckling line and into the relative peace of the arena itself, where the noise came from excited viewers eager to see their favorites perform, and set up in the corner of the rink a few yards off the ice. Whatever was happening outside the arena wasn't going to interfere with the program, and after the national anthem was sung, the skating began.

Tensions were running high between the young competitors on this final night of men's singles and pairs. I saw more than one angry look pass between Todd Allison and Jared Bright, but mainly they resolutely ignored each other as they ran through their routines mentally, meditated, prayed, whatever it was that each individual did before his dramatic entrance. Once on the ice, each of the young men went through an incredibly rigorous eight-minute program, each trying to include more drama, more passion, and more triple leaps than the others. Paul Cavanaugh overtook Jared Bright with a series of hard-hitting athletic leaps and came in second. But I wasn't surprised that Todd, the favorite, took the competition by storm; he included several triples and one quadruple axel, which made the audience leap to its feet with a collective roar of approval and loud applause. I nabbed a brief interview with Todd as he came off the ice, sweat pouring from his face, his black-and-silver costume drenched.

Then it was time for the pairs. The couple who had placed third, Elena Borovkin and Danny Slater, were the only real competition for the top two pairs contenders—Ari and Shannon and Susu and Paul. I watched eagerly as Borovkin and Slater went into a whirling, balletic routine that had the grace and speed it would take to grab the high marks the couple needed to pass either of those two other pairs. The routine went almost flawlessly until Danny tossed Elena into the air and she missed her landing. She fell on her right leg and slid; then, in an attempt to get up quickly and return to the program, she tumbled again.

"Ouch," Tony muttered beside me.

From our vantage point, I could see Elena holding back tears, but she and Danny went gamely through the rest of the program. They shorted two last jumps and made a tentative final move, which the crowd applauded with sympathy. But there would be no first or second place for them, unless genuine disaster struck one of the last two pairs.

It didn't. Ari and Shannon skated first, having drawn that spot in the finals event. Their performance was very, very good; they skated to three different Strauss waltzes and made the most of Ari's strength and Shannon's petite frame as they swirled around, Shannon held high over Ari's head. He threw her far out onto the ice and Shannon, unlike Elena, made a perfect landing.

Then, as the third segment of the music began, something happened to Shannon's concentration, and her rhythm went off; she and Ari missed a few of the fast, intricate side-by-side steps until she regained her focus. It happened again, on the last turn around the ice; when Ari tossed Shannon into the air, she lost her balance and fell straight down. She recovered well, but the program was far from perfect.

In contrast, Susu and Paul skated powerfully and made no mistakes. They wore striking red-and-black costumes, glittery and glamorous, with little attached capes that became part of the performance as they swirled and leaped to *Bolero*. They took first place by only a fraction of a point over Ari and Shannon, but a fraction of a point was all it took. Afterward, the Canadian pair looked thoroughly wrung out, wet to the skin, and ecstatic about their win.

In the hubbub backstage, after the prizes had been presented, I jockeyed for position with other news crews and got Susu and Paul's joy and relief on tape. It would make the happy, up story I'd been wanting to come out of this skewed competition all along, and it made me feel good. I knew it would do the same for the viewers.

"What do you think?" It was Channing Strummer beside me. "Will this take some of the onus off the crap outside?"

I laughed. It still felt odd to actually like Nick's ex-wife, but I couldn't help it; she was down-to-earth and she had a damned good sense of humor. "I think so," I said. "There's no downside to a story about struggling athletes and triumph." Then Channing asked how I was doing and I pointed to my painful arm and bruised face. "Better than I look," I said.

She frowned. "I can't believe that happened," she said angrily. "What's the world coming to?" Something in the grandstand caught her eye. "I'm going to call you next week about the interview, okay?"

As Channing left, I saw Melinda Parsons walking toward the exit and called out to her. She swiveled around when she heard my voice and came toward me with concern. "I heard about what happened to you," she said. I was beginning to feel like there had been no other news the night before. "Are you okay?"

I ran through the same brief explanation I had with Channing. "I'll be fine," I said. "But how are you? Nervous?"

"Not really," Melinda said thoughtfully. "At least, no more than usual." She shrugged. "I don't think I'm going to take first place, Miss Powell . . . Kit," she confessed. "Not this time—the competition is too stiff. But I'm getting there."

She was a pragmatic young woman. "No more junk in the mail or the lockers?" I asked.

Melinda shook her head, her nose wrinkling in distaste. "Even though I didn't want to talk about it at first, I have to admit it was really unnerving me. I think maybe the fact that it all finally got public scared off whoever was doing it. I'm glad it all came out," she told me.

"Well, you helped," I reminded her.

"What do you mean?" she asked, her expression puzzled. "I didn't do anything."

"You told Susu," I reminded her. "And after what happened to her, she decided to talk about it. That's why the story broke."

Melinda looked blankly at me. "I didn't tell Susu anything," she said. "Where did you get that idea?"

"But . . ." I regrouped my thoughts. "Are you sure you didn't mention the letters or the doll to her?"

Melinda shook her head firmly. "Of course not," she said. "I didn't talk to anyone but you about that stuff." She looked curiously at me. "What made you think that I had?"

I shook my head and pretended to be confused; it didn't take all that much effort. "My mistake," I said. "I must have mixed my information up." I smiled gamely and squeezed her arm. "Listen, I want to wish you all the best tomorrow night. You're terrific."

Melinda smiled. "Thanks," she said happily. "See you tomorrow night."

I stared at her retreating back, then over to the empty stand where Susu Jenrette and Paul Cavanaugh had just been holding forth. My brain had already run through all the possibilities in a computerlike fashion, but when it reached the end, there was only one logical conclusion, and it was as ugly as it could be. I went looking for Channing Strummer.

17

CHANNING AND I WAITED in Bill Bethlehem's luxurious suite at the Bethlehem Vista, where he'd agreed to meet us as soon as he wrapped up the night's competition business.

"I can't believe it," Channing said, perched stiffly in a wing chair, drumming her fingers on the arm. I had the sudden uncomfortable vision of her angry with Nick—she looked good even when she was pissed off. In pale gold silk, with her coloring and looks, she was strictly champagne; me, I'm beer. "I cannot believe she'd do something like that," Channing was saying. "I'm no stranger to competitive egos, either, but this is so . . . so . . ."

I supplied the word: "Revolting."

Channing popped up like a pissed-off jack-in-the-box as Bill Bethlehem strode into the suite, worry creasing his handsome forehead. "What's so urgent that we had to meet in secret?" he asked.

Channing nodded toward me. "Kit thinks she's found out who's behind all the hate mail, Bill," she said. "And I think she's right. And you"—she directed him to the conversation cluster of furniture—"you'd better sit down. You aren't going to like this at all."

Bethlehem's clear eyes clouded and I wondered if he thought coming to temperate, pleasant San Diego had been such a good idea after all. With all the negative press coverage, all the trouble surrounding both the industrial move to the area and the competition itself, it must have been a PR person's worst nightmare. But up until now, at least the participants in the competition had been beyond reproach. That was all about to change. Bill Bethlehem fixed himself and Channing a drink, but I declined. After this was over, I had to edit my skating piece and appear on the ten o'clock news.

"Okay," he said, sinking into a soft teal leather armchair. "Let's hear it."

I recounted my conversation with Susu in the hospital, and her claim that Melinda Parsons had told her about the doll in her locker. I also told him about Susu's allegation that she had just happened to see and overhear Ari Kotzloff telling Shannon Ngao about the swastika he'd received.

Bill Bethlehem nodded. "What's the problem?"

"Melinda says she never mentioned the doll to Susu," I said soberly.

It took a moment for the implication to sink in, and even then, Bethlehem did what I had done: search for alternative explanations. "And what about Ari?" Bethlehem asked. "Did you ask him about it?"

Channing and I exchanged glances. "We talked to him just before I called you," Channing told him. "And he says that Shannon is the one who came to him with the bowl of rice and maggots—that's when he told her about the swastika. And it didn't happen in her hotel room, it was during practice. They just sat on the bleachers away from the other skaters and talked about what had happened and what they should do."

"And Shannon confirmed that," I added.

"So it's . . . *possible* that they could have been overheard," Bethlehem mused, "by Susu or anyone else who happened to be around." He looked at me, already resigned to the truth. "But you don't think that's what happened, do you?"

"No." I shook my head. "I don't. Why would Susu bother to lie about *where* she overheard something if she admitted she was eavesdropping in the first place? And she was so clear about the details when she told me. . . ." I shook my head. "All the details that now prove not to be true at all. I hate it as much as you do, but I really think the only logical conclusion is that Susu Jenrette is the one who sent the doll and the rice and the swastikas."

Bethlehem's crystal tumbler hit the glass-topped coffee table with an angry thunk. "Goddamn it," he said softly.

"And she's had it planned for a long time," I continued. "This campaign began a while ago—Melinda Parsons got some pretty nasty letters before she even left Portland for the competition."

Bethlehem digested the information, nodding. Then he looked up at me. "But what about Susu's hit-and-run?" he asked incredulously. "You don't think she staged that, actually got herself hit by a car, do you?"

"Sure, I do," I said. "But not by herself. I think you ought to check Paul Cavanaugh's rental car—although she probably didn't even get hit hard enough to leave any evidence on the bumper."

Bethlehem shook his head again. "Hell and damnation," he said quietly. "All that nasty effort, and for what? They still couldn't guarantee a win for themselves. Why risk it?"

"Because it upped their odds hugely," Channing said.

I nodded in agreement. "Psychological terrorism is a very effective tool," I said. "And besides, they *did* win. Tonight, at least, in the pairs. And the publicity has been a real boost to their negotiating powers."

Bethlehem's face was a grim mask as he reached for the phone. "Please have security bring Miss Jenrette and Mr. Cavanaugh to my suite," he said. He paused. "I don't care if they're still celebrating. Get them here *now.*"

The winning pair appeared in the suite in less than ten minutes. Still in their glittery costumes, they wore expressions that were a mixture of excitement and confusion as they were ushered in to face the three of us. Bill Bethlehem took control of the situation, tersely rehearsing the facts as we now saw them, then waiting for a reply.

Paul Cavanaugh went dead pale when he heard Bethlehem lay out the accusations about the racist hate mail. Susu looked from me to Bill Bethlehem to Channing, her face a picture of innocent hurt. "I can't believe you could think I could do something like this." She turned to face me. "Especially you, Miss Powell. You know what I believe about someone trying to sabotage the competition—and you're trying to blame it on *me?*"

"You lied about where you got your information," I said.

"I didn't lie!" Susu said indignantly. "I got hit by a car, for God's sake—I was in shock! Maybe I got confused, but I didn't lie!"

Bethlehem sighed. "Miss Jenrette," he said, "I'm going to have to turn this over to the police and the USFSA."

Susu's expression of hurt turned to ice. "You do and I'll sue you until you don't have a cereal box left to your name!" she snarled. "Where's a phone? I'm calling my lawyer and my agent right now!"

"Be my guest." Bill Bethlehem gestured to a phone on the end table. He stared at Paul Cavanaugh. "How about you?" he asked. "Anyone you'd like to call?"

"I . . ." Paul glanced at Susu nervously. "We didn't have anything to do with the letters," he said softly.

"But that hit-and-run?" I asked, thinking how I'd tried to make Gary Held responsible for that.

"I was injured!" Susu interjected indignantly.

"Not so badly that you couldn't skate the next night," Bill Bethlehem said.

"I'm sure the car can be traced," I lied, staring Paul Cavanaugh in the eye.

Cavanaugh stared back, then crumbled. He wasn't made of the same stern stuff as his partner. His lip trembled. "I'm sorry," he said.

Bethlehem stared at him for a beat, then turned to Susu. "Did you act alone on the threats?" he demanded.

"Susu," Paul said, putting his hand on her arm, "if you had anything to do with that, just tell them the truth. . . ."

Suddenly the blandly stonewalling Susu Jenrette cracked. "Shut up, you fucking moron!" she snapped. "I haven't spent the past twelve years working my ass off to wind up as a has-been in some third-rate ice show!"

It wasn't an admission of guilt, but it was hardly a denial. And as it dawned on Paul Cavanaugh exactly what he might be implicated in, he suddenly couldn't wait to put some distance between himself and his partner. He wasted no time admitting that he had, at Susu's instigation, tapped her with his rental car, then run back into the arena and waited for the onslaught of hysterical reaction. He turned to his partner. "Susu, this is . . . You need help."

Susu smirked nastily at him. "But it worked, didn't it?" Then she looked at the rest of us. "I just screwed up at the end. If I just hadn't tried to add a little texture to my story, none of you would ever have known." She was almost gloating about her cleverness, wrapped up in her own vision of what she could have accomplished, not the reality of what she had brought down on herself.

I suspect that I looked as appalled as Channing and Bill Bethlehem; Paul Cavanaugh just looked like a stunned animal.

"But we do know, Susu," I reminded her.

"Know what?" She shrugged dismissively and tossed that perky blond ponytail. "It's his word against mine. Besides, what are you going to do about it?" She stared challengingly at Bill Bethlehem. "This competition has already had so much bad press, Mr. Bethlehem, that I just don't see how you can afford any more."

For just a beat, Bill Bethlehem wore such an unreadable expression that I wondered if he was actually going to cave in to Susu's form of public-relations blackmail. Then he rose to his feet. "That was another mistake, Miss Jenrette," he said in a powerful voice. "I have a strong aversion to threats." He glanced back and forth between Susu and Paul. "As of this moment, you are stripped of your titles and winnings in this event, and as soon as you've returned to your rooms to pack, I will be giving the judges a written statement to this effect so that they may inform the USFSA of your actions. I'm adding my strong recommendation that you be barred from competition for life."

"No!" It was that threat that finally got through to Susu Jenrette. "You can't! We'll never get a contract. . . ."

"And last," Bethlehem continued, ignoring her interruption, "as I indicated, I'm turning this entire matter over to the police. I believe several laws have been broken here."

There was a stunned silence in the room. Susu didn't blink. "You can't do that," she said flatly. Her tone was calm, but her face was more revealing—no longer cute, no longer perky, no longer quite so insulated by her crazy self-absorption.

"Please, Mr. Bethlehem," Paul said. "If you could just reconsider . . ."

Bill Bethlehem cut him off with a brusque gesture. "Don't," he said. "I've told you exactly what I'm going to do, and that's final."

"I won't let you take this away from me." Susu nearly spat the words.

Bethlehem shook his head in pity and disgust. "No one's taking anything away from you, Miss Jenrette—you did that all by yourself."

"I have the best sports lawyers money can buy, and I'm going to sue you until you don't have a penny left," Susu said through clenched teeth.

"Maybe," Bethlehem said grimly. "But believe me, by the time this is through, you'll be lucky to land a contract with the Roller Derby." He reached for the phone and called security again.

OKAY, SO THE LATE-NIGHT SPORTS SEGMENT wasn't exactly the upbeat, happy piece I'd thought it would be. Nothing even remotely involved with the Bethlehem Pro-Am was turning out the way it was supposed to. Who would ever have imagined a lead story about a violent protest would come out of it, let alone revelations of the kind of sabotage I'd just heard confessed? But the news is the news. Tricia did her thing, then I did mine, carefully couching the accusations against Cavanaugh-Jenrette in nonlitigious terms; after all, this had yet to be proven.

The shock waves that rolled through the station—and were reflected in the phone-ins afterward—were guaranteed to please Mr. Hoenig, who even now was probably sitting at home gleefully blessing my bruised face. No one wins, I thought, except the ratings. Even Ari and Shannon couldn't be all that overjoyed—default by scandal isn't the happiest way to get that coveted top spot.

I had two messages when I got off the set, one from Nick Strummer and one from Channing Strummer. How cozy, I thought ruefully. I phoned Mr. Strummer first.

"Did you see my report?" I asked.

"What? No," Nick sounded distracted. "I called to tell you that we lifted a set of fingerprints off the metal fastener of your seat belt—it wasn't charred enough to destroy them."

I fought off a feeling of panic as the image brought back the memory of being pulled from my car. "And?"

"They belong to one Mr. Coley Prideux," Nick said.

"Who's that?"

"One of Eugene Ebberly's lieutenants," Nick said with a certain grim glee. "With a lengthy record of assaults, armed robberies, and one attempted murder. We're going in, Kit, to Ebberly's ranch. We're going to arrest him for the attack on you. Tonight."

Feelings of relief and surprise at the expediency of this whole operation rolled through me, along with a serious shudder at what might have happened, given Mr. Prideux's record. But the attack on me had only been a fraction of the problems caused by White Nation. "What about the transient murders?" I asked.

"We're hoping that with enough applied pressure and the threat of a long-enough jail sentence for Prideux, we can make a deal for information about the killings," Nick told me.

"Nick," I said slowly, "do you really think someone like Prideux will fold for something like this charge? I mean, how heavy a penalty can that attack on me carry?"

"Not heavy enough," Nick told me. "But since Prideux's residence is Eugene Ebberly's ranch, we get to go in with a search warrant, and I'm hoping that Ebberly and his crew are just insane enough to have all sorts of illegal weapons and potential evidence against them stashed up in those hills. And don't forget, if we can find one iota of evidence linking them physically to Will Merriwether, we're talking death penalty here."

"Be careful," I said automatically.

"Always," Nick replied. "Now, what was it about your report?"

I told him about Susu Jenrette and the hate mail, and about the staging of her "hit-and-run" accident.

"Oh, for Christ's sake," Nick said in disgust. "All for a goddamned skating title."

"And for a guaranteed secure future," I said. "Financially speaking."

"Well, I suppose I'm glad the hate mail thing is cleared up, although I'd love to have pinned that on White Nation, too. Jenrette will probably get off with a slap on the wrist. What a poisonous little psycho." I heard him say something to someone else; then he came back on the line. "Gotta go, Kit," Nick said hastily. "I'll call you later and let you know when we've got these assholes behind bars."

I felt a wave of affection for him sweep through me as I made my next return call to his ex-wife.

Channing Strummer sounded as if she were about to come unglued. "Kit, I'm so sorry to keep dragging you into this mess, but can you come back to the hotel? There's something that's come up that I don't want to get into over the phone."

I glanced at my watch. It was nearly eleven and I was dead on my feet—reeling from the events of the last twenty-four hours, a little woozy from painkillers, ready to call it a night. "If it's that important," I said reluctantly. At the moment, I thought wearily, I'd almost prefer to hand a breaking story to Tricia.

"It's that important," Channing assured me. "I wouldn't ask you to come back if it weren't. We'll be waiting in Bill's suite."

"Okay," I said, wondering if Susu Jenrette had attempted suicide or if some other equally bizarre development had grown out of the latest discovery. I trudged wearily out of the station, got into my rental car, and drove to Pleasant Valley.

The Bethlehem Vista was beginning to feel like home to me. As I punched the button for the fourth floor and rode up in plush silence, I considered just checking in for the night. Or maybe a week. A luxury suite with a Jacuzzi and no phone sounded just about right to me. When I knocked lightly on Bill Bethlehem's suite door, Channing pulled it open and ushered me in with such alacrity that I thought she must have been hovering right inside it.

"What—" I began. Then I saw the Kistlers. They were sitting on the same couch I'd last seen Susu Jenrette and Paul Cavanaugh occupying.

"What's the matter?" I asked.

Ellen Kistler stared at me accusingly through red-rimmed eyes. "Where's Joelle?" she demanded. "Do you know?"

"No," I said. "Of course I don't. What's going on?"

Bill Bethlehem looked wearily at me. "Mrs. Kistler seems to think that something you said to Joelle got her upset, Miss Powell. Is that possible?"

Oh shit, I thought. "No," I replied. "I didn't say anything that would have upset Joelle. Anyway, what do you mean 'where's Joelle'? Is she missing?"

John Kistler nodded, his arm firmly around his distraught

wife's shoulder. He looked barely able to restrain tears himself. "She made some very . . . strange accusations to us, Miss Powell, and we tried to calm her down. She was hysterical. Ellen was so upset that I sent her to our suite, and I got a sedative for her."

I exchanged glances with Bill Bethlehem. Collectively, the Kistlers might prove to be of minimal help; they might prove to be no help at all. "And then what happened?"

"And when I returned to Joelle's suite she was just . . . gone."

"What did you argue about?" I asked. As if I didn't know.

"Never mind that, it's not important," Ellen Kistler said.

The Kistlers might want to preserve the make-believe world they had created, but I was too tired to play that game.

"Did she talk to you about Gary Held?" I asked.

John Kistler looked at me in shock, Ellen Kistler in fright.

"Who's Gary Held?" asked Bill Bethlehem.

"Joelle's natural father," I said evenly, not taking my eyes off the Kistlers.

"Joelle isn't your daughter?" Channing said to John Kistler in surprise.

"She's adopted," Kistler murmured.

"Is she, Mr. Kistler?" I asked. "Joelle seems to believe she wasn't ever legally adopted at all."

Ellen Kistler began to sob on her husband's shoulder, and the sobs became keening sounds of grief. Or maybe it was guilt.

"What does it matter now?" John Kistler said desperately. "All we care about is that she's safe, for God's sake!"

"Did she ask you to tell her the truth, Mrs. Kistler?" I insisted. Ellen was top dog here; if anyone was going to give me answers, it would be her. "Did she?" I repeated. She nodded, finally. "And you lied to her."

"What was I supposed to do!" she flared. "She's been upset enough about Terese, her entire performance has been off. She's been saying crazy things anyway, that she had no right to be who she was, that her whole life was a fake, that she was going to give up skating. I just tried to keep her mind focused. For God's sake, the finals are tomorrow night! Do you know how important those endorsements could be?"

She had psychologically melded her daughter's safety with her daughter's winning status. And she didn't seem aware that the two things had nothing to do with each other. I thought about Joelle's bitter comment that all the Kistlers wanted was a trophy, not a daughter.

"How did you learn all this, Kit?" Bill Bethlehem asked.

"I had a talk with Joelle," I said. Had it only been yesterday? Time seemed to be stretching like molasses candy.

"What did she tell you?" John Kistler demanded.

"Exactly what she probably told you," I replied. "She's very confused, Mr. Kistler. She's not thinking straight, and she needs to be told the facts about who she is and why you've kept the truth from her."

"We just did what we thought was best for her," he reiterated—the sad parental explanation for most courses of action, wise or unwise. A look of utter bewilderment crossed his face. "She said . . . she said she needed some time by herself, and that if we came after her, we'd never see her again."

"Do you think she could be with this . . . Held person?" Bill Bethlehem asked.

"I think it's a possibility," I said cautiously. I wasn't about to tell them what I thought really might have happened. "I also think we should call the police."

"No!" Ellen Kistler wailed. "No police, I can't take it! It will ruin Joelle's career!"

"Ellen," her husband said, but she just collapsed again, sobbing convulsively.

There seemed to be only one choice. "Let me see if I can find her," I volunteered.

John Kistler looked pleadingly at me. "Can you?" he asked. "Please, just bring her home to us, tell her we love her, tell her we'll do anything she wants, just tell her to come home!"

I nodded. I motioned Channing out into the lushly carpeted hallway with me. These seemed such unlikely surroundings for the drama that was being played out. I gave her the name of the street and a description of my rental car.

"Call the police," I told her.

192

18

M ARINE A VENUE WAS A SMALL dead-end street, part of a blighted residential pocket stuck in the middle of an urban war zone. It wasn't far from the halfway house I'd visited or from the freeway intersection where the last transient victim and Terese Steiner had been found. I drove slowly, looking for a car I recognized; without an address, it was all I had to go on. On one of the four blocks, loud salsa music blared from an apartment between two abandoned buildings, but most of the residents appeared to be locked away behind iron bars and security shutters. It wasn't a neighborhood I'd have chosen for an after-dark excursion by myself, and I hoped Channing had conveyed the urgency of the situation to the police. Having been married to a cop, she probably could make herself understood pretty easily. Having Strummer for a last name wouldn't hurt, either.

A banged-up older dark car halfway up the second block looked familiar, but as I slowed my rental to a crawl, I saw that its front two tires were blown and that the entire vehicle was resting on cinder blocks. It wasn't until I reached the very end of Marine and was starting to worry that somehow I'd wound up in the wrong place that I spotted the car belonging to the man who called himself Gary Held. It was parked in a dark driveway beside a shabby little house set far back on a shadowy corner lot. It was just far enough away from its neighbors to seem secluded in the middle of the city. I turned and cruised by again. The only light I could see in the place was flickering and low, the kind that comes from a television.

After parking my car a few yards down the block of the intersecting street, I sat there feeling jittery and exposed under the orange sulphur anticrime lights that didn't look like they were doing much good in this neighborhood. I didn't even have my tape-wrapped baton for protection, I realized; it had no doubt melted down in the wagon the night before. At least ten minutes crawled by with me watching my rearview mirror for the arrival of the police. Another five passed with no sign of help arriving. What if Channing hadn't gotten through to them? What if they couldn't find the place? Worry gnawed at my gut until, finally, I braced myself against the fear that threatened to paralyze me and forced myself to get out of the car.

I had no desire to engage in heroics, but I at least had to find out if Joelle was there, if she was alive. Keeping well hidden in the shadows, I skirted the draped front windows and peeling front door and crept quietly up the driveway beside the battered old car. I could hear nothing. A side door had a small glass pane in it, cracked but still intact. A piece of tattered calico cloth nearly covered it, but as I peered in, holding my breath, I could just make out the small, messy kitchen and a hallway beyond. I stood there in the shadows uncertainly, and then I heard the sound.

It was a high muffled noise, somewhere between crying and pleading. My blood froze. But I saw no one, and there was no movement from within the house, no shadows, no other sounds except the soft garbled ones that were intermittent and chilling. And as I stared hopefully down the driveway, no lights came up the street either, no longed-for cherry beacon rolled quietly up to take care of the situation. I padded around to the rear of the house in the direction of the crying. In the shadowy tangle of the overgrown backyard, weeds were thigh high, and thick branches of the huge old Eugenia bushes whipped at me as I pushed through the vegetation.

One of the double-hung windows had been painted black, and as I pressed my ear up against the pane, I could hear the crying more clearly. It was female, and I knew it was Joelle. At least she was still alive.

I winced as I heard the crack of a hard slap. "It's your fault," I heard a man say. His tone was almost conversational. "You have no one but yourself to blame."

There was a strangled sob.

"Considering the trouble you've caused me, you're actually a lucky little girl," he told his prisoner. "It will all be over soon. I'm gonna go out now and borrow me a different car to cart you off in, and then, honey, you and that nosy coach of yours can go skating into eternity together."

I waited, shaking, until I heard a door open and close, and the car door follow suit. I heard the sound of tires on asphalt fading and knew I didn't have any choice. This was where Terese Steiner had died, and this was where Joelle would die unless I did something. Shaking, I crept around to the side door.

It was locked. Taking a deep breath, I used my good elbow to knock the cracked pane of glass apart; the tinkling sound of the glass as it fell in on the linoleum floor sounded like thunder to me. I reached in gingerly and flipped the simple dead bolt. Then I went in, my heart thumping wildly. In the small living room the muted television lent an eerie glow to photographs scattered on the floor and the coffee table. It was obvious that there had been some sort of struggle. Photographs were ripped up and strewn around the room, a cheap Formica end table was tipped on its side, and the contents of a coffee mug had been spilled across the tattered green shag rug. One flat black ballet slipper lay in the middle of the room. My stomach twisted up even tighter when I saw it.

I heard the sound again and followed it down a short hallway, past a bedroom and bathroom, to a closed door at the back. I leaned forward quietly and listened, my ear to the door. The muffled noise was feminine. I pushed gently on the door, twisting the knob, but the door refused to open.

"Shit." The whispered sound of my own exclamation startled me and the choked wailing stopped abruptly; the person locked inside must have heard me, too. The sudden silence was as nerve-wrenching as the muffled sobbing had been.

Acting on instinct, I returned to the kitchen, rifling impatiently through an assortment of useless silverware and junky utensils in a drawer by the sink. The best I could come up with were a small serrated knife and a flathead screwdriver. They would have to do. Grabbing them, I went out the side door, and after casting a quick nervous glance down the driveway, I made my way back to the blacked-out back window. Without much hope, I tried pushing up on the bottom half with my good arm, but the wooden frame had been painted over so many times that it was wedged securely shut. It wouldn't budge.

I took the screwdriver and jammed it down into the frame between the glass and the wood. The benefit of growing up with a couple of brothers is that you learn to do all sorts of unfeminine things. I shimmied the tool carefully around, working first one side, then the other, loosening years of stuck paint and weather warp. Eventually, the paint flaked and chipped, the frame wiggled, and the window shook loose. I pushed up on it with all my strength, biting back a yelp as a sharp arrow of pain shot up my dislocated left arm. Then, without allowing myself any time to think about what I would find inside, I heaved myself over the sill and into a stifling, dark closet of a room.

I couldn't hear the whimpering noises emanating from the corner, but it wasn't until my eyes adjusted to the darkness that I actually saw Joelle. Curled in a ball on the floor in the corner, still wearing the leggings and sweater I'd last seen her in, the skater was filthy, her hair and clothing streaked with grime. Her wrists and ankles were bound. Her wide, terrified eyes stared at me above her taped mouth.

"Joelle," I whispered, "it's okay. It's me, Kit Powell."

She began to make a keening sound when she recognized me, and I murmured, "Shh, keep quiet," as I knelt to cut through the ropes that secured her.

My arm was throbbing, my breathing was shallow, and the knife was nearly useless. It seemed to take hours before I got her wrists and legs free. I looked at her questioningly in the darkness as I reached for the tape across her mouth. She understood and nodded but couldn't stop a sharp whimper from sounding when I ripped the tape off her mouth.

"Oh my God, Miss Powell, thank God you found me—you have to help me!" she said hoarsely.

"It's okay," I repeated, glancing toward the window.

"He's not . . . he's . . ."

"I know," I said. "Don't try to talk—we have to get out of here."

But Joelle was hysterical, and the words kept pouring out. "He killed Terese," Joelle sobbed.

"I know," I repeated. "Come on . . ."

"And he said he's coming back to kill me!" She clutched frantically at my sleeve. "Please help me!"

"Come on," I repeated, less patiently, trying to pull her to her feet. It was time to stop comforting and start moving. "The police are on their way, but we've got to get out of here now!"

Joelle tried to rise, but she immediately collapsed back down to her knees with a moan. "I can't," she sobbed.

"Goddamn it, Joelle," I said, fighting a wave of panic. "Get up!"

"I can't!" she said. "It's my ankle—he smashed my ankle when I said I didn't want to skate anymore. I think it might be broken."

The knot in my stomach got even tighter. One dislocated shoulder, one broken ankle, two unarmed females, no problem, I thought. We were a beautifully constructed double target. "Come on," I hissed, dragging Joelle to her knees. "I don't care if your ankle is broken, you can crawl!"

She stared up at me in shock. But young, terrorized, exposed to things unimaginable to her, she managed to rally. Grimacing with pain, Joelle nodded, and with me holding her arm for balance, she managed to drag herself across the floor to the window. She was a strong kid, I thought fleetingly, and a gutsy one. I had just begun to hoist her up so she could pull herself through when the door to the room opened.

The man who had called himself Gary Held had a gun in his hand. "Get your hands off that window," he told me, pointing the black muzzle at us. "You're not going anywhere."

I dropped my hands.

"Didn't what happened to you last night teach you anything?" he asked. I felt a wave of panic. I recognized the voice and, even in the faint light from the window, the dark glittering eyes of the man in the mask who had hit me. . . . Was it only the night before? "Well?" he asked.

"I'm a slow learner," I said.

"I'll say," he agreed, pointing the gun directly at me.

I studied his face in the dim room. Those obsidian eyes were definitely the ones that had laughed from behind the ski mask. I recalled Gary Held's description and mug shots. He had had blue eyes.

"Frank Pyne?" I ventured.

A glimmer of surprise showed on his face. "That doesn't matter," he said flatly.

"It might to the police," I said, trying to play for time.

"I don't see any cops here, do you?" He smiled a chilling smile.

Joelle whimpered faintly from her crouched position, and he looked down at her in disgust. "This is all your fault," he told her. "All you had to do was ask those rich parents of yours for some money, and all of this could have been avoided. Your coach would still be alive, and there'd be no problem."

When he glanced down at her, I shifted my hand slightly and rested it over the screwdriver I'd left on the window sill.

Joelle looked up at him, blinking back tears. "I can still get the money for you," she said, her voice shaking.

"It's too late." Pyne shook his head.

"I can get you anything you want, my parents will do anything. . . ."

I curled my fingers over the screwdriver and dropped my hand to my side.

"You should have thought of that before, you stupid little rich girl," Pyne spat contemptuously. "Before you ruined everything." He motioned at me with the gun. "Tie her back up," he said.

I moved slowly across the little room. Joelle stared at me.

"No!" she yelled as I bent toward her.

I stumbled back as Joelle rose to her knees and threw herself forward at Pyne. The unexpected move and the full impact of her body weight hitting his legs threw Pyne off balance, and he came flailing forward, arms outstretched. Joelle knocked herself into him again, and he stumbled toward me, gun to one side. I brought the screwdriver up and drove it as hard as I could into his throat.

There was a piercing scream—or maybe more than one—as blood spurted from the puncture, a dark jet of liquid arcing across us into the room. Pyne clutched frantically at the handle of the screwdriver as I dived for his gun hand.

But it was Joelle who yanked the gun from him, and it was Joelle who fired the shot that made the room go spinning in explosive red and acrid smells. Pyne's thigh was suddenly a pulpy mass of meat and bone, and he fell forward across Joelle, knocking me down with them in a bloody pile.

I wriggled desperately out from beneath him, my shoulder throbbing and my ears ringing, pulling Joelle along with me. Frank Pyne lay screaming in pain, bleeding profusely. I dragged Joelle out into the hallway, a slippery trail marking our passage. She still had the gun in her hand. The police chose that moment to arrive.

PYNE LIVED, and it didn't take him much time to cut a deal: in return for escaping the death penalty for killing Gary Held and Terese Steiner, he was willing to talk. In a raspy voice. Pyne agreed to confess to the attempted extortion of the Kistlers and to supply information needed to charge Eugene Ebberly and his White Nation inner circle with the deaths of the first four transients and Detective Will Merriwether. It wasn't an optimum trade as far as the police were concerned—they'd have loved to see Pyne pay the ultimate price. But they'd get some solid convictions from his information, and the men who had discovered the truth of Merriwether's identity and killed him would face the death penalty. And the mystery of what had happened to the real Gary Held was finally solved.

Pyne told the police he had first learned about Joelle when he and Gary Held lived in the Blasuccis' halfway house five years ago. Held's tale of hard luck had sounded like just another sad ex-con story until Pyne realized there was an angle to play—a monetary angle. Held told him all about the beginning—about how he had gone to pieces after the car he was driving drunk crashed into a big rig, killing his young wife. After two suicide attempts, Held did a six-month stint in the state head farm. When he was finally well enough to be released from the hospital, his baby daughter had been taken into foster care and adoption procedures were under way. Gary Held didn't object: his mess of a life and his guilt over his wife's death made him, even in his own eyes, unfit to raise a child. The baby would be better off with someone else.

The fact that the final adoption papers were never signed was not the fault of the Kistlers; it happened because Gary Held, released, dropped through the cracks of society and disappeared into a half-world of small-time crime and numbing alcoholic haze. Years later, at the halfway house, Gary Held told this all to his new friend, Frank Pyne. Told him all about the daughter he'd given up, the daughter whose life had turned out so blessed because of Gary's selfless action. Pyne, with the instincts of a predatory opportunist, pried deeper, learned that Held couldn't remember ever signing any papers, and spotted real potential in the scenario. He saw a golden opportunity for Held to get a large chunk of cash from John and Ellen Kistler, if only Gary would put forth his claim, a legal claim, to his daughter. Pyne worked on his buddy for a couple of years, while Joelle's fame grew.

But Gary Held was proud of one thing he had done in his sad mess of a life, proud that he had given his only child the chance for something better. And he clung to that shred of pride and dignity and refused to do what Frank Pyne wanted him to do. Eventually, it cost him his life. When Frank Pyne realized that Held couldn't be budged, Pyne killed Held in the same manner as White Nation—of which he was, indeed, an inner circle member—had killed the four transients. He got Gary drunk, strangled him, took his body to the freeway underpass, and set it on fire. Then he simply became Held.

It might have worked. Frank Pyne knew Gary Held had no family who would care to come looking for him. He'd been both lucky and intuitive when he targeted Joelle, rather than her adoptive parents: Joelle was emotionally vulnerable, a good route in to the Kistlers. Pyne also knew that Held had met the Kistlers, just once and over eighteen years ago. Still, he figured, why chance it? What if, despite his resemblance to Gary Held, they suspected something, they somehow realized that this might not really be the same man they'd once seen so briefly? Staying out of sight as much as possible was the savviest thing to do. And he had probably also been right when he assumed that John and Ellen Kistler would be so guilt-ridden and full of the fear of negative publicity that they would give him anything to get rid of him.

But the spin of events he had set into play wasn't that easy to control. He hadn't counted on Terese Steiner's protective instincts, on the coach's genuine concern for Joelle's distracted state of mind, to lead her to do the same kind of investigation I would do. He certainly hadn't foreseen a scenario in which Terese Steiner confronted him face-to-face and threatened to go to the police if he didn't leave Joelle alone. Pyne, who didn't hold human life in the highest regard, took what was for him the logical way out, and Terese became a victim.

The irony was that things went irreversibly wrong for Pyne because of his own skill. He played his part as Gary Held so well that Joelle, already off balance from Terese's death, seized on the emotionally loaded revelations about her real identity and went over the edge. When she ran off to join the man she believed was her real father, she told Pyne that she never wanted to skate again. Never wanted to see the Kistlers. Never wanted anything from them again. She didn't want to be Joelle Kistler anymore; she wanted to be Angela Held. There went Frank Pyne's monetary dreams. And there nearly went Joelle's life. And mine.

Not much of this information made it to the news in its purest form. After their raid on Eugene Ebberly's ranch, the police announced that eight members of the Aryan supremacist group known as White Nation had been arrested for the transient killings, and that they were also going to be charged in the murder of undercover detective Will Merriwether, who had infiltrated their ranks and been found out. My name was kept out of it, and the attack on me wasn't mentioned. Max reported the Joelle story as a stalker-and-extortion case, saying that Terese Steiner had stumbled onto the perpetrator and been killed because of that.

Me, I'm a sports color commentator, so on Saturday night, after yet another night of no sleep, I dragged myself to the women's finals at the Bethlehem Pro-Am.

The poised and immensely talented Greta Braun captured first place, and I could already envision her spinning figure on the front of a Bethlehem cereal box. Melinda Parsons took a strong second, sounding a warning to Greta. Shannon Ngao took third. Susu Jenrette was nowhere to be seen. Joelle Kistler, her ankle in a cast, watched from the front row. Her mother and father sat with her. I waved at Joelle but didn't try to get close to the Kistlers. Joelle waved back, her smile a little wobbly around the edges. At least she was alive.

After the late news, I went home, secure in the knowledge that those who wished me harm were behind bars. Dancer was in a mellow mood—he actually wanted to be petted before he was fed. I was perfectly happy to be alone. All I wanted was a hot bath, a glass of wine, and some jazz on the stereo. No guests, no surprises. No news.

Hot water running into the tub, glass of chardonnay in hand, I saw the light blinking on my answering machine. I pressed PLAY-BACK. There was a message from my sister Janet, reminding me about my niece Kelly's birthday party at the horrifying pizza palace. I remembered that I still had to buy new Rollerblades. There was a message from Mason, just checking up on the well-being of his expected baby's favorite aunt. I still thought the odds were that his adoptive process would be without problems. There was a message from a producer at an independent station up in Los Angeles who said she wanted to talk to me about my part in uncovering the scandal that was rocking the figure skating world.

There was a message from Nick Strummer, who wanted to know when we could get together, and a message from Sandy Harrow, who said pretty much the same thing. I decided that after my bath, I'd flip a coin to see which one of them I'd call first.